THE PORCELAIN DOLL

THERESA DODARO

Marilyn,

With warm wishes!

Theresa Dodaro

This book is a work of fiction. Names, characters, places, and incidents either are products of the author's imagination or are used fictionally. Any resemblance to actual events or locals or persons, living or dead, is entirely coincidental

Cover Designed by Lauren Dodaro @ http://laurendodaro.weebly.com

Edited by Melody Haislip @ greenladyediting@gmail.com

Proofread and Formatted by Jade Young @ http://www.theeducatedwriter.com

Manufactured in the United States of America

Library of Congress Cataloging-in-Publication Data

Dodaro, Theresa Ann

The Porcelain Doll/Theresa Ann Dodaro

ISBN: 1726400972

ISBN 13: 9781726400978

To Regina and Erika, two women who shared their stories with me. One who fled from the Soviet Army in 1945, leaving her broken porcelain doll behind, and the other, who survived the war by becoming a hidden child. And to all innocent children who suffer during war.

And to my mother, Faye Zimmardi (1922-2016). During your life, Alzheimer's may have taken your memory, but your memory still lives in me.

CHAPTER ONE

O*ver the past year, I have learned that it is one thing to live with grief, but quite another to live with guilt.*

I heard a sound in the apartment and told myself, "Old buildings in lower Manhattan always make odd noises." But this one sounded like his footsteps. I peeked into our bedroom one last time but, of course, there was no one there. After months of mourning, one thing was clear; it was time to let go of what might have been, and now, would never be. My own footsteps echoed on the oak wood floor as I wheeled my suitcase out the door.

I headed south toward The Great Smoky Mountains and my grandmother's camp for orphans. At twenty-six years old, I was on the road with everything I owned inside the trunk of my car and no idea of what the future held in store for me.

The drive was a long one, over twelve hours, and I had plenty of time to think about Brian along the way. We had met in college, Brian's major was finance and mine was a combination of both communications and theatre. After college, Brian found a job on Wall Street and I took intermittent internships in mid-town. We moved into a small one-bedroom apartment and enjoyed combing Greenwich Village and SoHo to find artwork for the walls and unique end tables to complement our eclectic style. I had yearned my whole life to have a place to call home. I thought I had finally found one with Brian. I thought I had found my fairy-tale ending. But neither of us knew then, how soon it would all be over.

My eyes were barely open by the time I reached the long winding road which led to my grandmother's mountain home. When I parked in front of her cabin, the porch light was on and the screen door was opening. I didn't even have a chance to lift my suitcase out of the trunk before her arms were surrounding me with much-needed love. Tears slipped down my cheeks as I bent to bury my face in her shoulder. She patted my back and said, "You are home now, mein liebling."

"Oma, I have missed you!"

"Ja, I have missed you too. It is good that you are here. Come inside, your room is ready for you."

The cabin smelled of pine wood. It was filled with rustic decorations, family pictures, and plaques with heartfelt sayings meant to inspire. It had been years since I was last here. With my father being in the Air Force, there were times when we lived in Nevada, Hawaii, and even Alaska. But I remembered that when I visited her as a child, she would take me on treasure hunts to find odds and ends to fill the empty spaces. One time she found an old spinning wheel in an antique store. With a mixture of sadness and joy, she told me, "Jace, this looks just like the one my Oma had." When we brought it home, she set it by the fireplace and said, "There, now it is where it should be." The memory brought a tired smile to my face. It seemed every bone in my body was aching for rest.

Oma looked at me, and I could see concern sweep over her features, "Come, come. You must be tired. Tomorrow we will talk. Tonight, you sleep." She led me to my bedroom and kissed me on my tear-stained cheeks before closing the door behind her. I didn't argue; I was both emotionally and physically exhausted. I collapsed onto the big bed without even taking the time to change my clothes. The dark was usually filled with nightmares about the accident, but for once, I slept soundly until the morning. When I awoke, I was disoriented and automatically reached across the unfamiliar bed for Brian, only to touch the cold sheets. The ache returned. I missed the warmth of his body next to mine. I missed the strength of his arms around me, and just being able to touch him.

The sun was well up in the sky by the time the smell of toasted bread, scrambled eggs, and sausage wafted under the door and enticed me to get out of bed. Barefoot, I found the bathroom and washed my face before following the delicious aromas to the kitchen. I pulled up a stool alongside the counter and watched Oma as she finished frying the sausage. She was humming a tune as she worked, and I couldn't help but notice that she was still a strikingly beautiful woman in spite of her advanced years. Although it had been far too long since I had last seen her, hardly a week had gone by without our talking.

Over the years, Oma's long honey-blonde hair had turned silver. But, as always, she wore it in braids on either side of her head, leading into a neat bun at the nape of her neck and her clear blue eyes still shone as brightly as crystals. Surprisingly, her skin was smooth. Not a wrinkle marred her unblemished complexion. I had been told that I resembled her; and looking at her now, I thought I could only hope to age as well as she had.

Placing the breakfast in front of me and filling a tall glass with fresh-squeezed orange juice, she said, "Eat. Fill your belly and you will think clearer. Then we can talk."

I loved her scrambled eggs and the way she always mixed them with lots of cheese. When I had finished, she cleared away the mess and said, "Jace, you are too young to spend your life grieving. Now you must start to live again. Come with me, I have something I want to give you."

I followed her into her bedroom. In the center of her bed was her doll. It had a soft body, but its head was molded porcelain. The doll had two hairline cracks running through its face and an old ribbon was tied around its head, holding it together. But even the fissures couldn't detract from its beauty. Oma lifted the doll and cradled it carefully in her arms. "Jace, do you remember my doll, Catrina?" I nodded. I remembered seeing the doll in her bed when I was little, but Oma always told me not to touch it.

Oma continued, "Well, she has been mine since I was five years old. I brought her with me when I left my home in East Prussia, and she has traveled with me across land and sea. She has been there to witness my most difficult days and to bring joy when I thought there was none to be had. Now, I want you to have her."

"Oma, why would you give her to me when she has been yours for so long?"

My grandmother lifted her hand to silence me, "It is time for her to travel along with you now. My own journey is almost at an end. But first I have a favor to ask of you, Jace."

"What is it Oma? Anything for you."

She sighed, "Ah, there are things I have seen in my life, and I want the story to be written down before it is too late. I'm afraid if I wait any longer, it will be lost. Will you write it down for me?"

This caused concern for her health, "Of course I will. But you're not going anywhere. You're . . . uh . . .you're not sick, are you?"

"No, no. But I can't live forever now, can I?"

Relieved, I turned away from her for a moment. Her bedroom was at the back of the cabin where the windows reached almost from the floor to the ceiling. Gazing out through them, I could see more mountains rising up in the distance beyond the valley. It took my breath away. The clouds hung just below the mountain tops and looked like a necklace of smoke adorning the range. I said, "Now I know why they call them the Smoky Mountains." Oma followed my gaze and said wistfully, "Ja, they are beautiful." Then she handed Catrina to me and left the room. I followed her back into the kitchen and placed the doll on the counter when she offered me a pen and a pad of paper.

I asked her, "Oma, I thought you lived in Germany, but you just mentioned East Prussia. Where is that?"

"Well, you see, after the Great War, oh, you would call that World War I, East Prussia became part of Germany. But then after the Second World War, it became part of The Soviet

Union. So, you see, it doesn't exist anymore and that is why my family had to leave our home."

"Oh, that's terrible. Is that how you ended up coming to America?"

Then Oma sat down and said, "Now, now, it is a long story, let me start at the beginning, let me start with Catrina."

CHAPTER TWO

1939

Eight-year-old Issy Brummel embraced her doll with a determination to enjoy their last day together. She knew tomorrow, December 6th, was Saint Nikolaus Day, and that, like last year and the year before, the doll would disappear and not be returned until Christmas morning. From the start, Issy had been mesmerized by the pure beauty of the porcelain face. The doll's blue eyes, pink rosy cheeks, and her tiny bow mouth were painted in fine detail. Issy had named the doll Catrina after her own grandmother. With one last hug, Issy placed Catrina gently into the doll's cradle beside her own bed. She pressed her lips to the doll's cool face and kissed her goodnight. She shivered, noticing the farmhouse was especially chilly, and so, she tucked a blanket securely around Catrina's soft body.

The bedroom was tiny and sparsely furnished, but Issy didn't mind. Behind her bed there was a crucifix on the wall, and across the room there was just enough space for her small wooden dresser. She knelt beside the bed on the hard wooden floorboards and said her prayers before turning down the gas lantern on her nightstand. She was aware her family wasn't particularly wealthy, but she had all that she needed. Their farm was about five kilometers from her school in Apfeldorf, a small village southeast of Königsberg. Her friends in the village enjoyed modern conveniences, such as electricity, telephones, and radios, but Issy's home had none of these. She climbed up into her bed, crawled under the covers, and then tucked the hot water bottle between her feet for extra warmth. Outside, snow was covering the ground, and she worried the animals in the barn would be too cold to sleep. Of course, she knew they had fur to keep them warm, but temperatures often fell well below zero in this part of East Prussia. Tonight, it seemed far too cold for any animal to spend a night in peaceful sleep. This made her think about the secret hiding place under their attic floor where her brother, Hans, sometimes hid. The heat from the farmhouse fireplaces and coal stove never quite made it all the way up to the attic.

When her father first built the false floor three years ago for Hans, she was told it was only a game. Her father told her that in order to win the game, she had to keep a big secret. She was never to tell anyone about the hidden compartment, and even more importantly, never to tell anyone that Hans was still living in their house. Issy did not like this game. She remembered when Hans was able to walk with her to school and play with her outside in the fresh air. She also regretted that this game meant her friend, Rebekah, wasn't able to come inside the farmhouse and play with her and Catrina. But her father said that if anyone found out Hans was in the house, somehow, they would all lose the game. Issy loved her father dearly, but she also knew his face could turn to stone in an instant when she disobeyed him. She shivered once again and decided it would be better to turn her thoughts to Christmas morning – to candies, doll's dresses, crinolines, and pretty bonnets.

Two weeks later, her father cut down an evergreen tree and the family prepared it for Christmas. The children made paper decorations and hung them while their mother carefully added hand-painted glass ornaments to the branches. After the tree was finished, thirteen-year-old Hans played with the nutcrackers and assembled them into a little army on the big wooden table. Her mother lit the last of the four candles on the family's Advent pyramid. Issy marveled at how the smoke caused the windmill at the top of the pyramid to spin as if by magic. On the base of the pyramid, little replicas of the Holy Family and barnyard animals twirled around as if on a carousel.

That night, they sat around the tree and sang Christmas carols as her father played his violin. The instrument was his pride and joy and he played it with ease. The curtains were shut tight on the windows as they sang Stille Nacht. Issy thought the lilting sound of the bow on the strings was beautiful. She leaned back into the lumpy chair and watched as her mother and Oma prepared a meal for the next day. She felt the antici-pation mount, as she always did on Christmas Eve. Issy thought, "Soon, Catrina will be back in my arms." Later that night, the children left their empty shoes by the stone hearth and bade their parents and grandmother a good night.

Early Christmas morning, Issy slipped into her stockings and knocked on Hans' door. "It's Christmas! Christkindl was here!" Then, without waiting for him, she ran down the wooden steps to see if any gifts had been left beneath the tree.

Her mother was already busy baking in the kitchen, while her father fed the animals outside. Issy implored, "Mutti! Come look!" Helga left the kitchen to watch her daughter discover the hidden treats. Issy was delighted to find chocolates and little cakes wrapped in paper inside of her shoes. Then, Issy jumped for joy when she saw Catrina under the tree in her new dress and apron. She touched the apron and cried, "It's lace!" She lifted the doll in her arms and exclaimed, "Christkindl brought you back to me! Oh, Catrina, how I have missed you!" She twirled around the room with the doll in her arms and nearly collided with her grandmother as she thrust the doll into the old woman's arms, "Oma! Look at Catrina!"

Oma exclaimed, "She's a beauty, your Catrina, just like you!" Her grandmother tapped the tip of Issy's nose with her finger.

Hans made his way down the stairs, and being taller than his little sister, and more interested in winning a prize, he set about searching for the pickle he knew would be hidden among the tree branches. It was their tradition to hide a pickle on the tree, and whoever found it on Christmas morning would receive an extra prize. It wasn't long until he announced, "I found it!" Oma took a ripe orange from her apron pocket and presented it to Hans as his reward. Next, he searched under the tree for his own present which was wrapped in simple brown paper. Inside were some colored pencils and drawing paper. Immediately, he sat by the fire and started to sketch. He preferred to draw or read, so this gift suited him better than a more traditional present for a boy such as a ball or slingshot ever could.

The house was filled with the aromas of Spritzkuchen, Streusel, and Stollen baking in the oven. Helga sat down to enjoy the moment and to watch the joy fill the faces of her children. Issy came to sit beside her mother to show off Catrina's new outfit and Helga pointed to a small box wrapped in brown paper.

"Issy, there appears to be another package under the tree for you." Issy's face lit up with excitement. She had never expected more than a new outfit for her doll. She sat beneath the tree and unwrapped the present carefully. When she opened the box, inside she found two necklaces each with a gold cross. Helga explained, "One for you, and one for Catrina, to keep you both safe." Issy felt very grown-up to have a necklace of her own and beamed with pride as her mother clasped it around her neck. Issy fumbled with the clasp on Catrina's necklace, so she asked her mother, "Mutti, please, help me put the other necklace on Catrina." Helga said, "You are a big girl now, Issy, keep trying, I'm sure you can do it yourself." Issy's fingers still fumbled, but with determination, she finally accomplished her task. It was a simple Christmas, but to the children, it was all they could have wished for and more.

CHAPTER THREE

1939

After a dinner of Christmas goose with apple and sausage stuffing, red cabbage, and potato dumplings, Issy asked if she could go to visit her friend, Rebekah. Helga bundled her little girl into a woolen coat and sturdy boots, "Be careful not to drop your doll in the snow," she warned.

"I won't Mutti. I promise."

Unlike Issy's house, which was made of stone with a wooden roof, Rebekah's house was made of plaster. It was decorated with wood trim and was crowned with a thatched roof. Issy thought the thatched roof made Rebekah's house look like a fairy-tale cottage. She knocked on their front door and Rebekah's father, Samuel, answered. When he saw Issy with her doll, he feigned surprise, "What do we have here?"

Issy responded proudly, "It's Catrina, don't you like her new outfit? Christkindl left her under our tree last night."

At Rebekah's house there was no Christmas tree, instead there was a menorah with eight candles glowing brightly. Rebekah wore a sweater over her dress with a yellow star sewn onto it. She admired Catrina's new outfit and then said, "She looks beautiful, Issy. Now look at what I got last night." Rebekah showed Issy that she had received a wooden spinning top as one of her eight nights of gifts for Hanukkah. Rebekah explained with a wink and a wise smile, "Opa enjoys whittling toys and painting them for me. This is called a dreidel or trundl."

Issy watched as Rebekah tried to spin it and asked, "May I have a try?"

"Of course, you can."

Issy handed Catrina to Rebekah while she tried to spin the top. Then they each took turns and attempted to get the toy to spin longer on the floor. Rebekah's grandfather watched them as Issy's honey-gold head and Rebekah's rich reddish-brown curls mingled together as they leaned toward each other in concentration. He called to his granddaughter, "Bring it here, Rebekah. I will show you how it is done." Rebekah and Issy brought the dreidel to the old man and he spun it on the table. The girls clapped when the top spun for much longer than either of them had been able to make it spin. He explained, "You must hold the dreidel like so and twist your fingers together before letting it go." He spun the dreidel again and it twirled across the table top as the girls shrieked with delight. Opa enjoyed having their attention and so he said, "Ah, now watch this, young ladies." And with that, he took a coin from his pocket and spun it on its edge. He then handed them each a coin to play with. While the girls practiced spinning them, Rebekah's grandfather went into his bedroom for a moment and returned with something else in his hand. He gave it to Issy. "For the doll," he instructed. Issy looked at what he had given her. It was a small dog carved out of wood. It was so tiny it fit inside the pocket on Catrina's new apron. "Oh, thank you, Opa! But I have nothing for you." The old man's eyes sparkled at the little girl's delight as he patted her head. "Ah, you are like another granddaughter to me, Issy. I am happy to see you and Rebekah together, like sisters, as it should be. That alone, is all I could hope for." But his last words brought a shade of sadness to his eyes.

Rebekah's mother, Hedda, called the children over to the kitchen for a special nighttime Hanukkah treat of jelly donuts. Rebekah's family was from Poland, and they called their jelly donuts, ponchiks.

That night, Rebekah walked Issy home and asked, "Why can I never play inside your house with you?"

Issy knew well how to play this game, so she told Rebekah, "You know why, because Oma isn't feeling well, and she needs to have quiet in the house at all times."

As they drew closer to the farmhouse, Rebekah noticed the chalk markings above Issy's front door. Helga had written the letters C-M-B and the numbers 1-9-4-0. Rebekah asked, "What are those letters and numbers for?"

Issy explained, "They stand for the names of the three kings, Caspar, Melchior and Balthasar, who brought gifts to baby Jesus. You see, as long as the letters and the new year are written above the front door before January 6th, the house is protected from harm. That's the day the kings arrived to honor baby Jesus. On that day, we will take down the tree and make a bonfire out of it."

"A bonfire! Can I come to see the bonfire? That would be so much fun!"

Issy knew it was the one night in the year that Hans was allowed to come out of the house, so she said, "I'm sorry, Rebekah. But the bonfire is just for my family."

Rebekah let go of Issy's hand, "If you were really my friend, you would want me to be here with you for the bonfire. And you would invite me to come inside your house sometimes."

Issy could see that Rebekah was hurt by this and so, although she knew it was forbidden, she decided it was time to tell her friend the truth.

"Rebekah, can you keep a secret?"

"Of course, I can!"

"Well, you see, the truth is, my brother, Hans is in the house at this very moment."

Rebekah looked confused and she said in surprise, "He's not in America?"

Issy shook her head, "He never did go to America to be with Onkel Peter." Issy's brow furrowed as she suddenly realized there must be more to this game than she knew. She was growing older and was beginning to question why this game was even being played in the first place.

"Oh!" Rebekah exclaimed and then she leaned in close to whisper in Issy's ear, "Is he hiding from the Nazis too?"

Issy asked, "What do you mean?"

"Don't you know, Issy?"

"Nein, please tell me."

Rebekah pulled Issy close to her and spoke ever so quietly, "Issy, the Nazis come, and they take the Jews away."

Issy blinked her eyes in her confusion and then opened them wide once again.

"Where do they take them?"

Rebekah frowned, "I don't know, but Opa says they don't come back."

Issy was full of questions, "Why are they taking Jews away? Is that why you don't go to school with me anymore? Do you think they want to take Hans?"

Rebekah reasoned, "I don't know why Hitler wants to take the Jews away and I don't think Hans is a Jew, so maybe I am wrong about him. But, Mutti and Vater said it is too dangerous for me to go to school anymore, so they are teaching me at home."

Issy decided it was time to ask her parents about this game. She had to show them she was no longer a child who played it without question. "Rebekah, I will ask Mutti if you can come to the bonfire. I will tell her I have told you the secret and that you have promised not to tell."

"I will never tell. I promise."

"Not even your parents, and not even Opa."

"No one. I promise."

"All right then. I will talk to Mutti."

Rebekah hugged her friend goodbye and opened the front door to her home. Issy walked inside with a mixture of feelings. She was afraid her parents were going to be very angry with her for telling the secret and even more frightened that she would finally find out the secret was indeed more than just a game. But she was also very determined to find out the truth.

CHAPTER FOUR

1939

Helga's smile crumbled as she listened to her daughter speak. "Mutti, Rebekah told me the Nazis take Jews away and they never come back. Is that why we hide Hans? Is he a Jew?"

Helga replied warily, "What have you and Rebekah been talking about?"

Issy took a deep breath before continuing, "Well, I told her about the bonfire and she asked if she could come." Issy hesitated before continuing, "I-I told her she couldn't come and when she didn't understand, I, oh, I had to tell her!"

Helga could see her daughter was close to tears. She felt a constriction around her own heart, "Tell her what?"

"I-I told her that Hans was secretly living in our house and that it was the only night he was allowed outside."

Issy watched as her mother collapsed back onto the kitchen

chair. In fear, Issy cried, "I'm sorry, Mutti!" Issy raced on, trying to explain, "I know you said it was a game and we shouldn't tell anyone that Hans was still here. But Rebekah won't tell anyone. She promised!"

Issy had expected her mother to be angry, but she hadn't expected her to cry. Helga put her hands over her face and tears spilled down her cheeks. "What is it Mutti? Tell me. I am right! This is not a game, is it?"

Helga reached for her daughter and Issy jumped back, afraid her mother was going to strike her. But instead, Helga hugged Issy and nearly knocked the breath out of her. When Helga finally loosened her grip, Issy stepped back dangling Catrina precariously from her hand.

Wiping away at her own tears, Helga faced her daughter and explained. "Hans is not a Jew. He is a German boy who the Nazis want to turn into a soldier. If they find him here, they will take him away and train him to fight." She turned Issy's small body around to look toward the fireplace where Hans sat drawing with his new pencils. Helga's voice cracked, "Hans is not a solider. He is my boy. If they take him, we may never see him again. They will force him to do terrible things. The German army is invading countries and fighting a war in which many will die. Not just other soldiers, but innocent people."

Rolf couldn't help but overhear their conversation. As his own mother slumbered in her rocking chair, he stood painfully and walked closer to the table where Helga and Issy sat. The hatred that existed between Germany and Russia had a long history. He had told Issy that when he was just a young boy, a bullet had shattered his leg as he was running away from a Russian solider. To this day, that leg still caused him discomfort. Issy looked directly at her father, her voice barely above a whisper, "And what happens to the Jews who are taken?"

Rolf waited for a nod from his wife before he answered, "They are being brought to camps in Poland. Der Führer does not feel they should mingle with the rest of the German population. He wants to eliminate them. Do you understand what that means?"

The heaviness of those words sunk deep into Issy's consciousness and her stomach felt as if she had eaten something rotten. Helga said, "Do you understand now why we can't allow Hans to be part of this?"

Issy turned to her mother and said, "Oh. I-I'm so sorry, Mutti. I didn't understand, but I do now. Will that happen to Rebekah? Will they take her too?"

Helga sighed, "Only God knows."

The next day, Helga took Issy with her when she walked over to Rebekah's house. Helga knocked on the heavy door and waited patiently for an answer. She saw the window curtain part as Hedda checked to see who stood by the door before opening it.

"Hedda, I need to speak with you and Samuel."

Issy stood uneasily at her mother's side and asked, "Where is Rebekah?"

Hedda answered, "She is in her room doing her lessons."

Issy understood this meant she was not to disturb her friend. Still holding her mother's hand, she impatiently shifted her weight from one foot to the other as she listened to the adult conversation. Samuel joined them and listened to Helga explain that they had been hiding Hans for the past three years. Hedda nodded and consoled her friend, "Don't worry, Helga. We will never tell." Samuel looked around the room to make sure Rebekah was not within earshot. As a tailor, he was impeccably dressed, and he held himself in a way that showed his confidence. He was also a man of imposing stature and strength. However, his handsome face was lined with worry as he spoke, "May I ask you something, Helga? If it comes to it . . . if they come for us . . . would you hide Rebekah?"

Issy felt her mother's body stiffen in fear but Helga did not hesitate, "Of course, we will. But I pray it never comes to that."

Samuel only nodded in response and then left the room. Hedda began to cry and Helga now tried to console her, "It won't come to that Hedda. I can't believe Hitler would even care about us. We are so far out into the countryside."

Hedda said, "From your mouth to God's ears."

On the night of January 6th, Rolf lit the evergreen tree and it burned brightly against the darkness. Not only did Rebekah join them, but so did Hedda, Samuel, and Opa. Forgetful of the fears of their parents, Issy and Rebekah danced around the fire, eating treats that had been hidden among the branches and enjoying the warmth on this frosty winter's night. Issy and Hans sang O Tannenbaum, as the tree continued to burn brightly.

It was mesmerizing to watch, and the tiny group huddled close to the flames as the fire turned from red and orange to white and blue. Rebekah held Catrina in her arms and asked her father, "Papa, do you think I could get a doll like Catrina for my birthday?" Samuel's smile crumbled. "I am sorry Rebekah, but the factories which once made toys are all closed now." Issy saw disappointment spread across Rebekah's face, so she suggested, "Why don't we let Catrina sleep over at your house sometimes? Then she can belong to both of us."

Samuel was so surprised by Issy's gesture, he gathered her into his arms and hugged her. "Danke, Issy. That is very kind of you." Issy explained, "Opa said Rebekah is my sister, of course we can share Catrina."

Samuel patted Issy on her head, "Ja, Rebekah is your sister."

The girls jumped up and started to dance around the flames again; the flames that were both warming them and threatening them at the same time.

CHAPTER FIVE

PRESENT DAY

When my grandmother stopped speaking, I looked up from the story I had scratched onto the pad. She put her hands over her face and hid her eyes from me for a moment. "Oma are you sure you're all right?"

"Ja, it's been a long time since I thought of these things. Sometimes my mind feels a bit cloudy." She nodded as if to reassure herself that she was doing the right thing, "This is good. But that is enough for now. We need to get ready for the campers. They will be coming soon."

Trying to alleviate some of the pain I saw in her eyes, I asked, "How many campers are you expecting this year?"

"Sixty. We have six cabins, three for the boys and three for the girls. Each cabin holds ten children."

"And how old are they?"

"They range in age from nine to seventeen." She sighed,

"When they turn eighteen, they are turned out of the orphanages."

"Oma, don't you think this is quite a lot for you to handle these days?"

"Nein, not at all. I have Bradley to run the camp, he's Marty's son. Do you remember Marty from when you used to visit? Poor Marty passed away last year, so this is Bradley's first year on his own. If he does half as good a job as his vater, I will have nothing to worry about. There's also, Murray, who cooks for the children and the kitchen staff, and then there's Hank, our custodian, and, of course, now I have you." She winked. "Oh, and I also have Tucker."

"Who is this Tucker person?"

My grandmother smiled mysteriously. "You will meet him when the time is right."

"Oma! You can't leave it like that. Please, tell!"

"All I'm going to say is, when you are ready to meet him, I will know."

I shook my head at her determination to be secretive. "Well, while we're at it, there's something else I've always wondered about. Why did you choose to open a camp just for orphans? It can't be very profitable."

"Ah, well, maybe it's that they need me; and then again, maybe it's because I need them. Not everything can be judged by the grand old American dollar. You will see this. It will be good for you, too. Now, you go find Bradley and ask him to show you around. It's been quite some time since you've been here, and a lot has changed. His cabin is the next one down the road from here."

I kissed Oma and brought Catrina to my bedroom, where I placed her on my dresser and then tucked the pad and pen in my nightstand. Rummaging through my suitcase, I found my camera and hung the strap around my neck before heading out the door.

The fresh mountain air was such a change from the smog that surrounded Manhattan. My cell phone buzzed, and I saw a text from my mother asking if I had made it to Oma's. I quickly replied and then shut off my phone. As I walked down the steep incline to the next cabin, I thought about my parents. Being raised in a military family, there were times when I felt like I had been drafted at birth. My father believed in a lot of structure and discipline; my mother was aloof. I often felt that she hadn't ever wanted to have a child. My parents were now stationed in Maine, and since the day I left for college, I assumed they were relieved they could go back to being just the two of them again. The truth was, I never did feel the closeness to them that I had always felt with my grandmother. Those visits with Oma when I was just a child had secured such a solid place in my heart, that even all the missed years in between couldn't change.

I approached the next cabin and knocked on the door. A well-tanned young man with dark brown hair and brown eyes answered. He had the muscular build of an athlete and the whitest teeth I had ever seen. My first thought was that he would look great in a television commercial. He looked surprised to see me, but then he quickly recovered and said, "Hello."

I introduced myself, "I'm Jace. Are you Bradley? My grandmother told me you could show me around the camp."

"Oh right, you're Issy's granddaughter. Sure, she told me you were coming." He put out his hand to shake mine, "But she's the only one I let call me Bradley. Just call me Brad." He smiled, and I could swear his teeth actually sparkled.

"Sure, Brad. I appreciate you being my guide. I haven't been here since I was thirteen."

"No problem. Let me just clean up a bit. Come on in."

Inside the cabin, I noticed that it was very well-kept. There wasn't a pillow out of place or a speck of dust anywhere. This surprised me, since I had spent so much time cleaning up after Brian. I followed Brad into the kitchen past the bare walls. There was a blender on the counter half-filled with a green liquid, "Do you want some?"

"What is it?" I grimaced; to me it looked like pureed frog.

He poured some in a glass for me and put an orange slice on the rim as if that was supposed to make it more appealing. "It's a spinach orange smoothie."

I took a hesitant sip and was amazed that it actually tasted good. I had never been big on vegetables, but I could actually drink this. I guess my face showed my shock, so I confessed, "Surprisingly, it's pretty tasty!"

"I'm glad you like it." He smiled, "You should try some of my other creations."

He emptied the rest of the contents of the blender into a plastic container and stored it in the refrigerator. Then he washed the blender in the sink and left it to dry. "Okay, just let me grab a set of keys and we'll be off." As I followed him through the cabin and back toward the front door, I passed by a bedroom and glanced inside. There was a simple bed, a dresser, and a set of weights on the floor in front of a full-length mirror. I turned to see him holding the front door open for me, and blushed when I realized he had been watching me checking out his bedroom. I picked up my pace and scooted out of the front door ahead of him.

He pointed to a cluster of cabins, "Those are for the campers. They're set up as dormitories, ten campers to a cabin." He pointed to each cabin and explained whether it would hold boys or girls, and the ages of the campers who would occupy it.

"Then the cabin over there is for the female counselors, and the one over there is for the male counselors. There are two counselors responsible for each cabin of campers."

"What orphanages do the children come from?"

"They come from a few different ones, but they are all in the Nashville area."

As he spoke, I noticed how he continually narrowed the space between us until he put one hand on my back and pointed with the other. His touch made me feel uncomfortable. It seemed as if he was being too familiar. I realized I must have missed something he said, so I asked, "Excuse me, what did you say?"

His smile widened, misinterpreting my distraction. "I said that is the mess hall where everyone eats."

"Oh, I see. How does that work, are they served or is it cafeteria style?"

He jingled the keys and said, "Let's go in and I'll show you." Inside, there were long tables with benches set up in rows. In the front, there was a rectangular opening in the wall that offered a view of the kitchen. A stainless-steel serving counter ran from one side of the opening to the other. Brad explained, "Murray's our cook. He places the meals on the counter and then his staff serves the campers. Usually the counselors stay at the table to keep the kids from having food fights." He chuckled. "They can get pretty rowdy at times."

"How do you keep them in line?"

"We have a point system, and if they lose points, they lose privileges. When they start to follow directions again, they can gain points and regain privileges."

"Okay, but I'm sure there are some who lose a lot of points. What do you do with them when they run out of privileges?"

"We send them back to the orphanage and they don't get to return here next year."

"Oh! That seems pretty harsh! After all, these kids don't have families. There may be reasons they are acting out. Do you ever talk to them first and maybe ask them why they aren't following directions?"

He shook his head and said, "Waste of time. There are rules, and either they follow them, or they don't. No need for a discussion."

I frowned. Brad could see the look of disappointment and concern on my face, so he continued, "They are fine. It's just like being at the orphanage; they know the rules."

I tried again to explain, "I'm just saying that maybe some of them need a little extra T.L.C."

Brad nodded, "They have your grandmother for that. They even call her, Oma."

Brad brushed my concern aside and continued with the tour,

"These are the showers and rest rooms. The campers in each cabin take turns being responsible for keeping them clean. Over there is the activities house. We spend a lot of time in there on rainy days. Then the sports fields are just beyond the swimming pool."

I remarked, "Wow, this camp really has grown since I last time I was here!" Once again, I regretted that it had taken me so long to come back. As a moody teenager, I stuck my nose in books and ignored everyone else in the world. But once I went to college and stayed in one place for four years, things changed. I had roots and friends for the first time, and I had Brian. Those college years were busy with activities, studies, and falling in love. But I should have made some time for Oma. I felt guilty now that I hadn't.

I could see a group of young people sitting around a picnic table near the pool. "Are those the counselors?"

"Yeah. They got here last week to help get everything ready."

"When are the children coming?"

"They arrive tomorrow."

"Okay, so how can I help you?"

He shook his head, "Everything is done."

I felt disappointed at that answer. I was ready to get my hands dirty and to find something to occupy my mind. He grabbed my hand and led me over to a babbling brook. I pulled my hand away and removed the camera strap from around my neck as I started snapping pictures of the clear blue water against the earthy tones of the rocks in the stream. Beyond it, there was a path that disappeared into the woods. "Where does that lead?"

"There's a lake about a half mile down the trail. We have rowboats and canoes for the campers. There are rivers higher in the mountain which feed down into the lake."

"Oh yeah, I remember that! It's all coming back to me now. So, is there a schedule of activities?"

"Yeah, yeah, but we don't need to worry about that right now. Why don't you take your sandals off and sit with me for a while?"

The water in the stream was colder than I had expected, but it felt good on my tired feet. I was glad the rocky terrain gave me a little personal space and that Brad was forced to sit on a different rock than me. There was no denying he was very handsome, but I really wasn't looking to find a new relationship right now. I just wanted some time to be by myself.

The silence stretched over the minutes, finally Brad said, "My dad ran this place since I was about ten. Sometimes I'd come with him for the day. I didn't really fit in with the other kids though." He picked up a small rock and threw it into the stream.

"Why?"

"I guess maybe because I had parents. I don't know." He shrugged, "It was like they all thought I had more than them. You know, I was different from them, we just didn't get along. So, anyway, I stopped coming. My dad needed help a couple of years ago and he asked me to be his assistant. I teach Phys. Ed. over in Knoxville, but I'm off for the month of July, so I agreed. But then my dad had a massive heart attack this past November."

I nodded, "Oma told me he had passed away. I'm so sorry. I

remember him from when I was little. What about your mother?"

"She's fine. She's still living in Knoxville."

"Do you like working here?"

He shrugged, "It's a job. How about you? What brings you here?"

I decided not to go into the whole explanation. Instead I said, "I just wanted to visit my grandmother."

"Well, that's good. Do you have anyone waiting for you in New York?"

I felt that familiar pain again, "No."

He smirked, "That's good, too."

"Is it? I'm not sure about that. Well, how about you? Anyone special?"

"Nah, no one special."

I put my sandals back on and stood up, "Well, I'd better get back to the cabin to see if my grandmother needs anything." I reached out my hand to shake his, "It was nice to meet you."

"Ah, come on now. We're friends, aren't we?" And with that, he reached his arms around me to give me a hug, saying, "Let me walk you back."

"You needn't bother. Really, I can find my own way back." But he wouldn't have it and said, "Don't be ridiculous, I have to walk that way anyhow." Again, I felt uncomfortable. When we reached Oma's cabin, I made sure I kept my distance from him and waved good-bye.

31

Inside, I called out, "Oma, I'm back!" The aroma coming from the kitchen was making my stomach growl, it smelled amazing.

She replied, "Oh good! I was just thinking I wanted to tell you more of my story. But let's have dinner on the deck first."

From the first bite, I was a big fan, "What is this?"

Oma said, "It's Tante Bridget's famous pot roast."

"Well then, you have to give me the recipe. It's delicious! And who is Tante Bridget?"

She replied, "She was the wife of my Vater's bruder, my Onkel Peter. As for the recipe, I've just got to take the time to write it down."

"Awesome!"

High stilted wooden posts and beams jutted out from the side of the steep mountain and supported the deck attached to the back of the cabin. The view was truly incredible. The sky was lit with reds and oranges as the sun dipped below the horizon. We talked as the full moon took its place in the sky and the mountain tops across the valley became shadows against the dark sky. Oma asked, "So what did you think of Bradley?"

"He seems to know the camp well."

She didn't let me off the hook that easily. She nudged me a little further, "He's very handsome, isn't he?"

"Oma are you trying to set me up?"

"Nein dear, I just thought he might be a nice diversion for you."

I laughed, "A 'diversion', that's a good way to put it!"

"Well, there are times in life when a diversion is welcome. It doesn't always have to be a forever love." Then in a sad voice she continued, "And if that forever love doesn't work out, it is still good to have someone to go through life with."

The sadness I saw in her face made me think of her little friend, Rebekah. "What happened to Rebekah, Oma?"

"Well, let me tell you more of my story. In time, I will tell you everything."

CHAPTER SIX

1940

Issy sat on a stool near the hearth, cradling her doll in her arms. She pretended to feed Catrina with an old baby bottle that had once been hers. It was the night before her birthday and she wondered if Rebekah and her family could come over and join in the celebration. Now that they knew about Hans, she couldn't think of a reason why they wouldn't be able to join them.

Rolf addressed his wife, "It is a good thing we do not have a radio. Der Führer has banned the BBC news radio station."

Helga shook her head, "What will be next? Will he ban music too?"

Rolf responded, "Today I heard that rations are being cut. We will have to make do with less. Perhaps we can use some of the farm produce to barter for more coal for the stove and oil for the lamps."

Helga replied, "Ja, we are lucky we live on a farm. Others are not so lucky."

Rolf took out his violin and started to play a sad tune. Oma was already asleep in her rocking chair and the loud snoring that was emanating from her open mouth seemed to accompany the violin as if she were trying to sing in her sleep. Hans caught his sister's eye and imitated their grandmother behind their father's back, which, in turn, caused Issy to laugh. Rolf was glad for the chance to hear his daughter's laughter, so he asked affectionately, "What is so funny, mein liebling?"

"Oh nothing, Papa." Then she thought, perhaps this was a good time to ask, "I was just thinking that maybe I could have a birthday party this year and we could invite Rebekah and her family. What do you think?"

Rolf teased, "Is it your birthday?"

"Ja, Papa! Did you forget? Tomorrow is June 10th and I will be nine years old."

He chuckled and said, "Well, I don't see why not. What do you think Helga?"

But before she could answer, there was a knock on the front door. Rolf stood up on his painful leg. With great care he gently set his violin on the side table and motioned for Hans to go upstairs and hide. The pounding on the door became more insistent and was loud enough to wake Oma. Issy's grandmother's eyes opened and she was instantly aware of the sound at the front door. Helga gripped her husband's arm, "Be careful, Rolf."

It seemed as if the sound of the clock ticking away the seconds echoed through the small stone house. Finally, Rolf moved forward, looking first toward his wife and then toward his mother and daughter. He dreaded opening the door and finding what might await him on the other side. When he was assured that Hans was well hidden, he gathered his courage and unlocked the door. The image that greeted his eyes was not the one he had expected. Rebekah stood there shivering in the cool summer night's breeze. Rolf looked behind her, but seeing the yard empty, he ushered her inside and quickly closed the door behind her.

She took a deep breath and cried out, "They took Mutti and Papa! E-even Opa, they are all gone!" Her face was flushed from fright and from running the distance between their houses. She looked wildly around the room as if she were a trapped fawn trying desperately to find a way out. Then she pulled a crumpled piece of paper out of her pocket and handed it to Rolf as she sobbed, "P-Papa put me out of the window and told me to run here. He gave me this letter to give to you."

She was dressed only in a white nightgown with tiny rose-buds, loosely covered by a thin white robe. There were no shoes or slippers on her feet, and her little body was shivering from both cold and fear. Finally, her eyes focused on Issy across the room. Rebekah ran to her friend and buried her face in Issy's shoulder, dissolving further into tears. Issy looked up to her father waiting to see what he would do. She felt a coldness rush through her veins and settle around her heart as the full weight of what Rebekah had just said sank into her young brain. She felt frozen with fear and completely unable to ask a simple question or even to put her arm around her friend. The Nazis had taken Rebekah's family. For the first time in her life, Issy knew hatred. She hated the soldiers who had taken her friend's family away from her.

Helga asked, "What does it say, Rolf?" Rolf unfolded the note and read Samuel's message. "It says, 'They have come for us. Surely, to take us to our deaths. I beg of you, please save our child.'" Tears threatened his own eyes, but he had no time for tears now. As soon as he finished reading the words on the paper, Rolf threw the note into the fire. He watched as the flames destroyed it and then ordered, "Issy, take Rebekah up to the attic and show her where to hide with Hans. Then put yourself to bed quickly. Whatever happens, Rebekah; whatever you hear, do not make a sound. And, Issy, do not let anyone who enters this house know where Hans and Rebekah are hiding." As the girls climbed the stairs, Helga reached her husband's side. "Rolf, will they come here?" He answered, "I think so. Let's prepare ourselves."

After bringing Rebekah to Han's hiding place, Issy had barely reached her bed before she heard another loud knock on the door. She picked up Catrina and jumped into bed squeezing her eyes closed and pulling the covers over her head. As the front door opened, she heard her father's voice say forcefully, "Heil Hitler!" A gruff voice returned the greeting. She heard the soldier ask, "'Where is the Jewish girl?" and her father respond, "I don't know what you are talking about. The only girl here is my daughter."

It wasn't long before there were heavy footsteps on the stairs and Issy knew what she must do. The German soldiers came into her room and one of them pulled her covers off. She feigned being woken up. Standing over her was a German officer. Looking at her with stone cold gray eyes, he demanded, "'Where is your friend?"

Issy's lip trembled but she commanded it to be stilled. "What friend?" she asked.

"The little Jewish girl? 'Where is she?"

Issy asked, "Do you mean Rebekah? I'm sure she's asleep in her own bed." The officer looked closely at her, trying to determine if she was lying to him.

In an even more menacing voice he continued, "Little girl, where is your friend? Did she come here? Are your parents hiding her?" Helga and Rolf now stood at Issy's bedroom door unable to move or even breathe, knowing all the while how little protection they could offer their young daughter at this moment. Issy saw the fear on her parents' faces, but she held onto her doll and looked the officer straight in his eyes. With an expression of stone, she spoke in a cool, even defiant tone, "I don't know where she is."

The captain stood there silently, watching her intently for what seemed like hours, but in fact, it was only a minute or so. He turned away from her and ordered, "All right men, search the house."

A moment later, one of the soldiers called, "Captain, there is another bedroom here, but it looks like it belongs to a boy." When the officer left Issy's room, she slid out of bed and into her stockings. Then holding Catrina tightly against her, she followed her parents into Hans' bedroom where the soldiers had gathered. The captain was leafing through Hans' drawings when he said in a grave voice, "How old is your son and where is he?"

Rolf answered, "He is thirteen and in America with his onkel. He is an apprentice learning how to work with electricity."

Still, the captain leafed through the drawings and then he examined the books on the shelf. Running his fingertips along the bindings of the dustless books, his keen eyes scanned the neatly made bed and a dresser drawer which was left opened, still filled with clothes. Bravely, Issy spoke up, "They are my drawings, I like to come in here and draw. Sometimes I even wear my bruder's old clothes; they make me feel closer to him. I miss him."

The captain seemed amused. "Hmpf, and these books? Are they yours too?"

She nodded her head, "Ja, Herr Captain."

"You must be a very precocious young lady. Here, read this for me." He pulled a book down from the shelf and held it out to her.

Issy gave her doll to her mother and reached for the book. She opened it and read the words from Goethe's *Faust* in a clear and loud voice.

"Only one of our needs is known to you;

You must not learn the other, oh beware!

In me there are two souls, alas, and their

Division tears my life in two.

One loves the world, it clutches her, it binds

Itself to her, clinging with furious lust;

The other longs to soar beyond the dust

Into the realm of high ancestral minds.

Are there no spirits moving in the air,

Ruling the region between earth and sky?

Come down then to me from your golden mists on high,

Give me a magic cloak to carry me

Away to some far place, some land untold,

And I'd not part with it for silk or gold

Or a king's crown, so precious it would be!"

The captain was impressed and laughed, "Ha, well done young lady!" Then he turned to his men and ordered, "Continue your search."

Issy stood there silently as the captain's eyes never left her face. She could hear the men searching the attic above and every moment that she waited for Hans and Rebekah to be exposed, seemed like an eternity. Yet she would not allow her fear to show while the captain watched her attentively.

Finally, Issy heard the men announce, "There is no one here. We've searched everywhere."

The captain seemed disappointed, but he said, "Very well." Issy handed the book to her mother and took Catrina once again into her own arms. Then the captain looked back at Issy, his eyes penetrating hers, before he ordered, "Go back to bed little girl." Then he turned to her parents, "I will see you downstairs." Helga and Rolf understood they were being ordered to leave their daughter behind. They hesitated for a moment, but then turned to climb back down the stairs. The other soldiers followed after them, but the captain walked into Issy's room and watched as she got back into her bed. He took Catrina from her and looked carefully at the doll and saw the gold cross around its neck. He lifted the cross in his hand and felt the weight of the gold, "What is your name, little girl?"

"My name is Issy."

"Does your doll have a name too?"

"Ja, it's Catrina. I named her after Oma." Issy watched him carefully and saw a wistful expression cross over his face. On an impulse, she asked, "Do you have a little girl, Herr Captain?"

He smiled at her perceptiveness, and his face softened. To Issy, he suddenly looked like any one of her father's friends. "Ja, I have a little girl. Her name is Frieda. She is about your age. How old are you?"

"Tomorrow is my birthday and I will be nine years old."

He nodded, "My little girl is seven. But I haven't seen her in months. She is in Sweden with her mutter." His gray eyes grew sad.

Issy asked, "Do you miss her?"

"Ja." He placed Catrina gently into her cradle and patted Issy's head, "Have a happy birthday, Issy. You are a remarkable little girl."

She didn't know what to say to that, so she just stared at him until he left her room. Then quietly, she left her bed and softly padded her way to the stairs. She peeked down from the landing and could see Oma sitting in her rocking chair and hear the soldiers rifling through the cupboards. She spied her parents standing there, her father looking longingly at the rifles over the fireplace. The Captain said, "Excuse the disturbance. If you happen to see the little Jewish girl, let us know."

Rolf responded, "Of course, Herr Captain, and it was no disturbance at all. We are at your disposal."

The captain sneered, "Ja, you are. And this, you should not forget."

When the soldiers left, Rolf and Helga locked the door behind them and ran up to find Issy sitting at the top of the stairs. She said, "He has a little girl like me. Why would he hurt Rebekah if he has a little girl of his own?" Her father didn't answer, he just gathered her up in his arms and crushed her small body against his. He let go of her when his heartbeat returned to normal and then he kissed her forehead.

"Are you all right, Vater? Did I do a good job?"

"Ja, you were very brave, now go back to bed, mein liebling. I will check on Hans and Rebekah; they will stay in the attic tonight."

She heard him climb the stairs to the attic and call out to Hans and Rebekah, "It's only me. It's all right." And with that, she heard him lift the boards which hid the children. "I think you are safe now but stay in the attic tonight just in case. Tomorrow, I will go into town, Rebekah, and see what I can find out about where they have taken your parents and grandfather."

In a small voice, Rebekah replied, "Danke."

CHAPTER SEVEN

1940

The following morning, Issy opened her eyes and stared at the ceiling in her room. This was her birthday, but she did not feel like celebrating. She heard muffled voices coming from the kitchen, so she tiptoed quietly and tried to sneak carefully down the stairs without causing them to creak.

She spied her parents before they saw her and as she entered the room, she saw the fear on their faces. In a shaky voice, she asked, "Papa, has something else happened?" Rolf reached out for her as she neared him, and he picked her up in his arms and sat down with her on his lap. He pressed his lips against her forehead and kissed her gently.

Rolf said, "I went into Apfeldorf early this morning. The Nazis rounded up many Jews last night and put them on a train. We have to be very careful, mein liebling. But I am very proud of you. You were a brave girl last night. We must keep Hans and Rebekah hidden and not let anyone know they are here. If they find Rebekah, she will be taken away and we will be sent to prison."

A scowl crossed Issy's brow as she tried to make sense of all that was happening. "Today is my birthday and I am nine years old now. I am not a baby anymore, Papa. I want to understand. Why do the Nazis hate the Jews? Why are they taking them away?"

Rolf was at a loss as to how to explain the twisted logic of Adolf Hitler to his young daughter. Helga pulled up a chair next to them and attempted to describe what had led Germany to this place. She reached out and gently touched her daughter's honey-colored curls, "There was a war twenty years ago, a Great War, and it left the people of Germany very angry. Papa was just a boy then, but even he couldn't escape being injured as the Germans and Russians fought over land they both wanted to claim as their own. That war grew into a world-wide war, which devastated Germany. Since then, the German people have struggled to find ways to take care of their families. They were looking for someone to blame for their hardships. Adolf Hitler saw a chance to gain power by blaming the Jews for all of Germany's troubles. Not everyone agreed, but if you did not agree, then you became another person to blame for the problem. So, people remained silent out of fear. Over time, Adolf Hitler became more and more powerful; and with that power, he became bolder, and soon the fear and anger of the German people grew into madness."

Tears were welling up again in Issy's eyes. Fear mounted and grew stronger within her as Issy spoke softly, "Mutti, what will they do with Samuel, Hedda, and Opa?"

Helga had to look away from her daughter; she could not answer. Issy could hear her own heartbeats in the silence.

Finally, Issy asked in a whisper, "Will they be killed? Like you said, will they be e-eliminated?"

With a heavy heart, Rolf decided his daughter needed to know the truth, "I think so, mein liebling. But we can pray they are returned unharmed."

"Papa, will they come and take you away? Where should I go if they take you? What should I do?" Rolf's heart broke at her words, and as he held her close, he promised her, "No one will ever take me away from you."

Seeing her father looking so broken, she tried again to show him that she was brave, "All right, Papa. We will hide Rebekah and she will be safe with us, and I will pray for her family to come home to her."

Helga said, "That is good, child. Now go tell Hans and Rebekah they can come down from the attic and have some breakfast."

Issy found them sitting on the attic floor. Rebekah's eyes were as round and red as Mutti's dinner plates and Hans' face was as white as Rebekah's robe. "Papa says you can both come downstairs now."

The children sat at the table as Oma piled hard boiled eggs, cheese and coarse bread with butter in front of them. "Eat children. You need to stay strong," she urged. Rebekah was still wearing her nightgown and robe, so after breakfast, Issy took her up to her room and gave her some clothes and shoes so she could get dressed.

Rebekah asked Issy, "Did your Vater find out where they took my parents and Opa? He said he was going to go into town this morning to see if he could find out."

Issy explained, "He only told me that they were put on a train. Others were taken too."

"Were they all Jews?" Rebekah asked.

Issy nodded.

Rebekah looked lost and Issy didn't know what to do. As tears spilled from her eyes and her lower lip trembled, Rebekah asked, "What will happen to me if my parents don't come back?"

Issy reached for her hand, "You will stay here with me and be my real sister like Opa and your Vater said." Issy reassured her, "You are safe here, the soldiers came last night and couldn't find you."

Rebekah then told her what it had been like to hear the soldiers looking for her as she hid beneath the attic floor. "I was so frightened, but I didn't move at all. I was glad Hans was there and that I wasn't alone. Really, it felt like I was in a coffin. I was thinking about my family. You see, when the knock came on our front door, Papa scribbled that note and placed it into my pocket. Then he put his finger over my lips to keep me quiet. He whispered, 'Go to Issy's house. Run, as fast as you can, and don't look back. Give my note to Issy's vater. You will be safe there.' Then he kissed the top of my head and said, 'Always remember h-how much we love you. Be strong, little one.' He lifted me then and put me out the back window. I ran as fast as I could, but I could still hear Mutti screaming, and the sound of gunshots behind me." When she finished, tears were pooling in Rebekah's eyes.

Issy looked down at the floor. She was imagining what Rebekah was describing. She hadn't known there were gunshots. She closed her eyes tightly against the scene that played in her head.

Rebekah continued, "Under the attic floor, I listened quietly as I heard the soldiers' heavy footsteps on the attic stairs. I didn't dare breathe as their boots pounded on the floor just inches above me. I was surprised when they didn't hear my heart beating with only a plank of wood separating me from them. Oh, Issy, the blood that was beating in my ears sounded as loud as a bass drum! I was so glad when Hans reached out to hold my hand. We just stayed as quiet as we could and waited for the soldiers to find us. We couldn't believe it when they left the attic without discovering us. When your Vater came and took us out, he hugged me. Your Vater is strong, but so was mine, and now he is gone. I am afraid no one can protect us, Issy."

They heard Helga call them to come down to the kitchen again. Glad for the distraction, the children returned. On the table they saw a birthday cake and a wrapped present. Helga said, "I know you don't feel like celebrating today, Issy, but sitting around and crying isn't going to change anything. We don't know what tomorrow will bring. Today is still your special day, and Rebekah's parents wouldn't want you to miss your birthday party."

So, they all ate cake, and Issy opened her present as Rolf played a tune on his violin. When the wrapping paper fell away, it revealed a set of watercolor paints along with a small set of paint brushes and paper. The two girls and Hans spent the afternoon painting at the big wooden table. Issy painted a ship on the ocean, sailing into the setting sun; Hans painted the fields outside his parents' farm; and Rebekah painted a train entering a dark tunnel.

CHAPTER EIGHT

PRESENT DAY

After hearing Oma's story, I had a difficult time sleeping that night. Although my bed was comfortable, I tossed and turned and reluctantly watched the sun rise through my window, just as I was finally about to doze off. Thoughts of Oma and her friend, Rebekah, kept flooding my brain. What had happened to Oma's brother, Hans, and to her parents? What had happened to Rebekah's family? I shuddered to think of how terrifying it must have been for them all and wondered why she had never mentioned any of this to me before.

But the morning once again brought the smells of breakfast from the kitchen. I showered and dressed quickly. I was surprised to see that, in spite of telling me her story, my grandmother seemed full of energy. Then I remembered that the children were coming today, and the thought filled me with enthusiasm too. After all, it felt good to have a purpose again. As I sat at the kitchen table and ate, I noticed for the first time that the morning sun shone through the stained glass above the front door. The stained-glass window was set high on the wall of the cabin, above the roof of the screened-in porch. The window filled the room with a magical rainbow of colors. Yesterday, I had awakened later in the morning and the sun was already high in the sky, so I had missed this amazing phenomenon. I studied the stained glass and saw the painted farmhouse. There was a barn and several small buildings in front of an apple orchard. Beyond that, there was an open field leading to woods. It was beautiful and serene, and I was surprised I hadn't noticed it before now.

"Oma, that stained-glass, it's beautiful!"

She smiled, "Tucker made it for me."

I had to ask, "Oma, is Tucker your boyfriend?"

"Oh, don't be ridiculous, Jace. He's not much older than you are, mein liebling." Then she walked out of the room, refusing to tell me any more about him.

By ten o'clock the buses arrived, loaded down with the campers and their luggage. The counselors helped the children find their cabins and assigned each to a cot. An hour later, Oma and I were standing in the mess hall and she was addressing everyone. "Most of you know me and have been here before. For those who haven't, you can call me Oma." Next, she pointed to me, "And this is my granddaughter, Jace. She will be helping out this year." The children smiled and politely chorused, "Hello, Jace."

After the rest of the staff was introduced, lunch was served. I sat at the table with the youngest campers. The little girl sitting next to me provided the necessary introductions. She announced, "My name is Haylie. This is Dalton, and that is

Maggie, and that's Benny." Haylie's bubbly personality shone through her smile and gestures. In a way, she reminded me of the stained-glass window. She sparkled with personality. Her big brown eyes widened as she told me about herself and her friends, "I'm ten years old. Dalton is the youngest, he's nine," she pointed to the quiet boy at the end of her table. "And then there's Maggie, she's ten, like me!" Maggie looked shy but her abundant red curls kept her from going unnoticed no matter how much she might have wished to do so. "Benny is the oldest, he's eleven," she said of the boy with sorrowful puppy-dog eyes. It was obvious from the start that Haylie was the leader of this little group.

"Well, I'm glad to meet you all. Have you been to the camp before?"

Hailey offered, "Benny and I were here last year, but this is the first time for Dalton and Maggie. We all come from the same orphanage in Nashville, so we already know each other."

"Okay, do you know some of the older children too?"

"Yeah, that's Olivia over there, she's twelve. She and the girl next to her, Ginny, are sisters. Ginny is seventeen. So, this will be her last year."

I looked closely at the two girls Haylie pointed to. Although Ginny was the older sister, she was rail-thin with a narrow-pointed face. Whereas, Olivia, was stocky, rounded, and quite developed for a twelve-year-old. From their appearance I would have thought they were closer in age than they actually were.

"And who else do you know?"

Haylie continued to point to children and tell me what she knew about them.

"Okay, let's see." I could tell she was really enjoying the attention. "That's Mack, he's thirteen. His voice is changing so he doesn't speak a lot. It bothers him when the other boys make fun of him. So, you should keep an eye on him, too. And that's Travis standing next to Mack. Travis is sixteen years old. Travis is funny, he always makes me laugh." While Mack had an athletic build, Travis was short for his age and overweight, but he also had a bright face with endearing dimples.

Finally, she said, "Those three girls over there are Mazie, Ella, and Vicky. They are very close to each other and never go anywhere alone. Mazie always entertains us though. She sings and also plays the guitar and the piano at the orphanage. Oh, I forgot to tell you that Maggie also sings. Just wait until we make a campfire, you'll find out! Ella's really quiet, she reads a lot. And Vicky is quite strong. If anyone picks on Mazie or Ella, Vicky takes care of them."

"Does that happen a lot? Are there bullies?"

She looked at me and crossed her eyes, "Of course there are!"

"Okay, well, Haylie, I'm going to depend on you to tell me what's going on around camp."

She brightened up and flicked her pointer finger at me, "I got you, Jace. You can count on me. Oh, wait, there's one more. That boy over at the end of the table, that's Wade." Haylie pointed to a muscular boy with blonde hair and brown eyes. "This is his last year too, he's seventeen. He usually has a lot of friends, but they aren't here anymore. Most of them had to leave the orphanage last year 'cause they turned eighteen." She sighed heavily and said, "It's a bummer. I hate when

51

people leave, but sometimes they come back the next year as counselors and we get to see them again when we come back to camp." That's when I realize that these children were each other's family.

"Thanks again, Haylie. This has been really helpful. But I think we might need to make some name tags; I'm never going to remember who everyone is." Haylie had a mouth full of sandwich, so she gave me a "thumbs up" in response.

Brad smiled as I approached him. He said, "Looks like you're making friends already."

I happily agreed, "Oh yes, that's Haylie, Benny, Dalton, and Maggie over there. They're a nice group of kids. I think this camp thing is going to be fun. But do you think we could get some of those stick-on name tags? There are so many names to remember."

"Sure, we've got some in the cabinet in the activities cabin. I'll get them later and hand them out at supper. But, don't let them fool you. They are all rug rats; every single one of them!"

I thought that was an odd thing to say and I took offense at it. "I really don't think that's fair."

He replied, "Oh, you'll find out."

The counselors looked like they had everything under control, so I took the opportunity to walk Oma back up to her cabin. I could see she was having a tough time walking on the uneven ground and the steep pavement. I would have to talk to her about getting a cane to help keep her steady when I wasn't there to hold her arm.

She asked, "How's it going?"

"I'm learning."

"And what about Bradley?"

I responded, "I'm reserving my right to judgment for now."

Oma laughed, "Oh, I see how it is! So, if you are up to it, how about I tell you more of my story when we get back to the house? We can sit inside the screened porch, so the mosquitoes don't get us, and we can enjoy some lemonade. What do you think?"

"Are you sure you want to do this Oma? I don't want it to upset you."

"Mein liebling, this story needs to be told. Too many people were silenced after the war because Germany was the enemy. Many brave people protected each other and hid children at great risk to themselves and their families. I want you to understand that not all people who lived in Germany were Nazis. Sometimes I don't think people see that. Believe me, I've done the same. I'm not proud of it. I too have judged people based on their ethnicity or religion. That doesn't make it right. I was just as wrong as others have been."

"All right, so tell me Oma, what was it like to live in Germany then?"

She corrected me, "East Prussia."

"Yes, yes, East Prussia."

She shrugged, "Well, we were part of Germany then." She thought for a moment before continuing, "Like Rebekah, there were others who were hidden children. Some of them are still so frightened they can only whisper their stories. In a way, they are still hiding after all of these years. We were just ordinary children, trying to survive a maniacal dictator. God preserve America and spare its citizens so they should never have to make the decisions we had to make then."

The anguish I saw in my grandmother's eyes was riveting. I knew there was more suffering to come in her story, so I braced myself to hear it all.

CHAPTER NINE

1941

Almost a year had passed since Rebekah's parents had been taken. Helga's face showed concern as she said, "Rolf, I have received a letter from my cousin, Nadja, in Munich."

"What does she say?"

Helga looked at her children who were sitting at the table reading. Issy turned pages and pretended to read her book but continued to listen intently to her parents. Helga lowered her voice as she browsed through the letter.

"Nadja says there is an institution for unwanted children in the city. The children suffer from afflictions and deformities. The Nazis have emptied it overnight. The nuns working at the institution said the children were ripped from their arms." Helga's voice faltered before she could continue, "And they were carted away as if they were animals. She believes the children are being taken to work camps, but she tells me that these so called "work camps" are nothing more than death camps. She warns us please to be careful. She says this is not the Germany that we have always known."

Issy turned another page in her book, but she had lost interest in the story before her. Real life and real worries filled her brain. She wondered what would happen next to her family and her country.

A week later, Issy arrived at school to find the nuns had been replaced by teachers who were approved by the Nazi party. They continually asked probing questions of the children and tried to uncover any failing allegiances to their cause. Fewer and fewer children filled the classrooms, but there were still several Jewish children present. Their families thought it would be more dangerous to keep them at home, fearing it would be seen as a sign of disloyalty to der Führer. These families were wealthier than most and offered services to the community that were needed. There was the village doctor, Dr. Ebrahem, the Chief of the Village Police, Herr Goldbach, and the Bürgermeister, Herr Rosenblum. The doctor's son, Josiah Ebrahem, was a small-framed boy with brown hair and large dark eyes. Josiah was Issy's desk mate and she had known him since they were little.

She remembered visiting his father's office when she was ill. Issy had been impressed with how Josiah assisted his father by handing him instruments. He told her, "Someday, I will be a doctor like my vater."

Recently, Issy had asked him, "Aren't you afraid the SS will take you?" He boasted to her, "No, I am not afraid of anyone."

Issy was struck by his bravery and when he said, "Girls need to be careful, but boys are here to protect them. As long as I am here, Issy, you don't have to be afraid." Issy's cheeks filled with pink as she blushed.

Today, Issy and Josiah were working on their geography project together. They were drawing a map of how Germany was growing. Their heads were tilted together, barely inches apart. She secretly had a crush on him, but at nearly ten years old, she had no intention of telling him so. They heard a commotion in the hallway and the next moment, soldiers entered their classroom. The students stiffened in fear as they saw that the men were in fact, the SS, the Schutzstaffel.

With guns drawn, one solider announced, "Jewish children are no longer allowed to attend school. If you are Jewish, please stand and form a line." The older students bravely held the hands of the little ones who were crying. Each of them had the Star of David sewn onto their clothing as Rebekah had once worn. Josiah took the hand of Kurt Goldbach, the young son of the Bürgermeister. Kurt was only six years old and had solemn gray eyes and curly red hair that was as soft as feathers. Josiah held onto Kurt and urged him to walk with him. Issy grabbed Josiah's arm and pleaded in a whisper, "Don't go Josiah." He spoke emphatically, "Don't worry Issy. No one would dare hurt me. My father is the only doctor in Apfeldorf."

As the line of children were led out of the classroom, Issy and the rest of the students who were left behind, ran to the window to watch their classmates. Several of the men, both Christian and Jewish, including Dr. Ebrahem, had congregated outside of the school. They tried to intervene as the children were marched passed them. Issy watched as the men were shot at point blank range and fell like rag dolls to the ground.

The SS continued to march the crying children toward the river. Beyond the tree line, they disappeared from view.

But within minutes, Issy heard their terrified screams and the roar of gunfire once again filled the air. She placed her hands over her ears, but the rat-a-tat-tat of the machine guns could still be heard. As she realized what had just happened, tears spilled over her cheeks and her stomach threatened to relieve itself of its contents. The girl next to her fainted right there on the floor.

The teacher, Frau Müller, lifted the girl up off of the floor and sat her, slumped in her chair, while ordering the remaining children to return to their seats. Issy looked around at her classroom; there were two chairs to each desk. The desks were lined in neat rows facing the front of the room with two large blackboards. A huge banner draped the wall between the blackboards with a picture of Adolph Hitler in the center and large swastikas on either side of his face. The remaining children obediently returned to their seats. Issy's legs were shaking but she followed the teacher's directions and returned to her own desk. Once seated, Issy counted the empty seats and uncontrollably wept. She reached her hand over to the chair next to her, which had so recently been filled by Josiah, and found it was still warm to the touch. When Issy continued to sob, Frau Müller loomed over her and rapped a long ruler loudly against her desk, "Stop that crying, we are all better off without them!" Issy choked back her tears and dutifully nodded and answered as she knew she must, "Ja, Frau Müller."

Then the teacher ordered her class to stand and announced, "There have been Jews hiding in their neighbors' homes. What you saw here today is how that act of treason is dealt with. Tell your families, if a Jew is found in their home, the same will happen to them. Now, all together, let's sing our National Anthem."

Together their small voices trembled over the words, "Deutschland, Deutschland, über Alles." They sang, "Germany, Germany, above everything."

Through the windows of their classroom, the children watched as the Chief of the Village Police, Herr Goldbach, and the Bürgermeister, Herr Rosenblum, along with their wives and the remaining Jews in the village, were marched to a waiting train.

Later that afternoon, the children were told to wear their finest outfits to school on the following day because there was to be a parade. The German army was en route to invade The Soviet Union.

When she walked home from school, Issy followed the path by the woods. She hoped she had been wrong; she wanted so much to be wrong. But what she saw turned her blood cold. The bodies of her classmates lay in the river. Even in death, Josiah was still holding Kurt's hand and the river had turned red with their blood. She vomited at the sight and then ran the rest of the way home blinded by her tears. When she reached home, she collapsed into her father's arms.

"Papa!" In hysterics, she rambled on and was barely understandable as she relayed the events of the afternoon. "Oh, Papa, they shot my friends, they shot Josiah and Kurt and all the Jewish children, and they left their bodies in the river. Oh Papa! It was so awful! The teacher yelled at me and told me not to cry. I was so scared, Papa! First, the soldiers said that Jewish children are forbidden to go to school and then they took them outside and they shot them! Frau Müller said that if any of us are found hiding Jews in our homes, we will be shot too. Oh, Papa." She said in despair, "They even shot Dr. Ebrahem! He's dead! And then they took Herr Goldbach and the Bürgermeister away."

Rolf held onto her as she cried. He had never been more frightened himself than he was at that moment. Although he would have given anything not to be forced to say the words that needed to be said, when her sobs finally abated, he told her, "You must act as if you do not care. I know this is difficult, but to survive, you must act your part. No one must ever suspect us, or they will come to search the house again. And Issy, don't tell this to Rebekah, she does not need to know this."

The following day, her mother told her to wear her white dress embroidered with blue forget-me-not flowers and her finest coat. Helga placed a white ribbon in her daughter's hair. Issy asked her mother, "Why must we to dress so fine today?"

Helga replied, "You know why, Issy. The German army is marching through the village on their way to Russia. The people have been ordered to line the streets to greet them and cheer the soldiers on to victory."

A worried expression crossed Issy's angelic face, "Mutti, what will happen if the German army loses the war?"

Rolf answered for her, "Do not ever breathe a word of fear that they will lose. Remember you must never let anyone see your feelings. Keep them hidden and locked inside of you when you are not within this house. You must tell others this war will be over quickly and that you pray it will be a victory for Germany."

Resolutely, Issy answered, "All right, Papa. I will continue to play the part." But her heart was completely broken. Rolf looked away from his daughter's eyes. He drove Issy to school that day in his wagon. When she climbed out, she didn't even say good-bye. She felt bereft of emotion.

Later that day, a teacher knocked on their classroom door and interrupted the children's daily English language lesson and instructed them to file out of school and to form a neat line as they joined the other villagers along the cobblestoned street. Issy could still see the bloodstains from the previous day, but the bodies of the men who had tried to intervene had been removed. The children waited patiently for an hour before the first sounds of the approaching army could be heard. Then, the ground shook under the weight of the Panzer tanks that rolled into view with a thunderous roar. At the same time, what seemed like thousands of aeroplanes of all sizes filled the sky. The deafening sounds as they soared by drew every eye in the crowd upward toward the flying machines. On the road before them, trucks passed by, laden with guns and supplies. After the trucks, came jeeps decorated with the blood-red Nazi flag with its huge black swastika. High-ranking officers sat in jeeps, confidence etched on their faces. But Issy could see the officers also watched the people lining the streets carefully, observing each person as they stood with outstretched arms in the mandatory Nazi salute.

The owner of the flower shop in the village, Frau Ackermann, handed out flowers to the young women lining the streets. They, in turn, threw sprigs of edelweiss into the soldiers' jeeps. As every German knew, this flower signified deep love and devotion. It grew naturally on steep mountains and fables told of many young men who proved their love and devotion to

THERESA DODARO

their sweethearts by attempting these dangerous and often fatal climbs to retrieve the delicate white flowers for them.

In one of the jeeps, Issy noticed the Captain who had been in her room the night that Rebekah came to hide in their house. She stared at him, until through some unknown phenomenon he sensed her looking at him. He recognized her then and taking a sprig of edelweiss that had been thrown into his jeep, he tossed it to her and she caught it. He smiled and waved to her as the jeeps rolled by, his head turning back to watch her until the line of jeeps which followed behind him, finally blocked her from his view. The voices in the crowd erupted in continuous cheers of "Heil Hitler" and together everyone joined in singing their National Anthem. Finally, the soldiers marched by clicking their shiny heels as they passed, while the older girls smiled sweetly up at them.

In spite of her fear, Issy was caught up in the importance of it all and the exuberance of those enjoying the pageantry of the parade. She knew she shouldn't enjoy this show of military force and immediately felt guilty at having a moment of excitement. She asked herself, "How could you, Issy? How could you, when the bodies of your classmates still lie in the river just beyond the trees?" She was disgusted with herself. She took a step back from the road and lowered her saluting arm. It only took a second, and her teacher was behind her sticking the ruler into her back, digging it deep into her soft flesh. In a threatening voice Frau Müller said, "Raise your arm young lady and be thankful that this is only a ruler sticking in your back and not a rifle." So Issy stepped forward and raised her arm once again.

After the parade, the teacher had them write over and over again, "Hold strong! Do not lose faith! Our victory is at hand!" After writing the words the children were ordered to stand, and Frau Müller directed, "Now children, repeat these words loud and clear."

The classroom filled with their small voices as they repeated over and over again to the terrifying cadence of the ruler against the teacher's desk, "Hold strong! Do not lose faith! Our victory is at hand! Hold strong! Do not lose faith! Our victory is at hand!" As Issy spoke the words, tears threatened to spill from her eyes again, but she fought valiantly against them. She would not show her fear. She would not show her sorrow. As her father had told her, she would hide deep inside of herself and never let anyone or anything ever touch her again.

Later that night, sitting on the attic floor, Issy described the parade for her brother and Rebekah, "Hans, it was terrible, but it was just as Papa said it would be. I played along as if I was an actor in a play and I had to make the audience believe everything I said and did was real. Even though we were all afraid, we stood there bravely and cheered as the soldiers marched by. Then we did as we were ordered to do. We didn't even dare to look at each other. We just did as we were told. And Rebekah, oh, that horrible Captain who came looking for you the night you came here; he was there. He saw me, and he threw a flower at me and smiled as he passed by in his jeep." Issy looked away as she remembered the moment she had felt the exhilaration of the crowd, regretful and embarrassed by her fleeting reaction.

Hans observed, "You did a good job, Issy. You need to keep doing that. It is harder for you than for us. You have to be careful of what you say and what you do, we only need to hide."

Rebekah shuddered after hearing the recounting of the parade. The fact that Issy had just seen the Captain, brought back all the terror of that night to her, the night when her parents were taken. She asked, "Issy, what do you think happened to my parents and Opa? Do you think they will ever come back for me?"

Issy felt for her friend; she knew how much Rebekah missed her parents and couldn't imagine being separated from her own family. She hadn't told Rebekah about what had happened to their Jewish classmates. But having seen what the SS was capable of, she was more certain than ever that Rebekah's family was dead. But instead of saying so, Issy answered, "I am sure they will come home and when they do, they will find you safe."

Issy smiled to reassure Rebekah, but Rebekah still looked forlorn. Issy hugged her doll close to her as if she could hold in all that was trying so hard to pour out of her. That's when she realized she was still acting; hoping Rebekah would believe what they both knew was not true. Issy was terrified that a soldier might one day walk Rebekah to a river and shoot her too.

Suddenly Issy had an idea, she unhooked the cross necklace which was around Catrina's neck, the one that matched the necklace she wore herself, and handed it to Rebekah. Issy said, "Rebekah, wear this. It will protect you. If you ever leave this house, let them see this around your neck. Let the world believe you are Christian. You too must play a part."

Rebekah took the necklace from her and fastened it around her own neck. She didn't need to be told what had happened to the other Jewish children; she understood now what world she lived in. She also knew that for her parents, she had to do whatever was necessary to survive; even if it meant denying her heritage. One day, she would search for them and she needed to stay alive in the meantime, so that if they survived, she could find them.

Rebekah asked, "Issy, can you teach me some of your prayers?"

"Of course, I can." And so, Issy taught Rebekah how to pray "The Our Father" and other prayers she hoped would protect Rebekah and allow her to pass for Christian in case it ever came to that.

CHAPTER TEN

PRESENT DAY

My stomach felt sour. I shivered and wrapped my sweater tightly around my shoulders. It was nearing night and I could see a campfire glowing brightly in the distance near the campers' cabins.

Oma's face was flushed when she finished. She took my hand in hers, it felt clammy and moist to the touch as she explained, "You should understand that the Soviets had been on the side of the Nazis in 1939. They committed many massacres against the Polish people in the early years of the war. But then Hitler turned against Stalin in 1941, and without warning, Hitler invaded The Soviet Union."

"Oma, I had no idea you knew so much about the war."

"I may have been a child when it happened, but I lived it, and what I didn't know then, I learned later."

She closed her eyes as if she could block out the images that undoubtedly were passing through her mind.

"Oma, perhaps you should take a walk with me and get some air?"

"Nein, Jace, you go."

I was hesitant to leave my grandmother after her sharing this part of her story, but I needed to see the campers. I was feeling claustrophobic and the word "escape" crossed my mind. I felt terrible to leave my grandmother behind, but she looked exhausted. So, I said, "Well, if it's all right with you, I think I will go for a walk now, Oma."

"Ja, you go. I will tell you more tomorrow. Enough for now."

Walking toward the campfire, I looked up at the wide sky filled with stars. I remembered when Brian and I had gone up to the Catskill Mountains on a camping trip. We were enthralled to see all the stars in the sky, so we moved our sleeping bags out of the tent and slept outside. I could still feel his breath against my cheek; still taste his lips on mine. I closed my eyes against the pain as my heart constricted. If we had left the party just a minute later or a minute earlier, would he still be here with me?

As I neared the campfire, I could hear the children singing. I couldn't help but think that the youngest of them were the age my grandmother had been when she witnessed the horrible events she had just relayed to me.

I heard one voice call out, "I said a boom chick-a boom."

The others responded, "I said a boom chick-a boom."

Again, the first voice called out, "I said a boom chick-a rock-a chick-a rock-a chick-a boom"

The group repeated, ""I said a boom chick-a rock-a chick-a rock-a chick-a boom"

"Uh-huh"

"Oh yeah"

"One more time…"

"Let's do that astronaut style."

"I said a zoom chick-a zoom, take a rocket to the moon a chick-a boom"

The children repeated and then all laughed as they continued the funny song.

I sat on a bench and watched them. But the chill still ran through me from the story Oma had just told me. What if someone marched these children off and did to them what had been done to Oma's friends? What would I do? What could anyone do?"

Brad sat down next to me, "You look gloomy."

I shook my head, "No, just thinking. I'm glad the children seem to be enjoying themselves."

"Yeah, it isn't hard to please orphans."

Once again, I was surprised by his callousness.

I heard a voice from the campfire say, "Let's do it janitor style" and I saw Maggie's red curls bouncing as she sang, "Like, I said, a broom, sweep-a mop-a, sweep-a mop-a, sweep-a broom!"

The children giggled as they sang in response.

Hank, the custodian, was passing by the camp fire. He walked with what looked like a painful limp. I asked Brad, "What happened to Hank? Do you know why he limps?"

"Oh, he was injured, years ago, in the Iraq War. I heard there's still some shrapnel in his leg which they never could get out."

"The Iraq War? When was that, like twenty years ago?"

He corrected me, "Actually, it was more than that. He's about forty, but he looks a lot older."

I was shocked. I would have thought he wasn't a day under sixty. It was more than just the lack of hair that made him appear much older than he was. It was how he carried himself and how his injury forced him to lean forward as he limped.

One of the counselors said, "All right everyone, it's time for a campfire story."

The children were sitting shoulder to shoulder and close to the fire in order to keep warm on this chillier than normal summer night.

Brad pointed to one of the counselors, "That's Lexi, she's our storyteller. The boy over there is Cole. He's sweet on her, but she hasn't a clue," he smirked, "a lot like someone else I know."

I tried to ignore him and instead, listened to Lexi as she told her story. Her voice was earthy and heavy, as she spoke just above the crackle of the flames. No one else made a sound; all were quickly enthralled in her tale.

"Did anyone tell you this camp was built on a Native American burial ground?"

I shivered as if an icy hand had just touched me.

69

Lexi continued, "Well, in 1830, President Andrew Jackson passed the Indian Removal Act and ordered the Cherokee to leave these mountains and walk across the country, over the Mississippi River, and all the way to what is now Oklahoma. But there were some Cherokee who decided to hide in these mountains and not follow along on what would one day become known as, *The Trail of Tears*.

Now, one of those who stayed behind was a boy named Crooked Crow. They called him Crooked Crow because he was born with a club foot and it dragged behind him as he walked. He knew he could never survive the long journey the others would be forced to endure. So, he hid in a cavern while his family and friends were led away. After hiding for days, he finally came out. For many years after that, he lived all alone and took care of the burial grounds. While doing so, he felt that he was given the protection of his ancestors. In his loneliness, he imagined they could talk to him; and so it was, that the dead kept him company.

He lived to be an old man, and when he died; his bones were left here unburied on top of his ancestors' graves. When this camp was being built, the construction crew found a few old bones. Knowing full well that they were the remains of a man, the workers tossed them aside and then bulldozed the ground, so they could build the cabins. But the bulldozing only exposed more bones. Realizing they had uncovered a Native American burial ground, they covered the graves again with fresh dirt and grew this nice green grass that we sit upon now. They built the cabins a few yards away and never told anyone what they had found; because if they had, they wouldn't have been able to build the camp."

Some of the campers shifted from where they were sitting before Lexi continued.

"I have heard that sometimes, late at night, campers have seen a shadow limping past their cabins. And they know it is Crooked Crow, still standing guard over the old burial grounds."

In the silence that followed her story, the crackling of the fire could be heard. In the distance, a deer must have stepped on a branch and the sound echoed over the campground. A shadow passed in the moonlight, a shadow of a man with a limp. The children screamed as Hank once again walked past the fire. Then the group exploded into excited chatter.

After roasting marshmallows and making S'mores, the children headed to their cabins for the night.

Brad asked me, "Would you want to take a ride down into Gatlinburg? You haven't seen much other than this camp since you've been here."

I wasn't ready to hear more of Oma's story, so I said, "Sure. That sounds nice."

The town of Gatlinburg was lit up with shops selling popcorn, ice cream, pizza, and pretzels. The streets were lined with game rooms filled with teenagers and store fronts where young couples sat on bar stools sampling a variety of moonshine. One store claimed to sell a pepper sauce made from the hottest peppers in the world. I dared Brad to put a tiny drop on a chip and touch it to his tongue. When he did, he immediately asked the salesgirl if they sold milk. She pointed to the refrigerator at the back of the store. He grabbed a small container of chocolate milk and drank it down within seconds. His mouth was still on fire as we walked through town a half hour later. He said, "I should kiss you now and share some of the pain."

I laughed, "No thank you. I'm fine just as I am. But maybe we should get some ice cream, instead."

As we walked, he pointed to a large home on a mountain that looked down on the town. There was something odd about the house. There was a light in the highest window, and yet the house was in terrible disrepair and obviously empty. It made a ghostly silhouette against the night sky.

He told me, "A few years ago, twelve people perished after some boys started a fire that ravaged that house and other homes on the mountain. A woman and her two little girls were trapped in one cabin. She called her husband who was in town with their son and told him the fire was getting closer. She said she and the girls were going to leave the house and attempt to climb higher to get away from the flames." Brad shook his head, "It took days before they were able to reach her cabin. They found a doll on the ground. A search party was formed and eventually they found their bodies. They hadn't been able to outrun the fire."

"That's horrible!"

He continued, "I was living in Pigeon Forge at the time, and we could see the sky had turned orange. There was ash falling down along the highway. Gatlinburg is still recovering. But, as they say, life must go on."

We were sitting on a bench alongside the river that ran through town when we saw a group of people staring at the store on the corner. I asked, "What are they doing?"

Brad said, "Oh, that's a Ghost Tour."

"A Ghost Tour? Are there real ghosts here?"

He laughed at me, "You see that store they are looking at? That is where the first store in Gatlinburg was built over a hundred years ago. Like the story Lexi told tonight, it was built on a burial site. But it wasn't an Indian burial ground; it was the grave of a townsman who drowned while crossing this river during a storm. In spite of that, the richest guy in town decided this was the best place to build his store. So, he promised the family of the dead guy that he'd remove the man's remains and bury him again in the cemetery. But the story is that he never really did. Instead, he only moved the headstone. Even now, people say strange things happen in that store and it's hard for the storeowner to keep employees."

"What kind of strange things?"

"Oh, like things flying off the shelves in the middle of the night. The workers come in the next morning to find a mess they have to clean up before they can even open the store again. Stuff like that."

"That's crazy!"

I looked at the store, but it didn't appear to be anything but normal. "Is there any truth to the story that Lexi told? Is the camp built on a Native American burial ground?"

He laughed, "No, not that I know of anyway. But, of course, the Trail of Tears thing is true. And there certainly were Indians who hid in the mountains when the rest were forced to leave. So, heck, you never know." He shrugged. "Across the mountains, is a town called Cherokee. It's in North Carolina and they perform a play under the stars every night which tells the whole story. It draws people from all fifty states, just to see the performance."

I was relieved to hear the story of the camp being built on a burial ground probably wasn't true. I decided to leave it at that. I had enough to keep me awake at night as it was. We drove home in silence; I was tired and started to doze off in the car.

When we got back to camp, Brad asked, "Can I walk you to the door?"

"Of course."

The night was quiet except for the sound of katydids in the trees and frogs in the stream. Surprised that I had enjoyed the evening, I said, "I had a nice time."

Brad asked, "Maybe we can do it again some time?"

"Sure. That would be nice." At that very moment, what sounded like the shrill scream of a woman came from the woods and I jumped. Brad took advantage of the moment and put his arms around me.

I asked, "What the heck was that?"

He chuckled, "Just a fox. You hear all sorts of noises in the mountains at night."

I rolled my eyes, "Great."

He smiled, "It is great, if it makes you jump into my arms like that."

He reached down and held the back of my head as he brought his lips to mine in a tender kiss.

Then he said, "See you in the morning, Jace."

I said, "Good night," and as I walked into the cabin, I thought that perhaps I had judged him too quickly. I started to think, just maybe, this distraction would end up being something good.

In the morning, Oma was waiting for me. She said, "I was thinking about the breakfasts my mother used to make for us and I want you to know I have good memories too, so I made some marmalade. I hope you like it!"

The table was laid out with bread and marmalade, sausage, cheese, and boiled eggs. I complained, "Oma, you are going to make me fat!"

Oma reminisced, "I remember how much Hans used to eat! You'd think he was a giant, but he was just a thin boy."

"Do you miss East Prussia?"

"Ja, I still miss it to this day."

"Have you ever gone back? To Germany, I mean?"

She shook her head, "No, never. When I left, there was no going back."

"What do you mean?"

"My home isn't East Prussia or even Germany anymore; after the war it became part of the Soviet Union. After you finish eating, I'll tell you more. This is a rainy day. It's a good day to tell you my story. So, when you're done, get your pad and pen, and we will get on with it."

"All right, Oma."

The breakfast was delicious, and I looked forward to a day of just staying in my pajamas. Even though it was still early in the morning, the gas fireplace was on and it made the cabin feel cozy on this gray and chilly day.

I sank into the big comfy sofa and wrapped a blanket around me. It was pouring cats and dogs outside and the sound on the roof was thunderous. Oma said, "Days like this make me miss my childhood home the most." She threw another blanket over my legs and stopped by the spinning wheel near the fire place. She ran her fingers along the old wood and spun the wheel once before taking her seat on the rocking chair.

"Let me see, where did I leave off?"

"You were telling me about giving Rebekah the cross that had been around Catrina's neck."

"Oh yes. Sometimes, I forget."

CHAPTER ELEVEN

1941

Issy loved the animals on her parents' farm, but none more than their horse, Hunter. One of her chores was to care for him. But to her, it wasn't a chore at all.

Hunter munched on hay while she brushed his coat until it was shiny. When she finished, he nudged her with his head as if to say, "Danke." Burying her face in his warm neck, she hugged him. Although he was meant to pull the plow or their wagon, her father sometimes let her ride him. It was the closest thing she had ever felt to flying. She especially enjoyed it when she rode him hard and fast, and they flew across an open field. But with all the snow on the ground, it had been months since she had been able to do so.

It wasn't even Christmas yet, but she could tell this was going to be a bad winter. The ice hanging from the barn was a testament to the frigid temperatures. Although her father had shoveled through a foot of snow for her to reach the barn, it wasn't long before the path was covered once again. It seemed they had had more snow already, in just the months of November and December, than during the entire winter last year. She patted Hunter gently and filled his stall with fresh hay. Hunter's ears perked up and a moment later, she heard her father outside trudging back towards the barn.

When he entered, he smiled at her and explained, "I was thinking I should fix that sled assembly, so I can attach it to the wagon. The snow will soon be too high for the wagon wheels." Issy's father looked tired and she knew it was because he was worrying about the war and the threats under which they lived. So, she tried to cheer him by saying, "I'll help you if you'd like."

He nodded to his daughter and was glad for her company. Together they worked through the morning and into the afternoon, repairing the old sled assembly. When they were finished, Rolf took off the old wheels and converted the wagon into a sleigh. The afternoon sun was waning when their neighbor, Friedrich Schultz, came riding up with his own wagon. He called out to Rolf, "Hey there, I was wondering if Helga could come to have a look at our boy. Vera says he won't eat, and his stomach is paining him."

Rolf answered, "Why don't you get back to your wife and son, Friedrich? I will bring Helga as soon as she is ready to leave."

An hour later, Helga climbed into the wagon with a bag full of herbs and a change of clothes just in case she had to stay the night. Issy begged, "Please can't I come with you, Mutti?"

"No Issy, it's best that you stay here."

"Oh, but I never get to go anywhere except for school and I hate school."

Helga looked at Rolf and he nodded his head, "All right then, get in Issy."

Issy was so excited that she climbed up into the back of the wagon and jumped onto the bed of hay with great exuberance. Rolf warned, "Now settle down my wild girl, we aren't going to a party. There is a sick child at the other end of this journey." Issy sobered up, "All right, Papa." As Hunter pulled their sleigh over the snow-packed road, her mood brightened again, and she thought about how lucky she was.

After all, there was no petrol to be had, so those with automobiles couldn't drive anywhere. The electricity her classmates had once enjoyed in the village, had become intermittent and unreliable at best and their houses had been difficult to heat this winter as coal became scarce. In the village, all the grocers were now out of food, so rations had become nearly impossible to find. But since she lived on a farm, she always had enough food to eat. And when they were without coal, she had wood for the fireplaces to keep her warm. Most importantly, she had Hunter and her papa's sleigh to take them anywhere they wanted to go.

She recalled the night in October, when she had been sitting next to her father on their wagon as they made their way through the village streets. They saw soldiers leaving houses with their arms laden down with radios and other household items they had confiscated. The soldiers threw them into a pile in the center of town in front of the giant clock tower. Furniture, paintings, and even books were added to the pile. They set the great stack on fire, and as a result, it became the largest bonfire Issy had ever seen. But few people stood around to watch it, most huddled unseen in their homes too afraid to walk out on the street.

Now in the sleigh, Issy unlaced her shoes a bit so that she could wiggle her toes. Remembering that their neighbor was a shoemaker, she asked her mother, "Mutti, do you think Herr Schultz could make me new shoes? I'm growing out of these." Issy was ten and a half now and growing like a weed. Bartering was becoming more popular than paying for what they needed. Since supplies of everything had become so difficult to come by as the shortage of goods spread across Germany, Reichsmarks had become almost worthless. Rolf called over his shoulder, "Ja, we will see what he can do."

They left their sleigh in the Schultzs' barn, and as they approached the house, the front door opened. Herr Schultz was anxiously awaiting their arrival and he quickly ushered them inside. He led Helga upstairs to the bedroom where his wife, Vera, was attending to their young son. For many years, Helga had helped the country women when their time came to birth their children. She was, in fact, a midwife of sorts, although she had never gone to university. What she knew, she had learned from her own mother and grandmother. But now, with no doctor in Apfeldorf, she was also called to help when someone fell ill. She had become the only medical support for many of their rural neighbors.

While Friedrich measured Issy's foot for new shoes, he and Rolf listened to his contraband radio. Issy wondered if Herr Schultz's radio might be the last radio left in Germany. Again, she thought, here was another reason living far out in the country was an advantage these days. If Herr Schultz lived in the village, surely his radio would have been burned in the bonfire. Rolf was saying, "Perhaps you can make two sets of shoes for Issy?"

Friedrich's eyes opened wider, "Such extravagance in times like these?"

"Well, the child runs wild and destroys her shoes in no time. It is best that we have two pairs for her, so there is one at the ready should she need it." But Issy knew that the second pair of shoes would do well for Rebekah who had also grown out of Issy's old shoes. In return, Rolf offered Friedrich a goat and a chicken, but Friedrich refused. "These shoes will be payment for your wife's services tonight. God help my little one!"

The announcer on the radio interrupted the music to say, "Yesterday morning, on Sunday, December 7th, 1941, The United States was attacked from the air. President Roosevelt said there was an unprovoked attack on their military base in Pearl Harbor in the Hawaiian Islands and their entire fleet has been destroyed. Stay tuned for further developments."

The men looked at each other in silence, both wondering what this meant for the war. Rolf wondered aloud, "Who attacked the United States?"

A short while later, the announcer again interrupted his program to say, "Pearl Harbor was attacked by squadrons of Japanese planes. This will surely mean war between the United States and The Empire of Japan. What remains to be seen, is if this will extend to a declaration of war against Germany." Issy listened intently, wondering what this meant for her family.

Friedrich said, "If the United States does not declare war on Germany, Hitler will surely declare war on the United States."

Rolf wasn't convinced, "Why, do you think that, Friedrich?"

Friedrich replied, "Because Hitler wants to get the Russians off of his back. He's going to think that if he declares war in unity with Japan against The United States, then Japan will finally declare war in unity with Germany against The Soviet Union."

Helga called down from Vera's bedroom, "Rolf, please take Issy home. I will stay here at least for the night. The baby is not doing well."

Rolf patted Friedrich on the back, "I'm so sorry Friedrich. But if there is anything that can be done, Helga will do it and please let me know if you hear anymore news."

Friedrich shook Rolf's hand, "No need for you to come back for Helga, I will take her home when she is done here, and I will bring the shoes."

Three days later, Friedrich brought Helga home. It was December 11th, and as Hans and Rebekah hid in the house, Rolf and Issy met him outside. Friedrich brought more news, "Germany has declared war on The United States." Rolf shook his head and helped Helga out of the wagon. He asked her, "How is the boy doing?" Helga said, "I have done all I can. It is in God's hands now."

Rolf looked straight at Friedrich, "I am really sorry. I will pray for your son."

Friedrich nodded, "The Lord has His own plans. But thank you for your prayers." Friedrich handed a parcel to Rolf, "Here are the shoes. Issy, I hope you wear them in good health."

Issy replied, "Danke, Herr Schultz."

Once in the house, Helga explained, "The child has severe

diarrhea and hasn't been able to keep anything down when he eats. I am afraid it is only a matter of days." Three days later, on December 14th, Vera's son died. Friedrich buried his child in a simple wooden box in the yard alongside the graves of his own parents.

CHAPTER TWELVE

1942

Issy was glad when the warmth of spring finally returned. She climbed onto Hunter's back and lifted the reigns. Mindful of her parents, she trotted slowly out of the barn and past the apple orchard. But once she reached the open field, she leaned down close to the horse's head and whispered, "Fly Hunter!"

The horse leapt into a full gallop and Issy's long braids whipped back from her face as Hunter flew through the open fields. When they reached the woods, he slowed down and walked the trail that wandered to the river. There was a man with a fishing pole standing by the water. Wary of whom the man might be, she whispered again to Hunter to halt. The horse's keen ears perked up at her command and instantly he came to a stop.

The man looked up at her, startled. Quickly, he turned his back toward her and faced the woods in the opposite direction. Issy followed his gaze and saw a woman and two children cowering behind a rudimentary lean-to. She could see that they were more frightened of her than she was of them. So, she called out in a friendly voice, "Hello." But still he stood there silently with a look of terror etched on his face.

Hunter quickly sensed the man's fear and started to prance forward and backward, unsure of the danger this man posed to Issy. Hunter lifted his head and whinnied, signaling a warning. Issy patted Hunter's neck and calmed the horse, "Hush, Hunter." Then addressing the man, she said, "My name is Issy. I live in the farmhouse past the apple orchard."

The man nodded as the fear slowly left his face. He introduced himself, "I am Verner Blumenthal. Please do not tell anyone you have seen me."

"What are you doing here Herr Blumenthal?"

"Issy, you seem like a nice girl. Please, keep our secret." Then he reached for his jacket and she could see the gold star that was sewn on it. She said, "You are hiding." It wasn't a question; it was a statement. She understood now.

He nodded again, "Ja. Please, do not tell. They will take us away and separate me from my family."

Issy knew better, she knew that wasn't all that they could do to him and his family. "I promise, I will not tell. Do you need anything?"

"We are fine, but danke."

Issy thought of what she could do to help them and said, "I could bring you apples."

"That would be very kind of you."

The woman and children slowly approached Issy and Hunter. The boy held a slingshot in one hand and a dead crow in the other. He was about the same age as Issy, but she had never seen him before. There was also a younger girl standing next to him. The boy said, "My name is Ezra. This is my sister, Chava."

Issy said, "I don't remember you from my school in Apfeldorf."

Ezra said, "We are not from Apfeldorf and my vater has kept us home from school for many years now."

Issy nodded sadly thinking of the massacre she had witnessed outside of her school, "That is a good."

She dismounted from Hunter and tied him to a tree. She kissed his muzzle as he whinnied again, nervous to have her leave his protection. "I'll be all right, Hunter. You stay here." Reassured, Hunter bent down to drink from the river as Issy followed Ezra to his family's camp. It was simple and crude, but it would do for now. Issy asked, "What will happen when the winter comes again?" Ezra shrugged. She watched as his mother plucked the feathers off the small bird and set it in a pot to boil along with some mushrooms and weeds. Ezra said proudly, "The crow will make a good soup for my family's dinner."

Chava reached out and shyly took Issy's hand. With a small tug, Chava said, "I miss our home. I miss my bed and my dolls." Issy's heart broke for the younger girl; she couldn't imagine being torn away from her home. Issy sat down next to Chava and Ezra as they watched the pot simmer over the open fire. She asked them, "How long have you been living in these woods?"

Ezra explained, "We move around a lot, but we left our house over a year ago. This is one of the better places we've stayed. We have shelter here, and there are plenty of fish and wild mushrooms. And sometimes, I can get a bird or squirrel with my slingshot."

Issy could feel how fragile Chava's hand felt inside her own. The child was too thin, and she had dark rings under her eyes. Again, Issy suggested, "I could bring you apples. We have a whole apple orchard by our house and I pass it on my way here."

Ezra said, "Chava would like that."

"All right, then I will bring some tomorrow."

Issy noticed their shoes. The soles of the shoes had been worn down until large holes had appeared in them. The dirty socks inside the shoes were also full of holes and dried blood caked their bare feet where their skin had been exposed to the thorns and rocks which covered the ground.

Ezra's mother took out some tin bowls and silver spoons and filled them with the thin broth that had been brewing over the fire. She offered some to Issy, but Issy shook her head, "Danke, but I have my own supper waiting for me at home." The woman nodded.

Issy felt guilty at having so much when they obviously had so little. She stood and said, "I'd better be going before my vater comes looking for me."

Issy climbed back up onto Hunter and said, "I will try to come by tomorrow." Ezra nodded, "Danke, Issy."

After school the next day, Issy took Hunter for a ride. She slowed Hunter down as they reached the apple orchard and she filled the basket which hung from the horse's neck with red and golden apples. She munched on a juicy apple as she led Hunter to Ezra's camp. But when she reached the camp, no one was there. So, she left the freshly filled basket on the ground by the cold ashes. The following day, Issy brought another basket of apples with her. At the old campsite, she found the basket she had left the day before. It was empty except for a sprig of wildflowers inside. After that, every day, Issy would bring a new basket of apples and pick up the old one. And every day, the old basket had a sprig of wildflowers inside for her. She never told anyone, not even her parents, what she was doing.

Then one day in late November, she heard gunfire coming from the woods and the sound of men shouting. An SS officer rode up to her farmhouse on his horse. Issy stood behind the doorway as the officer notified Rolf, "There are Jews hiding in these woods. If you have seen any, you must give us a complete description."

Rolf answered, "I don't know what you are talking about. I've never seen anyone hiding in these woods."

The officer watched Rolf with keen eyes and ascertained that he was telling the truth. He replied, "Very well." Then without another word, he turned on his horse and sped away.

Issy was terrified for her friends but there was nothing that she could do. The following day Issy mounted Hunter and was ready to gather another basket full of apples to leave by the river. But Rolf entered the barn and stopped her, "No more riding, Issy. It's too dangerous."

Issy begged Rolf to let her ride, but he would not give his consent. So, she reluctantly climbed down from Hunter's back. Although Issy never saw the Blumenthal family again, she often hoped and prayed they had made it safely to another part of the forest.

CHAPTER THIRTEEN

1943

Ever since the German army paraded through the village, Rolf had escorted his daughter to and from school. When the winter returned, Issy was again thankful for their sleigh. As Hunter pulled them across the ice and snow, the cool biting air whipped her cheeks. But she was warm cuddling under mounds of blankets. And her mother had heated some potatoes on the stove and placed them in two bags, one which was laid by Issy's feet and the other was held in her hands. The heat from the potatoes kept her comfortable on the ride, and later, she would eat them for her lunch.

After a long day at school, Rolf picked Issy up again and they stopped off on their way home to visit Friedrich at his shoe shop in Apfeldorf. While the village shops lined the streets on either side of the road, in the center of the ancient village was the giant clock tower which had a tunnel built into the base. The cobblestone road passed through the tunnel to the other side of town. Just a block beyond the clock tower, stood the shoe store.

A tiny bell above the shop door announced their entrance as Friedrich looked up from his work. He had a set of shiny black men's boots in front of him on his workbench and he was just attaching the new heels to the soles.

"How are you Friedrich? And how is Vera faring?"

Friedrich responded, "As well as can be expected."

Issy walked around the shop and looked at all the stylish shoes on the shelves as the men talked. She pretended to be interested in the array of shoes, but all the while, she listened closely. She had learned that if she acted like she wasn't paying attention to the men, then they were more likely to be careless with what they were saying in front of her. So, she picked up a pair of black boots and examined them closely.

She heard Friedrich say, "Hitler's army is freezing and starving to death in Russia. They've been stopped at Stalingrad and there are no more reinforcements to send to them. It seems fighting the British, the Americans, and the Soviets has depleted his army. They say General Paulus is pleading for supplies and more men, but there are none being sent. And there are hundreds of thousands, maybe even as many as a million corpses of German, Romanian, Hungarian, and Italian soldiers along the road leading to Stalingrad. Soviet forces have now crossed the frozen Volga River and surrounded the German army. With no way out, Hitler has ordered his tired, hungry, and frozen men to fight until death. They have been told that any surrender will end in their being designated as deserters, and thereby duly executed."

Rolf shook his head, "It is not surprising the Soviets are being merciless. It is a natural reaction when the path to Stalingrad has been littered with the victims of Nazi brutality. They should have thought of that first."

As the men continued their conversation in more detail, Issy hid behind a shelf and made herself as small as possible while she continued to listen.

Friedrich nodded, "Ja, they thought they were intimidating the Russians with their cruelty, but all they did was incite a thirst for revenge among the Soviets. And now Hitler has deserted his own men and left them to the mercy of their enemies."

Hearing all of this, Issy knew she had to report what she had just learned to Hans and Rebekah. The attic had become their place to speak openly about what was happening in the war around them without the adults being within earshot. So once Issy returned home, she joined Rebekah and Hans as they climbed back up to the attic and sat on the wooden floor. Before hearing what his sister had to say, Hans took a deep breath, "I am tired of hiding, Issy. I don't even fit in the space under the floor anymore. I wish this war would end. I am no longer a child, but I can't even walk outside in my own yard. This war is becoming very tiresome."

Rebekah said, "Hans, I'm glad you are here with me or else you might be in Stalingrad right now and I would be hiding here alone. But I know what you mean; I wish it would end too. I want to feel the sun on my face again." Tears of frustration came to her eyes.

Issy remarked, "Hans, I have to tell you what I heard today. The German soldiers are all but defeated in Russia; the Soviet army has surrounded and trapped them. The war *is* almost over, but what will happen to us when the Russians come across our land looking for revenge?"

Hans echoed the word, "Revenge? We haven't done anything to them. Why would they seek revenge on us?"

Issy confessed, "I do not always tell you all that I hear. Sometimes, I think I wish I did not hear some of the things our vater and Herr Schultz talk of." She shuddered, "Today, I heard papa and Herr Schultz say when the German army rolled through the Russian towns on their way to Stalingrad, they raped and murdered the citizens. They executed them and then hung their bodies along the side of the road as a warning to the other civilians. They didn't care if their victims were women and children, they didn't care if they were old or sick, they were vicious. Vater and Herr Schultz said when the Soviet Army makes its way into Germany, they will not care who is in their way, we are all Nazis to them." She thought now about her classmates that had been marched to their death by the river and knew it was time to tell both Hans and Rebekah.

"Remember that day the German army paraded through town on their way to Russia?"

"Ja"

"Well, the day before that, some German soldiers came into my school and marched the remaining Jewish children out to the river. They shot them in cold blood. I heard their screams and later, on my way home, I saw their bodies. If that is what they do to their own people, what do you think they did to their enemy?"

Hans understood. Although he was nearly seventeen, he had been so sheltered from what was going on around him that he had allowed himself to become selfishly bitter with his father for continuing to hide him in the attic. In his solitude, he had become frustrated at being confined and was only thinking of himself. He hadn't really allowed himself to think about what was happening to others outside the walls of his house.

Issy realized that it was time for them both to know all that she knew, "Hans, you could have been in Russia right now, starving to death. And Rebekah, you must understand that the Nazis have set up camps for those who are Jewish or for others who, for whatever reason, the Gestapo has decided are undesirables. There are some who say these camps are not just work camps, but death camps." She looked at Rebekah and reached out her hand to her before continuing. Rebekah grabbed onto Issy's hand and said, "Go on, I want to know what you know."

Issy whispered in a conspiratorial voice, "There are chambers where they tell the people they are going to have a shower, but instead they are locked inside as poisonous gas is added and they are left there to die, clawing over each other and into the stone walls desperately trying to breathe clean air. Others are used for medical experiments and are tortured in the name of medical advancements. The lucky ones, they say, are slowly starving and being worked to death."

Rebekah shuddered.

"I know you are both tired of staying inside this house and in this attic, but at least you are safe."

Hans' naturally pale face turned an even paler shade of white, "I didn't know."

CHAPTER FOURTEEN

1943

It was a beautiful summer day in late July and the church bells in Apfeldorf were ringing. The sky was a perfect blue and there was not a cloud in sight. As the months went by without the Soviet Army's entering East Prussia, Issy hoped that perhaps they would be spared the revenge that her father and Herr Schultz had spoken of. But whether the Russians came or not, one thing was certain, life in East Prussia was anything but normal. Issy and her mother were walking on the cobblestone streets in search of oil for their lamps. In their baskets, they carried eggs and cheese to barter with the townsfolk.

Food was still being rationed and there were long lines at designated areas where the meager provisions could be distributed, but there was never enough food for all those who stood in these lines.

As they walked, her mother asked people they passed, "Eggs and cheese for oil? Eggs and cheese for oil?"

One woman waiting in a line nodded, "I have oil, follow me."

They followed the woman through the streets to her home. Issy's shoes click-clacked on the cobblestones and almost sounded like music to her ears as she walked. The house was a handsome home painted green with an A-frame roof and yellow shutters around the windows. The green walls were crisscrossed with oak beams and there were empty wooden flower boxes under the windows. The door creaked as it was opened, and they were greeted by the cries of six small children huddled together, sitting in a circle on the bare wooden floor of the kitchen. They looked as if they might have been playing a game. But then one little boy whined as his mother entered, "We are hungry Mutti."

The woman instructed Helga and Issy, "Stay here. I will be right back."

After the woman left, one little girl picked up her baby sister and came over to Issy. The little girl's stomach grumbled with hunger. She looked in Issy's basket and asked, "Do you have any milk?"

Issy shook her head and looked toward her own mother. Helga nodded at Issy and the little girl and explained, "We do have milk, but there is none with us."

The girl said, "My little sister will only drink milk, she has no teeth to eat with yet. But there is no milk and my mutter's milk has dried up." The baby cried weakly in her arms.

The woman came back and handed Helga a stone jug with oil in it. Helga gave the woman the eggs and cheese that were in their baskets and said, "Danke, we will come back tomorrow with some milk for the baby."

The woman shook her head, "That is the last of my oil. I have nothing else to give you."

Helga assured her, "That is all right. This oil is more than enough payment."

The following day, they brought back the goat's milk. The woman poured some into a cup and Issy watched as the baby sipped listlessly. Issy worried that perhaps they were too late to save this baby, but the girl who had begged for milk yesterday said, "Danke, you saved my little sister's life." Issy hoped they had.

It occurred to Issy that the despondency she had seen on the faces of the villagers on the streets, had not adequately shown her how bad things were. It wasn't until she saw inside this bare home and heard the moans of these hungry children that she had fully comprehended the suffering that was growing in Apfeldorf. People were starving.

As she was walked back through the streets, she heard a man yell, "Hamburg has been bombed! Thousands are dead!"

Another man asked, "Dead soldiers?"

The first man shook his head, "Nein! Citizens. Women and children. The city is on fire. There is an awful storm raging and the winds are powerful and strong. The flames are spreading across the city. Everything is gone." The first man was sobbing now in disbelief, "The shipyards, the train yards, the houses, churches, and the schools, all gone!"

In the days that followed, Herr Schultz confirmed what the man had said. Over 40,000 civilians, many who were just trying to survive this war, were believed to have been killed in two British attacks on Hamburg in the last days of July 1943. Issy worried and asked her father, "Will they bomb us too?"

"No, mein liebling, we are too far for them to reach. The bombs are heavy, and the British planes cannot carry enough fuel to reach this far to the east and then still have enough fuel for their return trip."

She asked, "What about the Soviet aeroplanes?"

Rolf, surprised by his daughter's question, just shook his head. He had no more words of reassurance for her. She knew the time was growing closer now. The Soviet army had finally defeated the German army in Stalingrad and the eastern front of Hitler's war was crumbling. His army was retreating in spite of his orders to continue fighting. On the other hand, the Americans were sending reinforcements to England to join efforts to attack Germany from the west and it seemed that eventually, Germany would be crushed from both sides. The German army in North Africa had met its final defeat in May of 1943 and Italy itself was on the verge of surrender. It was only a matter of time until the allied armies found their way to her front door.

CHAPTER FIFTEEN

JUNE 1944

It had been four years since Rebekah had come to live in Issy's house. All of this time, she lived without feeling the warmth of the sun on her face. Issy couldn't remember the last time she had seen her friend smile. She was tired of waiting for this war to end and tired of feeling guilty that she could go out in the sun, but Rebekah couldn't. She thought perhaps, if they were careful and if they only went out for just a few minutes, maybe Rebekah would smile again. It was Issy's 13th birthday and a warm June afternoon in 1944 when the girls decided it was time to take a chance.

They came down from the attic to Issy's room where they retrieved Catrina from her cradle. Then they descended to the kitchen and Issy casually asked her grandmother, "Where are Mutti and Papa?" Oma was busy whirling thread on her spinning wheel and wasn't really paying attention to them. Distractedly, she said, "Your mutter isn't feeling well, and she is taking a nap. Your vater just went up to check on her."

With that, the two exchanged sly smiles and without Oma's noticing, they climbed out the large low-hung kitchen window. Outside, they ran quickly past the well and across the apple orchard until they reached the chicken coop. Rebekah waited there while Issy retrieved a horse blanket from the barn and laid it on the ground. The girls sat down and felt the sun heat their faces through the open slats of the roof.

Rebekah lay down on the horse blanket and stretched her arms and legs out as far as she could. It felt glorious and she giggled as Issy stretched out next to her. They stared up at the wooden roof of the large chicken coop. Issy could just make out the shapes of the clouds as they passed between the slats of wood. Then she sat up, holding Catrina's soft body in her arms. She wrapped the doll's blanket tighter around Catrina until only her perfect porcelain face peeked out. Oma had made the new brown blanket for the doll from her spun yarn. Rebekah asked, "May I hold her for a while?"

"Ja, of course, here you can take her." Rebekah cradled the doll and examined Catrina closely as she held her in her arms, "She is just so perfect. She's not afraid of anything and she knows she is loved and safe." Rebekah hugged the doll and kissed her painted face.

Issy wished she could find the words that would make Rebekah feel safe, but she knew there were no words that could allay her fears. Rebekah hadn't seen her parents since they had been taken away four years ago. There had been no word from them, or of them, and no one knew if they were still alive. As time went by, more and more horror stories had reached Issy's ears about life and death in the concentration camps. Now, at thirteen years old, she was more aware then ever of the dangers that surrounded them. But in spite of that knowledge, she still held onto hope as children often do.

"Someday" Issy said, "I'm going to sail to America. I want to see what it is like to live in a free land."

"I will come with you, Issy. We will go together and, of course, we will take Catrina with us."

"Ja, we will. And we will also take Oma and my parents and Hans." Then Issy added quietly, "And, perhaps we will find your parents and Opa after this war ends and they can come too." Rebekah smiled as she continued to listen to Issy and pictured this unlikely future.

Seeing her friend smile, Issy expanded on the dream they had talked so often about, "We will live next door to each other, and someday, you will marry Hans and become my real sister."

Rebekah blushed, "Oh, I don't know about that."

Issy stood and moved one of the chickens from its nest. She made a bed in the hay for her doll. "Rebekah, you can lay Catrina down here when you want." Rebekah placed the doll into the makeshift cradle.

Issy wiped the sweat off of her neck and complained, "It's so hot and I'm so thirsty!" The girls peeked out of the chicken coop to see if the way was clear. "Do you think we could make it to the well without being seen?" Rebekah asked.

"If we are quick about it, we should be fine. Oma is probably asleep by now."

Deciding it was indeed safe, they ran together holding hands and stifled their giggles as they cranked the handle until the bucket was lowered. It filled with water and then they raised it to the top once again. Using the ladle which was always kept at the side of the well, they poured some water over each other's heads and then took deep sips. In their amusement, they forgot the risk of being discovered and for a moment giggled loudly. This was followed immediately by clamping their hands over their mouths as if they could quiet the giggles that had already escaped.

Issy said, "We'd better get Catrina and go back inside the house before someone notices we are gone."

Rebekah pleaded, "No Issy, just a little bit longer. We can hide in the chicken coop. Please, no one will notice we are gone."

Seeing how much a few more moments meant to Rebekah, Issy agreed, "All right, but we can't stay too long, besides, we left Catrina there anyway."

They ran back across the apple orchard to the chicken coop and Issy was just picking up Catrina when Rolf's shadow blocked their path to the doorway.

Fear at the danger the girls had put themselves in by coming outside in broad daylight caused his anger to flare. With the escalation of the war and knowing that the Soviet army was on the move toward them, Rolf was cracking under the pressure. His face was contorted as he demanded in a measured and threatening tone, "What are you girls doing?"

Neither girl could speak for the fear that clutched them. Issy backed away from her father while holding Catrina. Rolf crossed the space which separated them and reached for the doll. In his anger, he threw Catrina to the ground and instantly, two cracks appeared on her porcelain face.

Issy cried out, "Catrina!" but she was too afraid of her father to move.

Rolf's anger blinded him to his daughter's cry, "You think we hide Rebekah in our house for no reason? There are German soldiers, deserters, survivors of the battles in Russia swarming our roads, and believe me, the Soviets will not be far behind them. Earlier this week, the United States landed troops in France, they are on the ground in Europe now."

Issy shuddered with fear as Rolf went on, "The closer they get, the easier it is for them to reach us with bombs and artillery. If the Gestapo doesn't find Rebekah first and put her in a concentration camp and the rest of us in prison, and if we are all lucky enough to live to see the end of this war, then we will be left to the mercy of the Soviet army. And believe me, we will find no mercy with them."

As the words spilled out of his mouth, Rolf knew he was not only saying them to the girls, but to himself as well. Although he knew he had already said too much, he could not stop himself from continuing. The stress and fear had overwhelmed him for far too long. He had no way of knowing that Issy was already aware of the risk she and Rebekah had decided to take. So, he explained, "The Soviet army will not come here looking to liberate us. They will come here to kill us. They do not care if you are Jewish or Christian, to them you are German, and to them all Germans are Nazis. They hate us all for what the German army did to the Russian people. They are coming sooner, rather than later, and yet we are still being ordered by der Führer to stay here and wait for them." Rolf finally stopped talking as he regained his composure and saw the terror on Issy's and Rebekah's faces. He became disgusted with himself for frightening the girls and as he looked at the broken doll on the ground, he collapsed next to it as if in shock.

Shaking, Issy hugged her father, "Please, Papa, please, get up and come into the house with us. We will be good. Rebekah won't go outside anymore."

He reached for the doll and handed it back to Issy and said softly, "I'm sorry mein liebling." He pulled her onto his lap and hugged her, almost crushing her in his arms. Rebekah stood next to them trembling with fear. Rolf pulled her into his arms as well and held onto both girls. When he finally released them, Rebekah stood up first. She reached her hand down toward Issy and helped her friend to stand. Then both girls reached down to help Rolf.

Rolf stood and took a ragged breath. He hugged them both once again and said, "Go inside now, I will be there in a minute."

But it was a long time before Rolf joined them. By the time he came back into the house, the sun was already down, and the sound of crickets filled the night's air. His dinner was cold on the table when he finally sat down to eat.

Having already finished their meager meal, Issy and Rebekah sat once again on the attic floor with Hans. They told him what Rolf had said to them and what had happened in the chicken coop. Hans reprimanded them, "Well, you shouldn't have gone out. You should be more careful, Rebekah."

Hans often spoke with his father now about the war. He didn't want to be kept in the dark any longer. After all, he was a grown man now.

Rebekah asked him as she had a hundred times before, "Do you think my parents are dead, Hans?"

Gently he said, "Ja, Rebekah, more than likely they are. But you must already know that by now and you still have us." He put his arm around her to comfort her.

Rebekah looked at him and knew he was telling her the truth, "Will we die, Hans? Will the Russians kill us?"

He answered honestly, "I hope not."

Issy looked at the cracked face of her doll, and a stubborn determination came over her, "We will not die. We will go to America as we planned. We will take Catrina with us and we will fix her there."

Rebekah nodded; it was her turn now to act, and so she pretended she believed this dream of theirs was still possible.

CHAPTER SIXTEEN

1944

O rdinarily, the doll would have been sent to Nuremberg to have her head replaced, but all the toy factories had long ago been turned into munitions factories, and now most of those had been destroyed by bombs and heavy aircraft artillery. So, Catrina lay untouched in Issy's bedroom in her cradle. Issy was afraid to even lift her, afraid the cracks in her head would spread and completely shatter her face.

Every German knew by the end of August that the war was lost for them. Still, they were not allowed to say so out loud. On the last few days of August, Königsberg was bombed. There was a huge loss of life as people were instantly incinerated in the historic center of the city. The quarters of Altstadt, Löbenicht and Kneiphof were completely reduced to rubble. The bombs destroyed the Dom Cathedral, the castle, all the churches in the city, both the old and the new universities, and the entire warehouse district.

The Brummels and Rebekah watched the distant tower of smoke fill the air. Although they were 40 kilometers from Königsberg, the air turned acrid as the black cloud blew in their direction. They all understood that if the British and American bombers could reach Königsberg, then now they could reach them as well. The fear was so real they could taste it. But they were still forbidden to leave their homes without its being seen as desertion.

Issy continued to perform her chores as usual. She brushed Hunter and cooed soothing words to him, "You are my beauty." Then she fed him an apple she had picked up on her way to the barn. She spoke to him as if he could answer her, "I wish there was something I could do to cheer up Rebekah. I know she is lonely for her parents and her Opa." Hunter raised his head as if he understood. She continued, "If only I could brush her worries away, like I brush the flies from your coat." Suddenly, she heard a movement in the hayloft at the top of the barn. She stood stock still, listening intently. A moment later, Issy heard a moan. Someone was up there.

Issy quietly put down the brush and looked around the barn for a weapon. She found her father's axe, but as she tried lifting it, she realized the iron head made it too heavy for her to wield. Next, she found a walking stick that Oma sometimes used to help keep her steady on the uneven ground. Issy picked it up and moved toward the ladder which led to the hayloft. As she walked, the goats parted for her to pass.

Like a ghost, she ascended the ladder. But she stopped when she heard another moan. It took her a while to move again; her legs were trembling and threatening to collapse underneath her. She commanded them to move up just one more rung on the ladder. When she neared the top, she adjusted her grip on the walking stick to get better leverage should she need to use it. She peeked above the hay on the floor to see a man lying on his side, facing her. It only took a moment for Issy to recognize him. She remembered him clearly from the night that Rebekah came to hide in their house. It was the same captain who had asked her to read Faust, it was the same captain who had ordered his men to search her house, it was the same captain who then smiled at her and told her that he had a daughter about her age, and it was the same captain who had thrown a sprig of edelweiss to her as the German army marched toward Russia.

His gray eyes watched her as she raised herself onto the floor of the hayloft and stood above him holding the walking stick over her head. Then he said, "Hello, my friend. I see you have grown up while I was away." He was a bit surprised to see the vision before him. Issy's hair was free of its braids and formed a wild mess around her face, but it did not hide her striking beauty. Her angry eyes flashed at him and a warm pink color tinted her naturally fair skin.

He moved his right hand away from the left side of his stomach to reveal a huge blood stain that had soaked his jacket. He continued, "You have nothing to fear from me, my little friend. As you can see, I am injured and in no shape to harm you. Not that I would if I could."

Issy asked him, "What are you doing here?"

He tried to smile, but winced in pain. "I would have knocked on your door, but I was afraid your vater would shoot me and finish the job for the Russians. So, instead, I climbed up here to rest before I continue on with my journey. I didn't wish to disturb your family. I thought I would be gone by now, but I am weaker than I thought, and I can't seem to get to my feet."

Issy didn't trust him. She looked him over carefully, "Do you have a weapon?"

He showed her the empty palms of his hand and said, "I do." He pointed to his leg and Issy saw the glint of metal. She was afraid to approach him, but was also afraid to ask him to touch his own weapon. He could easily turn it on her rather than discarding it. He could see her indecision, so moving very slowly and very carefully, he took the revolver from his pant leg and pushed it toward her across the hay-covered floor. She bent down without taking her eyes off of him. Then she dropped the walking stick to pick up the gun. Aiming it at the captain, Issy questioned him again, "Do you have a knife?"

His eyes widened, "You really are a very surprising young lady." He then took the knife that was hidden in his boot and slid it gently to her as well.

She kicked the knife and walking stick toward the wall as she backed away from him and called out the window to her father, "Papa, there's someone in the barn!"

Rolf crossed the yard as quickly as his old injury would allow. He had no weapon with him, so he reached for the discarded axe as he entered the barn. When he saw Issy standing in the hayloft holding a gun, he felt his heart in his throat and climbed quickly to the top. Upon seeing the man lying there, he stood between the two of them and said, "Well done, Issy."

He could tell right away that the Captain was severely injured. "Hand me the gun Issy and go back in the house and tell Mutti what you have found here. Tell her to bring whatever is needed to treat a gunshot wound."

Issy ran to the house and burst through the door. Hans, Rebekah, and Helga looked up in surprise from where they were sitting by the fireplace. "Mutti, the German Captain, the one who came to search our house for Rebekah, he is in the barn. He's been shot. Papa said you should bring your medical supplies." Helga sprang into action and collected bandages and hydrogen peroxide and a small sharp knife. She said, "Issy, go fill this bucket with water and heat it on the stove until it boils, then put the knife into the water and clean it well. When you are done, bring the knife to me."

Oma came out of her bedroom as Helga left for the barn. Oma asked, "What is going on?"

Issy said, "Remember the German Captain from the night that Rebekah came to live here? Well he's in the barn. He's injured, and Papa thinks it's a gunshot wound."

Oma nodded, "Very well." She pulled out a small bottle from her apron pocket, "Here take this, Helga, he might need it."

Hans' eyes widened in surprise to see his grandmother holding a bottle of whisky, at the sight he exclaimed, "Oma!"

She shrugged her shoulders, "So what? I am an old woman, and it helps me with my aches and pains."

When Issy had finished boiling the water she sterilized the knife as her mother had instructed. Then she brought the knife and bottle of whiskey to the barn. Helga approved of the whiskey, she took the bottle and handed it to the captain. She ordered him, "Drink." He drank the whole bottle down in an instant. Then Issy watched as her mother cleaned the wound with the hydrogen peroxide. Even with the whiskey, the Captain winced as the antiseptic bubbled up on the open wound. With care, Helga examined her patient. She could see the bullet had shattered when it hit near his hip bone and split into several small pieces. She gave the captain a piece of wood to bite down on as she retrieved the bullet and its fragments as best as she could with the sterilized knife. She then stitched his torn flesh back together with a needle and thread. Finally, she doused the wound with more hydrogen peroxide and bandaged him up.

When she was finished he said, "Danke, Frau Brummel."

Rolf instructed, "Issy, go get the Captain some water, a chunk of buttered bread and a blanket."

Issy brought the food to the barn and left it by the Captain's side. It seemed that he had passed out after all. When she left the barn with her parents, she asked, "What will we do with him, Papa?"

"We will feed him and care for him until he is well enough to leave."

"But what if he finds Rebekah and Hans in the house?"

"He won't say anything, Issy. He is a deserter and is only trying to get back home to his own family. He won't give us any trouble. This war is over for him."

She said, "I wish the war was over for us as well."

Her father replied, "It will be soon enough, Issy. One way or another."

The Captain stayed in the barn for a month. One morning, Issy went to the barn to do her chores and she found him gone. But he had left something for her. It was an old blood-stained and frayed copy of Franz Kafka's *The Metamorphosis*. Inside, he had written a note to her on the first page.

Dear Issy,

There are those of us who are monsters on the outside, but who are not so on the inside, and vice versa. We all struggle between how we see ourselves and how we are perceived by others. Please forgive me.

Captain Hugo Breitstadt

Issy brought the book into the house and put it on her shelf. Although Hans had quite a selection of books, her own shelf of books was comprised solely of her school books. No one had ever thought to give her a book as a present. She stood looking at it thoughtfully for a few moments and then took it down from the shelf again. She sat on her bed and started to read. *"One morning, when Gregor Samsa woke from troubled dreams, he found himself transformed in his bed into a horrible vermin."*

CHAPTER SEVENTEEN

JANUARY 1945

T he bombs continued to fall across Germany throughout the rest of 1944 and into the beginning of 1945. It was mid-January 1945 when Rolf returned from a visit with Friedrich and Vera. Issy sat unnoticed, as he addressed Helga, "Friedrich says that Vera is close to her due date and is hoping you will go to her when her time comes."

"Ja. Of course. Poor dear."

Rolf agreed, "This is no time to be bringing a child into the world. We heard on the British radio broadcast that although der Führer continues his demands for us all to stand strong and not leave our homes defenseless, the war is all but over and that the Soviets are on our doorstep."

Helga stood there with raw dough on her hands and asked, "Well then Rolf, when will it be time to leave?"

"I think we should all pack our bags and be ready, just in case."

"Ja, I think you are right." Helga called the children into the kitchen, "Each of you, go pack a suitcase. Not so much that it is too heavy to carry on your own back if it comes to that. Only what you need."

Issy asked, "Are we leaving? Where are we going?"

Helga said, "We are getting prepared to leave. I do not know when, but the time is coming, and we must be ready."

Helga told Issy and Rebekah, "First bring your warmest woolen dresses to the kitchen. Oma will sew silver coins and spoons into the lining." She told the girls, "When you leave, you wear these dresses." After bringing the dresses to Oma, Issy and Rebekah went to their room and packed their bags. Since the girls wore the same clothes, they could share what was packed in either satchel, so they divided them evenly. As the girls had grown, and with the shortage of cloth, Issy's clothes had been extended until neither girl could possibly fit in them anymore. Recently, Helga had taken her own clothes and tailored them to fit the girls since they were now almost as tall as she. Issy closed her bag and then looked at Catrina in the cradle. She opened it again and hid the doll gently between the folds of clothes. As a last thought, she also took the book off of the shelf that the Captain had given her and hid it in her bag as well.

That night, Issy and Rebekah lay side-by-side in Issy's bed and listened to the sound of the wind whipping through the bare branches of the apple trees outside. The chill seemed to come right through the walls of the house, so the girls hugged each other for warmth. Issy recited the plans they had spoken of many times over the past five years as if they were a prayer, "We will walk to the west. We will find your family. We continue to walk until we find a ship that will take us to America. When we get there, Papa will find work and we will all be safe."

Rebekah did not reply; she only listened in silence.

The sounds of Rolf's violin softly filled the house and a sense of peace came over Issy to hear her father play. All could not be so terrible if her father was playing his violin. Rebekah soon fell into a deep sleep, but Issy continued to stare up at the ceiling of her bedroom. The night might be cold outside, but they were still warm within the walls of her parents' farm house. Whatever was to come, there was nothing to gain by worrying about it now. Instead she wanted just to concentrate on this moment and on the sound of her father's violin. She listened also to the sound of Rebekah's even breaths. Issy's heavy eyelids soon closed and although it was hours later, it seemed to her that she had just fallen asleep when she heard the banging on the door.

The loud knocking woke the entire household. Rolf appeared at Issy's bedroom doorway and ordered Rebekah to join Hans in the attic. Rolf made his way down to the front door with Issy following close behind him. Oma appeared downstairs in her bedroom doorway and pulled her robe tightly around her body. The cold had stiffened her joints and the fear at hearing the loud knock on the door at dawn had caused her to move quicker than she should have. She lifted her hand to hold her head to still the dizziness that had been caused by her quick actions. Rolf opened the door cautiously to see Friedrich standing there. Issy heard Herr Schultz say, "It's Vera's time."

Rolf nodded, "Issy, go fetch Mutti."

Helga dressed in her warmest coat and boots and climbed onto the wagon that Herr Schultz had brought with him. Before he left, he told Rolf, "I am afraid the Soviets are almost here. You should prepare your family to leave today."

Rolf nodded and locked the door behind them and then crossed the room and stoked the fire into a blaze. He called Hans and Rebekah to come down from the attic and told them all, "Take these sacks and fill them with eggs, bread, cheese, and potatoes. Take all that will fit and don't forget to pack the tin cups. Mutti has gone to the Schultzs' to help Vera because the time has come for her child. We will be leaving as soon as she returns."

"But Vater," Hans reasoned, "the roads are covered in snow and ice. The wagon will not make it far through this snow."

"Ja, Hans, come with me, we will put the sled assembly onto the wagon." As the men walked to the barn, Issy watched from the door. She saw Hans stop for a moment and tilt his head up to feel the snowflakes as they landed on his face. She realized how long it had been since he had been outside. Even the bonfires on the Epiphany once a year had stopped after 1940. Issy left Rebekah and Oma to fill the sacks and, instead, followed the men into the barn. Hans helped Rolf lift the empty wagon off of the wheels and then fastened the sled assembly to it.

When they had finished, Rolf attached two goats to the wagon on leads and then instructed Hans, "Hitch Hunter to the wagon. Issy, pack sacks of oats and hay for Hunter and the goats. Also fill a sack with apples." When Hans asked, "Don't you think the goats will slow us down?" Rolf explained, "With the goats, we will have milk to drink if nothing else. Water will freeze."

When they were done, Hans, Rolf, and Issy loaded the wagon and then left it in the barn. When they returned to the kitchen, they saw that Oma had placed bacon, cheese, and bread on the table. Rolf ordered the children, "Sit and eat. Fill your bellies for the journey."

Hans asked, "But where are we going, Vater?"

"We are going northwest toward Königsberg and from Königsberg to the Vistula Spit. We will go to Pillau to see if there are any boats leaving. If not, then we will continue on to Gotenhafen."

Hans asked, "But Königsberg is destroyed. Why are we going there?"

"It is the straightest road to take us where we want to go. We will approach it with care and see for ourselves. If we cannot stop there, we will continue on until we find a place where we can stop."

Issy asked, "Where will the boat take us?"

"We will get on a boat and cross the Baltic Sea to safety, perhaps in Denmark. Friedrich said there are refugee camps being set up there." Rolf took out a map and showed Hans the way.

Hans pointed to the map, "Vater, how will we cross the channel at the spit?"

Rolf said, "It will be frozen over. That is about the only advantage to these freezing temperatures."

Hans pointed to the map, "Vater, that is such a narrow strip of land that leads from Pillau to Gotenhafen, won't we be trapped with the sea on both sides of us and nowhere to run in case the aeroplanes come?"

"It is the only way, Hans. Everything else has been cut off by the Soviet army and their allies." He pointed to the rest of Germany on the map, "The Soviets are east, south, and west of us already. This is the only route left to take. I have been planning this for a long time. If anything happens to me, Hans, you must take the family northwest till you reach the sea and then find a boat to cross the Baltic." Rolf folded the map and with a pen he wrote down the address for his brother, Peter, on the cover and then returned it again to his pocket. He explained, "When we get to safety, we will send a letter to my bruder and secure passage to America."

At the suggestion that something might happen to her father, Issy started to cry. She hugged Rolf and he held her close. "You must be my brave girl now, Issy. Just like you were when you found the Captain in the barn. We will try our best to stay together, but if we are separated, we will meet in Pillau. Do you understand?"

Through her tears, she said, "Ja, I understand Papa."

"Remember the English you have learned. It will help you speak to people who are not like us."

With that, he took down the two bolt action rifles from above the fireplace and loaded five bullets into each of them. They had only just finished eating when they heard a commotion outside. Rolf handed one of the rifles to Hans and then waved to him. He pointed to the stairs and quietly told them all to go up to the attic. Issy kissed Oma on her cheek. The old woman sat down by the hearth and picked up her knitting as if the world was not shattering around them.

In the attic, Hans told the girls to hide under the floor while he sat on a chair just inside the attic door and waited. Through the floor below them, the girls listened for any sounds they might be able to hear.

They heard the door open and it was immediately followed by the sound of gunshots, and then, terrifyingly so, utter silence. Issy wanted to run down the stairs, but she knew she must remain absolutely still. All the rest of that day and through the night, they waited in the cold attic for Rolf to call to them or for the Soviet soldiers to open the attic door and discover them. Finally, the next morning dawned without either happening. Hans instructed the girls to follow closely behind him, and without a sound, they walked down the stairs to the kitchen.

The first one they saw was Oma. She was slumped in her rocking chair, the spinning wheel turned on its side. While her hands remained motionless, they still held her knitting needles. Lifting the barrel of his rifle before him, Hans slowly turned the corner to have a better view of the front door. Issy and Rebekah held onto each other as their eyes took in the carnage in front of them. Rolf lay in a pool of blood beside the wooden table. Two Russian soldiers, one middle-aged and one as young as Hans, had collapsed just inside of the house and the door was still open to the outside. Snow mixed with blood and covered the bodies of the men and the wooden planks of the kitchen floor. The fire in the hearth had been blown out by the wind and the chill pervaded the house. Hans went to his father first and verified that Rolf was indeed dead. Then Hans checked the soldiers, there were no signs of life. He took the rifles from their frozen hands and unclipped their bullet cartridges from their belts.

Already knowing it was too late for his grandmother, Hans walked back toward Oma anyway and checked for a pulse, but there was none. Once again, he returned to his father's body and this time, searched Rolf's pocket. Hans took out the map and placed it inside his own shirt.

All this time, Issy stood motionless. Shock setting in at first, until Rebekah started to cry. Then taking the blanket that was still clasped around her body for warmth, Issy fell on the floor next to her father and desperately tried to sop up the blood that had pooled and started to freeze around his body as she repeatedly sobbed, "No Papa, no Papa."

Hans spoke calmly, "Girls, put on your coats and your shoes. Then we will go to the Schultzs' to find Mutti."

Issy cried and looked around the room desperately, "Where's Papa's violin? We must take it!" Hans saw it before she did. It was on the floor next to Oma and it had been shattered to pieces by a bullet. "Oh no!" Issy sobbed, distraught at the sight of the broken instrument that her father loved so much.

Hans tried to imitate his father's authoritative tone, "Issy! We cannot wait. There may be more soldiers. We have to leave now! Get those sacks we filled with food then put on your shoes and coats. Let's go." Hans carried all four rifles to the wagon that was still hidden in the barn. He tied two more ropes to it for the girls to hold onto so they would not get separated from the wagon as the sky was filled with snow and sleet.

Hans looked through his father's bag and found a pouch of money and his father's hunting knife. He opened his own bag and among his books, he hid the pouch of money and put the knife in his boot. Then he took the bags that had belonged to his father and Oma out to lighten the wagon. Finally, he buried three of the rifles under blankets and slung the fourth over his shoulder. At the last minute, he grabbed a couple of chickens, put them in a crate covered with chicken wire, and placed it in the wagon. The girls held onto the ropes as he led Hunter to the road which led to the Schultzs' home.

CHAPTER EIGHTEEN

1945

At first, when Friedrich opened the door, he didn't recognize any of his visitors. Then he realized the young blonde girl was Issy. She was crying, her hair was soaked, and her cheeks were raw from the cold. There was also blood smeared over her clothes and mittens. He asked, "Issy, what has happened?" But the girl did not answer. Instead the young man with her said, "Herr Schultz, I am Hans, Issy's bruder. Russian soldiers came to our house and killed Vater and Oma. We are here for our mutter." Friedrich was taken aback. There was so much about this encounter that didn't seem right, but he couldn't get past the word "killed" to even try to understand the rest.

Friedrich repeated the word, "Killed?"

"Ja, the soldiers came and Vater told us to hide. Then we heard the gunshots and when we came down, they were all dead, Vader, Oma, and the soldiers."

Friedrich looked past them and saw their wagon by his barn. Shaken and aware of imminent danger, he told them, "Come, come in." He had remembered Hans from when he was a little boy, but he, like all the other neighbors and acquaintances of Rolf and Helga, had thought Hans was in America. Rolf had never told him that Hans was still in the house. Friedrich locked the door behind them and asked, "Are there more soldiers, Hans?"

"Not that I have seen, but we heard tanks in the distance as we made our way here."

Then Friedrich glanced at Rebekah and it took a moment longer for him to recognize her, "Rebekah?"

She nodded.

Friedrich remembered the night the little Jewish girl went missing. The German soldiers had also come to his house looking for her. With relief he said, "Ah, you escaped. I knew your vater, Samuel, well. He was a good man."

Rebekah cringed at the word "was."

There was a movement behind Friedrich, Helga was standing on the stairs. She had overheard the words that had been exchanged. She stood there in a daze, not quite focusing on the scene in front of her. Issy broke away from the group and ran to her mother, "Mutti! Papa and Oma! The soldiers, they killed them!" Issy's whole body shook as she held onto her mother and finally Helga woke from her trance. Helga hugged her daughter as she came back to her senses. She reached her arm out toward Hans and Rebekah and they climbed the stairs toward her. She wrapped her arms around the three children and held them for a desperate moment. She knew that there was nothing she could do for her husband or his mother, but she had to think now what to do for her children. They were out of time.

Hans spoke up, "Mutter, we have to go. Vater told us to pack the wagon and to head toward Königsberg. Your bags are on the wagon, let us go now."

She wanted nothing more than to flee, but she shook her head, "No Hans. We cannot go yet. Vera and the baby cannot travel. She is weak and has lost a lot of blood and the baby is too small." Hans tried to protest, but his mother silenced him before she continued. "We will wait a day or two to make sure they can travel. We will all stay here, together."

Friedrich helped Hans and the girls hide the wagon and put the animals in the barn. When Friedrich saw the chickens, he slaughtered them and brought them into the house. "Helga, cook these chickens. There may not be a place to cook them while we are traveling and the cold will keep them."

Helga slept in Vera's room with Vera and the baby that night. Rebekah and Issy slept in the spare bedroom and the men remained downstairs ready to defend the women and children if it came to that.

The next day, Hans and Friedrich stacked the Schultzs' wagon with their belongings. Helga handed them more blankets to pack, saying, "We will never have enough of these for the journey."

When darkness approached, they sat around the radio listening to the broadcasts. On the BBC radio station, they heard the announcer urge, "The war is over, Hitler has lost. His own men are deserting him. Lay down your weapons and surrender."

Still, in spite of everything, on the German broadcast channel, the announcer still promised a victory and warned its citizens to continue the fight or be treated as traitors. Hans and Friedrich could hear aeroplanes above them, flying west, and knew they were Soviet planes. They also knew that there were already Soviet tanks on their roads. Friedrich said, "We will leave tomorrow."

Helga protested, "But your wife and son are not ready yet for such a journey."

Friedrich answered, "I know." He was fully aware of the risks they would be taking by trying to flee in subzero temperatures in an active war zone. But he also knew that staying where they were, was no longer an option.

The following morning Friedrich and Hans were in the barn when they heard the women scream.

CHAPTER NINETEEN

PRESENT DAY

I looked outside and saw the rain hitting the glass door. I couldn't see the mountains or even the railing of the deck that stood just feet away from where I sat at the kitchen table. The gray day matched the mood in the room. I tried to imagine how Oma felt, being a child and having to leave behind everything she knew. How could she have handled losing her father and grandmother in such a violent way and at such a tender age? I pulled the afghan closer around me.

Her loss reminded me of my own loss. There had been times when it felt as if a pile of bricks were crushing my chest, making it difficult to breathe. Difficult to move. And yet, I couldn't deny that lately, there had been whole days without a thought about Brian. But then the guilt would settle in again, and I would berate myself for having forgotten him, even for such a short time. I was learning that the pain of loss could be buried, but it never quite disappeared. It existed ominously just under the surface, ready to be uncovered at any moment.

The guilt over living with momentary lapses of grief, piled on top of the guilt at causing his death, was suffocating. But placing my own sorrows aside, seeing my grandmother relive the pain from her own childhood, made me feel protective of her, and that somehow helped me to deal with my own loss.

"Oma, perhaps we should eat something. Let me make a meal for you." My grandmother was lost in her reverie and so she simply nodded her head. I opened her refrigerator and saw she had taken out some pork chops. There was applesauce and salad. That would do. As I prepared our meal, I kept an eye on her. The story was taking its toll on her, but I could tell it was a story she needed to tell. I hoped it would help her to purge it from her life. That was what this really was, a purging. I only hoped that at the end, she felt relieved of the burdens she had been carrying for so long.

I turned the gas fireplace on and the red glow of the flames warmed the room. In spite of filling our bellies and the warmth of the hearth, I was becoming more and more afraid to hear what was coming next.

She grabbed my hand, "You know, Jace, there have been so many times when I have wondered if I could have done one thing differently, maybe they wouldn't have had to die. If I had asked if we could all go to the Schultzs' house with my mutter, would they have left? If I had gone down to the kitchen immediately after the shooting, could I have saved them?"

"I know Oma. I understand."

She nodded sadly, "Ja, I know you do. But please, Jace, let's continue."

"Are you sure, Oma? This can wait until tomorrow."

"Nein, it can't. I need to get through this next part."

This was really frightening me. After all, I wondered, how much worse could the story get? Her father and grandmother had been killed while she hid in the attic of her house with her brother and friend. At thirteen, she was forced to leave the only home she had ever known and was made to strike out into a terrifying world in subzero temperatures. But she was insistent on continuing so I said, "All right." I put the dishes in the sink and returned to the table again.

Perhaps I was stalling, but I said, "Oma, I remember you had a dog when I was little. What was her name?"

She smiled, "Sassy, and she lived up to every bit of her name."

I laughed, "Yes, I remember you couldn't leave anything on the counter because if you did, she'd get it. In fact, one time you had bought chocolate chip cookies for me and I remember we had just opened the box and I had only had one. I must have left them on the kitchen table when I went outside. When I came back, all that was left was crumbs."

Oma took a deep breath; it was good to see her smiling. She said, "I remember that. We found her in the middle of the mess and she looked around like she was trying to find the culprit. Ha! Those big brown eyes, they helped her get away with a lot of mischief."

"She was a German Shepard, right?" Oma nodded. An idea was forming in my brain. "Oma, maybe we should get you another dog? Wouldn't you like the company?"

She said, "I don't know. I'm not sure I'm up to caring for another living creature. Besides, any dog will surely outlive me, and then what would become of it?"

"What if I stayed, Oma? What if I made this my home?"

She perked up, "Nothing would make me happier, Jace. But I don't want you to do it on my account. I only want you to make that decision if it is the right one for you."

"Okay, we'll table this discussion for now. Let's give it the rest of the summer, then we'll talk again."

"All right. Now settle down so we can continue."

"Yes, Oma." But I really wished I didn't have to hear any more.

CHAPTER TWENTY

1945

While Hans and Friedrich were in the barn, the front door of the Schultzs' house burst wide open. The women screamed as four Russian soldiers entered the house. In an instant, one grabbed Helga and pushed her to the floor as he ripped at her clothes and climbed on top of her while opening his belt. Another pushed Issy up against the large kitchen table. He slapped Issy's face hard with the back of his hand. The ring on his finger, gauged a hole in her cheek and blood trickled into her mouth. She gagged on the blood as he slapped her again, this time with the palm of his hand. Her head twisted with the force of the blow. A third solider pushed Rebekah up against the wall and ripped the bodice of her dress away. Vera was on the stairs holding her baby and letting go of a bloodcurdling scream while the fourth soldier tried to yank her son from her arms.

Issy felt the punch to her stomach that followed the slaps. She would have doubled over in pain if she could have, but he held her against the table with his left arm. Her back was being bent at an unnatural angle and the edge of the table cut into her spine as the soldier leaned all of his weight against her. Just as she thought her back would break, she heard the shots ring out.

Catching the soldiers off guard, Hans lifted his rifle and shot the one who was raping his mother. At the same time, Friedrich shot the soldier who was grabbing for his baby and then quickly turned the rifle and shot the man holding Rebekah.

The soldier who held Issy, pulled her body in front of his to shield himself. Then he took out his pistol and put it to Issy's head. In Russian he ordered Hans and Friedrich to put their rifles down.

The soldier holding Issy, backed away still holding a gun to her head. Warily, he watched as Hans and Friedrich laid down their rifles. He turned the pistol away from Issy's head and pointed it directly at Hans. But as soon as he did so, Rebekah came up from behind him and stabbed him in the neck with a large kitchen knife. With a squish, the soft tissue of his neck gave way to the blade and blood spurted from his artery. The soldier fell to the ground and the pistol discharged without injuring anyone. Hans retrieved his rifle and walked over to the dying soldier. He pointed the rifle directly at the Russian and unloaded another bullet into his chest at point blank range. Over his shoulder he said, "Go to the wagons, we leave now."

Crying, Issy and Rebekah gathered their clothes together and did as Hans said, while Friedrich helped Vera and the baby to his own wagon. Helga stood in the middle of the room, looking around her at the dead Russians as if she were in a trance. Hans took his mother's hand and gently coaxed her, "Mutti, we have to go. Come with me." He led her out of the house and helped her to climb up into the wagon.

The wagons made their way on the road to Königsberg. The girls walked along, one on each side, and held onto the ropes. Each was lost in her own terror as they walked blindly forward. Issy still tasted the blood in her mouth and she couldn't forget the smell of the Russian's sour breath. Rebekah kept remembering the feel of the knife cutting through the soldier's neck until it hit solid bone. She had killed someone. But what choice had she had? Each of them moved in a daze, letting the biting wind and cold blister their faces and sting their eyes.

It wasn't long before their wagons met up with others. Together they made a small convoy. Progress was slow because of the wind, snow, and ice. They moved during the day and tried to sleep at night. At first, Friedrich, set small fires at the side of the road when they stopped to rest. But on the third night, a deafening sound split the sky as fighter planes came into view. With a roar, artillery pummeled the ground around them. Bodies flew into the air like ragdolls. Entire wagons splintered like toys, and when the aeroplanes soared away, they left behind the sound of tortured screams which filled the void. In the aftermath, bodies lay across the road and alongside of it. The wounded cried out in pain as their families tried in vain to attend to them. The next morning, many had to be left behind as their families moved on. Without wagons, they were unable to carry their injured loved ones with them.

After that, Friedrich made no more fires on the open road. Instead, they huddled together in freezing temperatures and tried to keep each other warm beneath the heavy blankets. They ate when they could and were glad for the milk which the goats provided to ease their thirst. Others were not so lucky, and Issy saw that thirst was almost as vicious as the cold in its unrelenting torture.

The snow was deep and the Schultzs' wagon wheels often became stuck. With their hands, Hans and Friedrich dug out the wheels to free them. When they finally made it to the outskirts of Königsberg, they found the city heavily damaged. Friedrich pointed to a warehouse, "Over there, let's stop for the night." The warehouse was large enough for the wagons to be led inside.

There were still German soldiers in the city, but they had other concerns that were more pertinent to them than the refugees. After all, the Soviet infantry was about to enter the city. So, when Hans and Friedrich led the wagons into the warehouse, the soldiers paid them no mind.

As Hans unloaded only the necessities from the wagons, Friedrich started a small fire within the warehouse walls. Vera sat close to the fire, grateful for its warmth, and held tightly onto her baby. She rocked him as she softly sang a German lullaby. The child's weak cries could be heard when Vera finished singing. Vera put him to her breast and hoped that he would take her milk.

They were already dangerously low on food. With six people in their party, it hadn't taken long to go through the food they had brought with them. The girls changed their clothes and Helga began sewing their torn dresses. Issy and Rebekah decided to explore the warehouse, hoping to find something to eat or other useful supplies for their journey.

Issy complained, "Rebekah, I can't feel my legs. I touch them with my hands and I can feel them with my hands, but my legs feel nothing."

Rebekah said, "Try to think of something else. It helps if you fill your mind with other things like finding food." Then Rebekah climbed on top of a beam which had fallen to the ground and balanced her weight as if walking on a tight rope. She pointed to what looked like a pile of clothes in the shadows against the far wall, "What is that?"

As the girls got closer, they saw a little boy of about six years old. His brown hair was a sharp contrast to his pale white skin. He was wrapped in several blankets and holding the cold hand of a dead woman. Next to the little boy was a basket of potatoes. His eyes implored them as his parched lips spoke the words, "wasser, bitte."

Rebekah said, "He wants water." Rebekah climbed over the debris to reach him while Issy ran to get some goat's milk. "Mutti, we found a boy. He's very thirsty. Can I give him some milk?"

"Is he alone?"

"He is holding his mutter's hand, but she is dead."

Helga found a tin cup and poured some goat's milk into it. She followed her daughter to where they had found the boy. Rebekah was murmuring comforting words to him as he cried. Helga saw the sad state that he was in, "Oh, you poor thing."

Helga held the cup to his lips and he drank eagerly. When he had had his full, she gently pried his hand from the frozen fingers of his mother. She asked him, "What is your name?"

The little boy looked frightened as he said, "Markos."

Friedrich reached the group then, and seeing the situation at hand, he lifted the boy in his arms. Markos started to cry out, "Mutti, Mutti." It broke Issy's heart to hear his desperate pleas for his mother. Friedrich carried him back toward the fire as Helga retrieved the basket of potatoes. Rebekah and Issy took one of the blankets which had fallen off of Markos as Friedrich had lifted him. They covered his mother's frozen body with it. Issy spoke to the dead woman, "Do not worry. You can rest now. We will take care of him."

Friedrich rubbed the boy's limbs by the fire to bring back some pink in them as Helga held him close to her own body to give him more warmth. The child had nearly frozen to death. Helga held the cup of goat's milk to his lips and again he drank. Marcos spoke weakly, his voice still hoarse from thirst, "Danke." Helga smiled, "No need to thank me child, drink some more." She fed the milk to him as if he was a little bird and he took it gratefully. Vera looked on blankly, holding her own son close to her under the many blankets which surrounded them. Helga worried that Vera's child had sounded so weak, but Vera would not let anyone else near the baby. Helga spoke quietly to Vera, "This is Markos. His mother is over there, but she did not make it. We will take him with us." Vera looked at Markos briefly and then returned her gaze to her baby, she started to sing softly once again.

Friedrich and Hans examined the map and discussed which roads to take next. Helga instructed the girls, "Boil some water and cut up three potatoes. Put them in the water and let them cook. We will have potato soup tonight."

When their meager meal was finished, Issy fed some hay and oats to the goats and Hunter. She rested her head against the horse's neck and felt the pulse of blood beneath his skin.

When she closed her eyes, she could almost make believe she was back on her farm taking care of Hunter in the barn. His body warmed her until feeling returned to her legs with pins and needles. Hunter knew how to soothe her by rustling his head gently against hers. She whispered, "You are a good boy, Hunter. I am glad I still have you."

The night was long. They heard the bombs that continued to be dropped on Königsberg. The next day, they heard the roar of tanks getting closer and decided it was time to continue on with their journey. Just as they left the city, they saw the first tanks approaching with the Soviet Army following close behind.

CHAPTER TWENTY-ONE

1945

Issy was exhausted. Each cold night, Issy had fitful dreams that were splintered by the sound of the artillery which surrounded them. Each morning she woke, she found herself surprised at still being alive. On the road to Pillau they passed many weary travelers. They moved ever forward, their eyes only leaving the road to glance uneasily at the sky. When they reached the hills, traveling became even harder as they urged Hunter to pull the sleigh over the snowy roads.

When they crested one hill, a woman walking on the side of the road caught Issy's attention. Her head was hung low with her dark hair covering her face. She wandered about in aimless circles, not paying attention to anyone else around her. The woman's thin clothes were torn into tatters and exposed the black and blue marks on her bare skin. When she finally lifted her head, Issy could see that her face was also battered and bruised. Ice crystals filled her hair and hung from her nose. For a moment, their eyes locked and then the woman lowered her head and her hair covered her face once again. As they passed the woman, Issy turned to look behind her and continued to watch her. Issy saw her walk toward the edge of the hill that ended in a cliff which overlooked the valley below. Then, without a sound, the woman's body fell backward and disappeared from view. Issy looked forward after that and tried not to make eye contact with anyone again.

The roads were littered with abandoned automobiles whose engines had frozen and seized. It sleeted all day and their blankets became encrusted in ice. At night they clung to each other trying to find warmth. Their clothes were wet and had frozen to their raw skin. One morning, Friedrich ordered, "Get up." In spite of their frozen limbs, Issy and Rebekah stood and grabbed onto their ropes, but Helga did not rise with them. Issy called to her mother, but Helga still did not move. She walked back to her mother and shook her. Helga's body fell over onto the ground. "No, Mutti!" Issy cried. Hans came to her side and examined his mother. He shook his head, "I'm sorry, Issy. We must keep going. If we don't keep walking, we will die too. The exercise will keep the blood pumping in our veins. No more sleep, we must keep walking until we have reached Pillau." He pulled her away from their mother's body. Issy begged, "Let me stay with her Hans. I don't want to walk anymore. I don't care what happens to me. Please, let me stay."

Hans wrapped his arms around his sister and said, "Issy, you are all I have left. I need you to keep walking. Without you, I will die." Rebekah joined her and whispered in her ear, "We are walking like we planned. We will find a ship that will take us to safety. Issy, you need to keep walking." Obediently, Issy nodded and again took hold of one of the ropes.

They reached Pillau two days later and were glad to find the German army was still there. One German soldier heard they had come from Königsberg and asked them what they had seen there. Hans told them that as they were leaving, they saw tanks and long lines of Soviet troop approaching. The soldier said, "Ja, I heard that there are upwards of 1,500,000 troops expected to reach Königsberg by today. Issy and Rebekah watched as Panzers lumbered out of Pillau toward Königsberg, in the direction they had just come from. Anti-aircraft guns shot into the night sky as the Soviet aeroplanes returned fire and flew by with an ear-splitting roar. They took shelter in a bunker on the side of the road and slept for the first time in several days.

The next morning, Friedrich asked if there were any ships leaving from Pillau which could take them to safety, but he was told that the inlet was frozen, and no boats were able to leave. A soldier pointed west, "You should keep going toward Gotenhafen. You will have better luck there." So, they gathered their belongings and proceeded to cross the ice on the frozen inlet of the Vistula Lagoon. A line of refugees extended as far as they could see, both in front of them and behind them. The horses slipped as they tried to pull the wagons across. The sled assembly fared better than the wheels on the Schultzs' wagon, but both had a difficult time crossing on the churned-up ice.

Issy no longer felt the cold. She felt nothing at all as they walked and walked and walked in the sub-zero temperatures. Her feet were completely frozen, so she didn't feel the pain where her skin had been shaved away. She thought her feet resembled sliced raw meat. They passed by many frozen bodies left behind by friends and families. The food they had packed and the potatoes they had found with Markos were gone except for the apples. The Vistula Spit was a narrow peninsula which stretched out across the Baltic Sea. Behind them the German army continued to shoot at the sky as the fighters roared above. But they were no match for the Soviet bombers that now approached. All of a sudden Issy heard the screech of a bomb falling through the sky and she watched as it impacted indiscriminately with the earth behind her. The road disappeared, and bodies were incinerated in a cloud of fire.

They pushed on, but they could only move at a snail's pace. The road was crowded and more aeroplanes returned to shoot at them once again. People fell around them and yet, somehow, in the random selection of those who live through war, Issy and her group continued on.

They walked like this for four more days, not stopping to sleep. When they finally reached Gotenhafen, the sight that greeted them was one of utter chaos. There were wagons and horses left stranded as their owners had abandoned them to board ships to cross the Baltic Sea. Hans took the pouch of his father's money and went to try to buy tickets for their passage on a ship to Denmark. Although Denmark had once been a neutral country, it had been occupied by Germany since it was invaded in April of 1940.

Issy had learned all about the invasion of Denmark in school and knew that the Royal Guard in Copenhagen had resisted, but Denmark had been too small to hold out for long against Germany. So, the Danes surrendered, and occupation occurred rather peacefully compared to other countries invaded by Germany during the war. However, she knew that the Danes had no love for the German people who now ruled over them.

There were many tiny ships, but only one great ship in the harbor. Hans was told that the last tickets had been sold for the giant vessel, The Wilhelm Gustloff. It was set to leave the following day for its destination, Kiel, Germany. Hans offered to pay twice the going rate for each boarding pass, but to no avail.

That night, while in a bunker, the girls met two sisters, Erika and Regina, who were set to board the great ship in the harbor the next day. Erika was nine years old and Regina was six. Their father, Gregor Van Nustrand, was an officer in Nazi Germany's Navy, which was known as the Kriegsmarine. Regina was holding onto a doll that looked much like Issy's own doll. When Issy saw it, she carefully took Catrina out of her satchel and showed it to the girls, "See, I have a doll just like yours."

Erika asked, "How did your doll get broken?"

Issy explained, "My Vater accidently dropped her."

Regina's eyes widened, "Well then, why didn't you get her fixed?"

Issy said, "Because, as you must know, the factories are all gone."

Erika nodded, "Ja, the bombs destroyed the factories."

Regina hugged her doll, "I don't want my doll to get broken."

Erika assured her little sister, "Just hold onto her, she'll be fine. We are leaving tomorrow on the biggest ship in the harbor. Soon we will all be safe." She asked Issy, "Are you going to be on the big ship too?"

Issy replied, "No, they said there are no more boarding passes. There is no more room."

Erika looked concerned, "The Red Army is coming, you have to get away before they get here."

"I know," Issy said. "But there is nothing we can do about it. We have to wait our turn for another ship. There were many people here before us."

Regina asked Rebekah, "Do you want to hold my doll? She looks just like you with her red hair."

Rebekah smiled at the little girl, "Thank you, I would like that." Rebekah took out a brush from her bag and brushed the doll's hair until it was smooth and shiny, then handed her back to the little girl."

"Oh, she looks beautiful now!" Regina exclaimed, "Danke."

Someone yelled above all the people chattering, "Lights out," and with that, the darkness engulfed them.

The children slept soundly that night from pure exhaustion. The next morning, the people with boarding passes lined up to embark on the Wilhelm Gustloff. Issy and Rebekah watched as the ship was loaded with its passengers. First to board were the Nazi officers and their families. Next were the wounded soldiers and the women's naval auxiliary. Finally, thousands of civilians crammed the deck as the ship was loaded well beyond its capacity. At the last moment, weary refugees without boarding passes pushed their way onto the ship in desperation. The Wilhelm Gustloff may have been only one of many ships that was participating in what the Germans called, Operation Hannibal, the code name for the evacuation of German troops and refugees in the wake of the approaching Soviet Army, but it was also the largest.

Rebekah and Issy located Regina and Erika by the ship's highest railing and waved to them. The little girls waved back, their faces flushed with excitement. Just after noon, the ship set out to sea as all aboard cheered. The passengers were crowded together, especially on the lower levels of the ship. Issy watched as the Wilhelm Gustloff left port and wished she could be among those on board. Although she noted to herself that not everyone looked as happy as Erika and Regina. There were tearful children who had been separated from their parents. Older children held smaller children in their arms. There were women with wounded souls looking out through tormented eyes. There were others who jostled for enough room to breathe; they panicked and shoved each other as they were crushed together by the sheer number of bodies that had boarded. The ship had been loaded with over 10,000 desperate passengers, five times its capacity and more than half of those passengers were children. But Issy and Rebekah would have to wait for another ship.

As they spent the night again in the bunker, Issy could hear Friedrich and Vera argue. Vera refused to let him hold their baby. Finally, he ripped the child from her arms and as he looked down into his son's face, he cried. "Vera, it's too late. He's gone." It was as he had suspected; the baby had died days ago on their journey. Vera screamed as she tried to grab hold of the baby once again, "Give him back to me!"

With tears in his own eyes, Friedrich begged, "You must let him go."

"Nein! Give him back!" She let out a piercing scream as he struggled with her.

Exhausted and pushed beyond his endurance, Friedrich slapped her across her face. She stopped screaming then and looked at him with sorrowful eyes. Quieter, she begged, "Bitte, please, Friedrich." Her plea was so pitiful that he handed the dead baby back to her, and after that, she held it in a vise-like grip. She whispered, "Danke."

The following day they heard about the disaster of the Wilhelm Gustloff. It had been sunk by a Soviet submarine the night before and it was reported that there were very few survivors. A few days later, word reached Gotenhafen that the ropes holding the lifeboats had been frozen to the ship and so the crew was unable to lower most of them to safety. They believed 9,000 people, mostly children, had lost their lives that night in the Baltic Sea. The Captain had made a crucial mistake and had chosen to stay far away from the coast because he knew it was littered with mines. Instead, he chose to set out into deeper waters. Unfortunately, that was where the Soviet submarine had found them.

Issy and Rebekah re-wrapped their bloody feet in rags before slipping them into their ruined shoes. They looked out over the peaceful Baltic Sea which had become a grave to so many refugee children. Thinking now of the mournful fate of Regina and Erika, the girls grasped onto their crosses and prayed for safe passage to Denmark. Over the years of staying with Issy's family, Rebekah had learned the Catholic prayers. She somehow found strength in them and much of what she had known as a small child about her own religion was now lost to her. As she prayed, she realized that in all ways except for being baptized, she had become a Christian and she no longer needed to just play the part. She hoped that if her parents were looking down on her now, they would forgive her.

CHAPTER TWENTY-TWO

Night had fallen while Oma told her story, and the unforgiving rain was still tormenting the mountain. I realized that my grandmother had lived through all of this by the time she was the age of the campers she now cared for. In fact, it occurred to me that Oma had become an orphan herself at the age of thirteen. There was so much I had never known, and I wondered now, why my mother hadn't ever told me. "Oma, have you ever told this story to my mother?"

"Ja, a long time ago."

I shook my head, "Because she never mentioned any of this to me."

"Well, it has always been my story to tell and she knows that. However, now I need you to write it down, so you can tell your children someday. Maybe you can even tell others after I am gone. You could write a book or something, people need to know that living in Germany during the war didn't make us all Nazis, and maybe enough time has passed so that they can listen. Ja, there were some terrible people who committed awful crimes against their neighbors, but there were also many of us who tried to help each other and protect those who were most vulnerable, especially the children. And there were innocent children like Erika and Regina who died in the icy waters of the Baltic Sea along with thousands of others. Somehow, history has forgotten them because of the atrocities that Hitler perpetrated against his own people. I am not minimizing what Hitler and his followers did to millions of people, I am just saying that in war, there are innocent victims on all sides. I was not a Nazi, but I am German just the same."

I almost corrected her and said, East Prussian, but I decided perhaps it was best not to. Instead, I said, "I am sorry, Oma, for the deaths of your friends. I have to be honest, I've never heard of the Wilhelm Gustloff. I've always thought the Titanic was the greatest maritime disaster of all time and I bet most people do."

Oma agreed, "Ja, this is true. Today, our world has all the information needed at the touch of our fingertips. Look it up on your phone, and you will see for yourself."

The following morning, the sun rose once again in the sky and was welcomed into the cabin like a long-lost friend. My eyes were drawn once more to the stained glass above the front door.

"Oma, is that your parents' farm?"

"Ja, it is. Tucker made it for me."

"Tucker? When are you going to tell me who this Tucker is?"

"Ah, Tucker," she smiled, "we have something to do today. Get yourself ready, we are going for a drive."

She directed me toward town and I recalled passing this same way with Brad. Just before Gatlinburg, there was an artists' community. We passed little craft shops of all kinds along the sides of the road, and every now and then, we passed a quaint wedding chapel with the mountains rising majestically behind it. Finally, Oma told me to turn into a driveway. There was a sign out front that said, "Tucker's Glass Works."

Inside the shop, there was a wonderland of colored glass. There were stained glass windows and blown glass bottles, bowls, and vases lined up on shelves. The young man at the counter smiled broadly at my grandmother. "Oma! So nice to see you!"

"Tucker, I want you to meet my granddaughter, Jace. She's come all the way from New York to visit me."

He was very pleasing to look at with dimples that gave him one of those eternally boyish appearances like Dick Clark or Ryan Seacrest. He reached out his hand and I took it. His touch seemed to ignite a fire inside of me which I hadn't felt since Brian's death. Immediately, I felt guilty that my body was reacting in this way to another man and quickly withdrew my hand.

Disconcerted, I stuttered, "I-It's nice to meet you." Somehow, he didn't seem to notice the effect he had on me.

Tucker remarked, "Well, what brings you two lovely ladies here to my shop today?"

Oma explained, "Jace has taken a liking to the stained glass above my front door, so I thought I would bring her here to see your beautiful work."

With a nod and a loving smile, Tucker said, "Ah, Oma, your parents' farm."

"Ja. I have been telling Jace the story of my life in Germany."

He looked at me with compassion as he said, "Your grandmother is a very special lady and she has had an extraordinary life." I was unsettled for a moment to realize that Oma had told him her whole story before she had told me.

He said, "You know, if it weren't for your grandmother, I wouldn't have this shop."

I asked, "What do you mean?"

He motioned for us to follow him, "Come ladies; let me give you a tour."

Behind the store was a workshop filled with tables and equipment. He explained, "When I'm not selling my pieces up front, I am back here working. Over there you will see some stained glass which I am currently working on. And in the back, along the wall, are ovens where I blow glass." As we walked I admired his artwork in various stages of completion.

He asked, "Would you like to make some stained glass?"

"Sure." We sat on stools at a large table and he handed Oma and me simple patterns, sheets of colorful glass, and some cutting tools. Step by step we followed his instructions, until we had cut each piece to fit the pattern into a frame.

He explained, "Now comes the hard part, soldering."

After dropping a bit of solder to connect each piece of glass to the next, he held my hand steady to help me spread it along the edges of the glass and join the pieces together. First, we did the front of the piece, and then we turned it over to secure the back.

I was amazed by the difficulty and intricacy of the work, and yet he made it seem so easy. I said, "I had no idea that so much precision went into making a simple piece of stained glass!"

"It gets easier the more you do it, and I find it . . . therapeutic."

I liked his smile, it was easy and real. There was no bravado or boasting in his expression as there was in Brad's. He was just content and confident in his work.

I asked him, "What did you mean when you said you wouldn't have this shop if not for my grandmother?"

Before he had a chance to answer, Oma took it upon herself to explain, "Jace, I've had some difficult times in my life; but life is long, and I have had happiness too. I survived the war for a reason. I had to believe that, or I couldn't have lived with the fact that so many others didn't. I was given a second chance at life. There have been many times when I felt I didn't deserve all of the good that followed. I questioned why I survived when so many of my loved ones didn't. The only way I could continue on, was to find ways to repay God, or fate, or whatever it was that saved my life."

I was stunned. I had no idea my grandmother felt this way about her life. But listening to her now, it all made sense.

Tucker put his arm around Oma and kissed her on her head. "Your grandmother was the one who saved my life. I was an orphan. But then the orphanage sent me to your grandmother's camp one summer. I was already ten or so by then, headstrong and angry at the world. But she took an interest in me and, eventually, convinced the orphanage to let her be my foster mother. They didn't want to give me to her, thought I'd cause trouble and then she might close her camp to the other orphans. But she kept on fighting for me, and in time, I came to live with her. When I grew up, she bought this little shop for me and said it was an investment in my future because she believed in me. I live upstairs in an apartment over the workshop. She gave me a future I never would have had on my own." Tears came to his eyes as he spoke. He shook his head to ward off the emotions that threatened to overwhelm him, "I can never repay her for all she has given me."

Oma replied, "Seeing you happy, and living a prosperous life, is all the repayment I need. Now Jace, I think we had better be getting back, I'm feeling a little tired."

I could see that she needed some rest, but I wasn't ready to leave yet. I had too many questions and all this was a lot for me to absorb, "Wait a minute, Tucker, when did you start to live with her?"

Again, Oma answered for him, "He became my foster child when he was sixteen."

I wondered how it could be that I never knew my grandmother had taken in a foster child. Was I so consumed with my own life that I didn't know this important piece of information? I looked at him and asked, "And how old are you now?"

"Twenty-nine."

Thinking back to my visits when I was a child I said, "Well

then, I may have met you when you were a camper here. You do look sort of familiar."

He made a non-committal shrug. Immediately, Oma exclaimed, "Really, Jace, it's time for us to go."

I slid off of the stool and watched as Tucker held Oma's arm to steady her while we walked to my car. Concerned that she looked so pale, I asked, "Oma, are you all right?" My unanswered questions were forgotten as my fear for her increased.

"Just a bit dizzy. I'll be fine. When we get home, I will lie down for a while." I looked over at Tucker and saw the apprehension on his face. After seating her in my car he said, "Wait a minute, I have some cold bottled water in the store, let me get you one."

I sat in the car next to my grandmother as he ran back into the shop. Her head was leaning against the back of the car seat, but she turned to look at me with a smile on her face. "He's nice, isn't he?"

"Yes, Oma, he's very nice. I'm just surprised that I never knew you took in a foster child."

"Well, you stopped coming down to the camp around then." She explained, "When Tucker came to live with me, I stayed home with him for the holidays until he was twenty-one, and by then, he was independent. He started his little business and the holidays became a busy time for him. I hope it doesn't bother you that I took him in."

"Of course it doesn't." And I realized I really meant that. I said, "I'm glad you haven't been alone all this time."

Tucker was back a minute later with a cool bottle of water. He opened it for her and she took a big drink. "Oh, that's much better! Thank you, Tucker."

As we drove away, I could see in the rearview mirror that Tucker was still standing where we left him, watching us until we turned off the road.

CHAPTER TWENTY-THREE

1945

As more and more people were exiled from their homes, the line of desperate families increased. Tickets to cross on a ship were sold at a premium. Without money or valuable goods to trade, many refugees waited hopelessly, while those who could pay, secured passage. Issy remembered the silver coins and spoons which her grandmother had sewn into their dresses and she ripped hers at its seam and showed the silver to Hans. Rebekah did the same. Thankfully, the silver was finally enough for Hans to acquire tickets for their entire group to board a ship bound for Denmark.

Hans had to hand over the guns before they could board. And they were only allowed to take what they could carry. They were lined up to board when Issy said, "There's something I have to do first." She left the others and ran toward Hunter who had been left hitched to their wagon just in case they needed to leave on foot. Issy had been caring for him and the goats while they waited to secure passage. But now she was faced with leaving him behind. She hadn't allowed herself to think about this moment. She untied the goats and freed Hunter from the straps that anchored him to the wagon. She reached into her pocket for her last apple. Issy fed it to her horse and whispered in his ear as the tears fell freely down her cheeks, "Fly Hunter." But the horse only looked at her with sorrowful brown eyes. Without her on his back, he was not about to go anywhere. She kissed him and nuzzled his mane one more time. Then, it took everything she had to walk away from him.

As the ship pulled out of port, Hunter still stood there, waiting patiently for her to return. Issy shouted in desperation as loud as she could above the noise of the ship's engines, "Fly Hunter, please! Go! Find a grassy meadow to live in!" But the horse only watched as the ship sailed further away from land.

Over the next two days, the ship inched closer to Copenhagen. The captain stayed near land as his crew diligently searched the waters ahead of them for Soviet mines. Dangerous sheets of ice surrounded them and floated by on the surface. Issy, Rebekah, and Markos huddled together under a woolen blanket trying desperately to stay warm. Every inch of the ship was taken up by refugees. There was barely enough room for the children to sit on their suitcases. At night, they leaned against each other and tried to sleep.

The next day Issy's stomach grumbled louder. She hadn't eaten since she had left Gotenhafen the day before. But there was no food for the refugees on the ship. She would have to wait until they disembarked at Copenhagen.

When they finally arrived in Denmark, Hans said to Issy and Rebekah with relief, "We made it!" Hope filled all of the refugees on board. Rebekah and Issy each held onto Markos's hands as the ship pulled into port. But with their first full view of the shore, they saw a great ship, much larger than theirs. It was lying on its side, half sunk, in the harbor. Hollowed out buildings greeted them and lined the streets to remind them that Germany had been the aggressor and had invaded this country which had tried so valiantly to remain neutral. Although Germany was still in control of Denmark, Issy worried they would soon become unwelcome guests in a foreign land. But as they walked off of the gangplank, she hoped and prayed that they had finally found peace.

Once on land, Issy, Rebekah, and Markos were ushered into a building where German inspectors searched them over and directed them into different lines. These lines determined which camp destinations the refugees would be sent to. A German soldier lifted the cross necklace from around Rebekah's throat and examined it. He looked again at her face before letting go of the cross. He pointed to the line where Issy and Markos stood waiting. They were thankful that the three of them were allowed to remain together. Then Hans joined them, and Issy hugged her brother as tears left dirty trails down her cheeks.

A moment later, they heard Vera scream as the German soldiers ripped her dead baby from her arms. Issy watched helplessly as Friedrich had to physically force Vera to come with him as they were instructed to join the rest of their group. But Vera continued to scream like a mad woman until the terror on Friedrich's face finally silenced her. After that, Vera followed along quietly.

They were loaded onto open trucks and driven to Klovermarken, which was mostly an open field full of clovers.

Hastily erected tents and cabins had been built to house the refugees. Vera, Issy, Rebekah and Markos were placed with other women and children in one of the cabins, while Friedrich and Hans were placed in a long tent with other men.

Rebekah found four empty cots and quickly took possession of them. She said, "Here, Issy, sleep next to me." She arranged the beds so Vera could sleep next to the wall, with Markos next to her, followed by Issy, and then Rebekah. Looking around the room, as it filled up with tired and desperately hungry women and children, Rebekah felt protective of her little group. Vera curled up immediately on her cot, she wrapped her arms tightly around herself and stared blankly at the wall.

A German soldier came into the cabin and announced, "A meal will be served once a day at noon. If you miss it, you will go without food." Issy's legs felt shaky, she sat down on the cot. Her head felt cloudy and her body started to tremble violently. Rebekah saw her face and sat down next to her, "What's wrong, Issy?" "I'm so hungry and thirsty." Rebekah put her arm around Issy to comfort her. She remembered the many times in the attic when Issy had done the same for her. "I know, Issy. Me too. My head is throbbing, my stomach hurts, and my legs feel like rubber. My feet are screaming at me for walking so far and I've been cold so long that it seems the chill has become part of my bones. We need to think about something else."

"But, Rebekah, when I let myself think, I think about Mutter and Vater." Tears spilled down Issy's face and soon tears filled Rebekah's eyes as well. They held onto each other, each knowing that without the other, they would be swallowed up by the waves of hopelessness.

Rebekah wiped the tears from her own face, and started to recite their old plans, "Issy, we are going to find a boat to take us to America. We will grow old together, you and I."

Then Rebekah remembered Catrina. She stood up and opened Issy's suitcase. Inside lay the porcelain doll. She found a ribbon among Issy's clothes and wrapped it around Catrina's head. The ribbon held the doll's face together and closed the larger of the two cracks that had been spreading. She then wrapped the doll in the little brown blanket that Oma had made and handed her over to Issy. "Here you go."

Issy looked up at her friend and saw the desperation in Rebekah's expression, so she took Catrina from Rebekah and continued the story, "And we will take Catrina with us. We will find a way to fix her in America."

Rebekah smiled as she saw Issy's tears abate, "Yes, we will fix her in America."

At noon on the following day, Issy, Rebekah, and Markos were ushered into the main dining room for what would become their only meal of the day. Vera had refused to come with them. The room was filled with long tables surrounded by hard benches. In the front of the room was the largest table. Female German soldiers stood behind it with ladles in their hands and steaming pots set on the table in front of them. Lines were formed, and as each refugee passed in front of the women, they were handed a bowl of thick gruel. Issy choked as she spooned the food into her mouth too quickly. When Hans and Friedrich joined them, they were worried to find that Vera hadn't come. Issy said, "Don't worry, we will bring food back to her." Rebekah added, "It will take some time, Herr Schultz, we will attend to her." Friedrich knew that food alone would not make his wife well again. He was thankful

Issy and Rebekah were there for her, and he knew they would do all they could to help his wife regain her strength. But he wondered if there was anything that would help Vera regain her will to live.

Back in the cabin, Issy tried to hand Vera a bowl and spoon, but Vera refused to hold either. "What will we do, Rebekah?" Rebekah scooped up some gruel with the spoon and lifted it to Vera's mouth. "Vera, you need to eat something or you will get sick." Vera's face showed the despondence that filled her as she turned away from the spoon. At a loss for what to do next, Rebekah placed the bowl near Vera's cot and left it there.

In the middle of the night, Markos woke from a dream crying, "Mutti! Mutti!" The sobs were wrenched from deep in his soul. Issy and Rebekah jumped up from their cots to console him, but found that he was already in Vera's arms. He had crawled into her bed seeking comfort. Vera rocked him as she softly cooed and tried to soothe him. And then Vera started to sing. It was the same German lullaby that she had been singing to her own child. Rebekah grabbed onto Issy's arm and gently pulled her friend back toward their cots. She whispered to Issy, "Vera will be all right now." Vera held onto Markos all night, cradling him in her arms. The next day, Vera held Markos by the hand as she followed the girls into the main dining hall for breakfast.

CHAPTER TWENTY-FOUR

1945

For the first time since she came down from the attic to find her father and grandmother dead, Issy had a moment to herself to think about all that had happened. She lay on her cot awake, surrounded by darkness. The sounds of other refugees crying around her could be heard above the continuous coughing. She buried her own sobs in her sleeve as her heart broke again and again. She yearned to feel the protection of her father and the devotion of her mother and grandmother once again. She realized that she had mostly taken their presence in her life for granted. She wondered how she was supposed to go on with her life after leaving her own mother's body, frozen, along a desolate road. She shivered. Quietly, she spoke to her parents and grand-mother in the dark, "Mutti, do you forgive me? Vater, please protect us, keep Hans and Rebekah safe. Oma, I love you and I will never forget you. I love you all and miss you so much! How am I going to live without you?"

The sadness was too much for her to contain and her sobs grew louder. Rebekah woke up and heard her friend crying. At first she wasn't sure if she should intrude, after all, she had had many nights where she had cried herself to sleep and understood there was nothing that could take the pain of loss away. But she left her bed and sat on Issy's cot, "Hold my hand, Issy. I am here."

Issy sat up and the two girls hugged each other. Issy laid her head on Rebekah's shoulder and asked, "Rebekah, how can you be so brave? You lost your family too."

By thirteen, Rebekah had learned that feeling sorry for herself did not solve anything. So, she said in a stoic voice, "I have had enough taken from me. I will not lose what I have left. If my family is still out there, I'm going to find them. If they aren't, if I am alone, then I know they would want me to survive. What good would it do for me to give up? I need to have the strength to fight for what I have left. And I still have you and Hans." Issy admired Rebekah's indomitable spirit and hoped she too could find the strength to continue living after so much loss. But for now, she wanted some time to mourn.

At noon the following day, they met Hans and Friedrich in the dining hall. As they were eating, Hans began to cough. When he saw the look of concern on his sister's face he assured her, "I'm fine Issy. It's just a cough. Everyone in the camp has it, haven't you heard them?" But her instincts told her she should keep a close eye on her brother. It worried her that she was not able to see the inside of the tent where Hans and Friedrich were living. But there were strict rules that the men were not allowed to enter the cabins that the women and children were living in and, likewise, the women and children were not allowed to enter the long tents where the men were housed.

When a coughing fit hit him again, he coughed into his sleeve attempting to muffle the sound. But Issy's keen eyes saw the tiny spots of blood which appeared on his arm. She watched him as he nonchalantly rolled up his sleeve to cover the blood.

When the children started dying, there was an increase in the demand for those who were still healthy to work. Some dug graves, while Hans and Friedrich were assigned with others to build additional housing for the refugees who continued to pour into the camp. Issy and Rebekah were sent to work, building separate living quarters for the German officers and their families, along with separate dining halls and privies. The work filled their days and the weeks passed. Finally, as April approached, the snow started to melt, and the frozen grip of winter began to abate. But in spite of the warming weather, conditions in the camp continued to get worse by the day.

Many of the refugees had been in such poor physical health when they arrived, that disease quickly took the lives of a quarter of the children housed in Klovermarken. Unable to keep up with the demand for graves, the bodies of the children were thrown into piles. Issy and Rebekah were taken away from their work on the soldiers' quarters and told to help dig mass graves just outside the camp. The stench from the decaying bodies became unbearable as the everything thawed around them. In addition, the human waste which was being carried by the constant rain, turned the insufficient drainage systems into rivers of sewage throughout the camp. Diseases spread and more lives were lost.

Then one day in May, they awoke to find all of the German officers, guards, and their families gone. They had left in the middle of the night. The first Danish officials entered the camp several days later. Hungry and fearful, the inhabitants gathered together in the courtyard to hear what the officials had to say.

The Danish Officer announced in German, "On May 6th, 1945, the Germans surrendered to the Allied forces. The war has ended, and the Danish people are thankful to the British for the liberation of Denmark from Germany's Third Reich. While you were taking refuge on our land, the German Army was evacuating thousands of Danish citizens to concentration camps and prisons across Germany and Poland. Now your officers and soldiers have deserted you." He spat tobacco onto the ground.

Issy felt his chilling words and understood immediately, their position now was more precarious than ever.

The Officer continued, "You are to remain here until further arrangements can be made to move you back to your homelands. In the event that you cannot be repatriated, then you will be moved to other camps within Denmark until we can find a country that will take you. The Refugee Administration has been set up by the Allied Forces to oversee all phases of this transition and we will be documenting your information to distinguish your nationality and to determine which camp you should be transferred to in the future. Inoculations against diphtheria, typhoid, paratyphoid, and dysentery will take place over the next month. But make no mistake; the Danish government does not hold itself responsible to treat the residents of these refugee camps for any diseases or illnesses once contracted. With that said, you are forbidden to leave this camp unless you obtain a pass to do so. Consider yourselves to be quarantined. Finally, there will be no fraternization between the refugees and the Danish people, most certainly, including the guards who will now be stationed at this camp.

God Bless Denmark!" He then spat at the crowd gathered before him and took his leave.

In June everyone had to have their heads shaved to combat the lice which were infesting the camp. Issy and Rebekah had gone from being innocent children caught up in a devastating war, to fleeing certain death as refugees, and now they had become prisoners and the enemy in a foreign land.

CHAPTER TWENTY-FIVE

PRESENT DAY

During the second week of camp, we took the children to the lake for the day. We brought fried chicken, sausage and peppers, corn on the cob, salads, and all the fixings with us. It was late-afternoon and I was enjoying setting the tables for supper with cheerful checkered tablecloths, plates, cups, napkins and utensils. Thankfully, it wasn't a windy day, and everything was staying in its place.

Shelby and Josie, two of the counselors, were unpacking trays from the coolers and lighting the Sternos to warm the food. Josie's shirt ended in fringes around her waist. Her colorful leggings turned her legs into works of art and her shoes were bedazzled with sparkles. The girl stood out in a crowd and wasn't afraid to do so. I liked her authenticity. As I glanced over the tables, trying to assess whether anything was missing, Brad touched my arm and startled me. "Oh!" I grabbed onto the table and nearly knocked it over as I took a quick step and tripped over a rock.

He said, "Whoa! Hey, sorry!"

I assured him, "It's all right. I'm fine."

He smiled with his perfect teeth and said, "I haven't seen you around the camp much lately."

I took a step back from him, "Well, I caught that 24-hour stomach virus which was going around, and I thought it was best if I kept myself away from the children until I knew I was better. Thankfully, my grandmother hasn't caught it yet, but I'm still keeping an eye on her."

"Ah, things like that are always running rampant at camp. Don't worry; I'm sure the worst is over. After all, they've all had their shots." He sounded like he was talking about pets rather than children, and for a moment, I thought of the children in the refugee camps who had died without proper medicine. He continued, "Well, it looks like you have everything under control here. How about going for a ride in one of the canoes with me?"

I had never been in a canoe before and thought I would like to give it a try, but still I hesitated.

Josie said, "Go ahead, Jace, we can handle things here."

So, I agreed and soon I was sitting in the canoe as he pushed it off from the shore. Brad paddled past the children who were laughing as they rowed around the lake. I could see Haylie, Benny, Maggie, and Dalton all in one rowboat together. In spite of Haylie's yelling out orders, the boat was going in circles. In another boat, were the older girls, Mazie, Ella, Ginny, Vicky and

Olivia. They were rowing around the island in a race against a boat with the older boys, Cliff, Wade, Travis, Mack and Tanner. They all rowed in unison, two sat on the back bench, two on the middle bench, and one in the front of the boat. Wade was on the back bench putting some muscle into it that propelled the boys' boat far ahead of the girls'. The girls screamed as the boys passed them and the boys crowed like roosters.

Brad rowed our canoe beyond the small island and out into the body of the lake leaving the children far behind.

"Where are we going?"

"Just finding a quiet spot away from the kids."

Ignoring the slight alarm bells that went off in my head, I said, "Oh, okay."

He said, "I've missed you."

I was taken aback by this declaration. "Oh, well, I'm here now."

It was hot in the sun and Brad stopped rowing for a moment to take off his shirt. He was well tanned from being outside every day, and as he started to row again, his muscles flexed. His body was well sculpted with defined lines and my heart took a little leap at the sight of his bare chest and arms. It had been so long since I had seen a man's bare chest. I closed my eyes against the pain which inevitably followed any thought of Brian.

He rowed until we reached the shore of a peninsula on the far side of the lake. A mountain stream made its way over a gentle waterfall and emptied itself into the lake. Brad jumped out of the boat and guided it onto the rocky shore. "Come on. Follow me and let's explore a little." He reached into the boat to help me out. Then he pulled the canoe further up on land so it wouldn't float away while we were gone. My sneakers were wet from the water in the bottom of the boat and dirt collected on them as I walked. Brad took my hand when we reached a rocky stream further inland, and then, never let go. Holding hands, we climbed along a path to find a larger waterfall. It was beautiful, dangerous, and peaceful, all at the same time. He guided me over smaller slippery black rocks until we reached a rock large enough for us to sit on. The water cascaded off the cliff above and landed alongside us as I sat there intoxicated by its beauty.

Brad ordered, "Take off your sneakers."

I took them off and put my feet into the water. He ran his fingers slowly over my calf, "You have beautiful legs. You should wear short shorts more often."

I blushed and wrestled with the conflicting feelings that were building up within me.

He stood up and walked into the water. "Here, take my hand. Let's walk in a little further."

Although I felt afraid, I joined him. As we walked toward the rushing water, he said, "Don't worry, I won't let you fall." But he was holding my hand too tightly in his grip. I tried, unsuccessfully, to pull my hand from his. In response, he loosened his grip just a bit, "Oh, I'm sorry. Did I hurt you? I just wanted to make sure you didn't fall."

He kept moving closer to the waterfall, and the closer I got, the more frightened I became. I said, "I think this is close enough now."

With a throaty voice, he coaxed me, "Just a little closer."

We were so close that I could feel the force of the water as it fell from the rocks above. The spray doused us, and my clothes became wet and stuck to my body. He said something that I didn't quite hear. The water roared loudly just inches from us.

I slipped on a rock and twisted my ankle. Quickly, he caught me in his arms. He pulled me to him, and was crushing my body against his, he lowered his lips to mine. I couldn't push away from him without falling, so I was forced to cling to him. Tears spilled from my eyes and I felt trapped and frightened. Thoughts of Oma as a little girl in the hands of the Russian soldier passed through my mind.

Since he couldn't possibly hear my words, saying anything was pointless. So instead, still holding onto him with one hand, I pointed to the dry land with the other. Reluctantly, he helped me back to solid ground.

As soon as I was safe, I pushed him away from me and angrily asked, "Why did you do that?"

He said, "Do what? You were never in any danger, Jace. I had you."

I was so annoyed with him I snapped, "Can we go back, please? I'm sure that supper is ready by now."

"Yeah, sure."

On the canoe trip back to camp, I tried to compose myself. I didn't want the children to see that I had been crying. Brad didn't seem to notice. He was smiling as he rowed and looking rather satisfied with the way things had gone.

When we got back to camp, he reached in to help me out of the canoe. I didn't take his hand this time. Instead, I got out on my own. I felt like running back to my grandmother at her cabin but decided not to. I wasn't a child anymore and I wasn't going to let him completely ruin this day for me either. I brushed away the tears that snuck out of my eyes.

As the sun started to set low in the sky, the children gathered around to eat their supper. Haylie sat next to me and exclaimed, "We had fun today, even if we kept going in circles!"

"I'm glad you had fun, Haylie."

"I saw you with Mr. Brad. Do you like him?"

I wasn't sure of how to answer that question at the moment and she saw me hesitate. Then she said, "I don't like him either."

That startled me, "Why, Haylie?"

She tried to brush it off, "Oh, I don't know."

I asked her again, "Haylie? Why don't you like him?"

She shrugged, "I don't think he likes us."

Worried about her response, I pressed her further, "What makes you say that?"

"Just stuff."

"What kind of stuff?"

"Well, one time I saw him get mad at Benny. You know Benny, he's my best friend." I remembered the small boy with the large brown eyes. She continued, "I don't know how to explain this."

"Okay, just try. Just say what you're thinking. What did you see?"

Haylie made a huffing sound and let out a deep breath, "The boys make fun of Benny and tease him, and they call him a girl. They call him other names too. Even at the orphanage, the other boys tease him all the time."

"Did Mr. Brad call him names?"

"No. But the older boys where making fun of Benny and, like I said, they were calling him names. So, I told Mr. Brad because I thought he would help Benny. But instead, he came over and grabbed Benny by the arm and dragged him away from everyone. I ran after them because Benny was crying, and I said, 'You're hurting him. Stop it!' but Mr. Brad didn't stop. He was shaking Benny and I saw Benny's arm go to a funny angle and it made a popping sound. Benny screamed, and I could see he was really hurt. But then Mr. Brad looked at me and he looked pretty scary. He told me I shouldn't tell anyone what happened or Benny and I would be sent back to the orphanage. Then he grabbed Benny's arm again and pushed it back into his shoulder blade. At least, that's what it looked like. He told Benny that it was his fault the boys called him names and that he should 'man-up' and 'take it like man.'" By the time Haylie had finished telling me the story, she was crying angry tears.

I hugged her and tried to calm her down. I hadn't meant to get her so upset. "Okay, Haylie, I'm glad you told me."

She sobbed, "But he said not to tell anyone and now I'm afraid. Are we going to get sent back to the orphanage?"

"No. Don't worry, honey. It will be all right. I promise. You're not going anywhere."

I kept my composure for the rest of the day and made sure the children were all back in their beds before returning to my grandmother's cabin.

"Oma, I have to talk to you."

"What is it dear?"

"I think we have a problem with Brad."

"What do you mean, Jace? What kind of problem?"

I told her what had happened to me at the waterfall and then I told her what Haylie told me about Benny.

My grandmother may be elderly, but the thought of children being harmed brought out the fire in her. She was angry, "Oh my! Well, that's it. Bradley can't stay."

"I was hoping you would say that."

"Jace, do you think you could take over? I know you haven't even been here for very long yet, but it's too late to hire someone else to run the camp."

"Oma, there is such a great team here who would help me, and I have you in case I need some advice. I would love to take over this camp. I just can't imagine what else has been going on that we don't know about, and I don't think we can trust him with the children now that we know what's been going on."

Oma nodded, "I agree. I will tell him first thing in the morning."

CHAPTER TWENTY-SIX

The following morning, Murray, the cook, was already in Oma's kitchen when I woke up.

I asked, "What's going on here?"

Oma explained, "Hank just went to get Bradley, and they are on their way up here. Hank was here earlier, and I spoke to both him and Murray. It seems they too have seen some bizarre behavior from Bradley. I've told them of our plans to replace him with you and they are in agreement."

Murray spoke with an Irish brogue, "My dear, Issy, I should have said somethin' a'fore this. I thought maybe I was rushing to judgment. His father was a good friend of mine and I kept hoping he would shape up."

Oma reassured him, "It's all right Murray; you have a good heart. I'm only sorry that I didn't see it myself and sooner." Murray beamed at Oma and I realized there was more going on between them than I had ever imagined. Although Murray was probably close to ten years younger than my grand-mother, he was obviously sweet on her.

Murray continued, "You and I have been doing this for a long time, Issy. We've got this camp working like clockwork. We don't need him here messing things up."

She responded, "All right, then, it's settled."

There was a knock at the door and I opened it to find Hank and Brad standing there. I pulled my robe closer around me. As Brad came inside he could tell something was up and he gave me a penetrating look. Protectively, Hank stood between us. Evidently, my grandmother had also relayed to Hank what had happened between Brad and me.

Oma began, "Bradley, I'm sorry, but this isn't working out the way I had planned. I would like you to take your things and leave immediately. I will pay you for the rest of the week."

Defensively, Brad replied, "What do you mean? Why am I being fired?"

Oma explained, "Bradley, some things have come to my atten-tion about how you have handled yourself with the children and with my granddaughter. This is not acceptable behavior."

He looked at me in disgust, "What did you tell her? Did you tell her how you flirted with me and led me on and then turned to ice? You're nothing but a tease and a whore!"

The words hit me as if I had been slapped in the face.

Hank interceded, "That's enough, Brad. Let's go take a walk and get your things." Hank tried to grab Brad's arm, but truthfully, Hank was no match for him.

Brad shook him off, "I'm going; I don't need no cripple

walking me anywhere." And with that, he turned on his heels and left the cabin.

Hank stood guard at Oma's front door as Murray went to explain what was happening to the rest of the staff and counselors. Grandmother looked drained from the stress of the situation. She said, "I'm sorry, Jace. That was a terrible thing for him to say to you. I guess I really didn't know him at all. I made an awful mistake and you and the children had to suffer for it."

I protested, "You couldn't have known, Oma. And as soon as you were made aware of it, you handled it."

Hank nodded, "You're a force to be reckoned with, Issy. I'm proud of you."

I left her in Hank's care while I took a shower and got dressed for the day. Once Murray came back to say that Brad had left the premises, I took a walk down to the activities cabin. The air already seemed somehow lighter now that he was gone.

Still, I felt vulnerable, and the last thing I wanted to feel was vulnerable. Even though I knew I didn't deserve it, being called a tease and a whore was hurtful. I told myself I didn't need a man in my life and that I was fine on my own. Stubbornly, I thought no one could ever live up to my memory of Brian anyway. But a moment later, I realized that in the year which had passed since his death, I had built up our relationship to be this perfect thing in my mind. I had managed to only remember the good times we had, and my carelessness that had ended in the accident that took his life. The truth was that as much as I loved Brian, our relationship was flawed. It wasn't the fairy-tale I had wanted to believe it was. I just hadn't wanted to admit it because I didn't want to be alone again.

I was surprised to find Tucker in the activities cabin with the campers. He was having them trace out patterns and helping them to make simple stained-glass pieces. He looked up when I entered, and our eyes locked for a moment until I looked away. The hurt I had felt at Brad's ugly words was still evident on my face. As I walked around the room, I realized the counselors all knew what they were doing. They had obviously helped the campers with this type of project before.

Two of the counselors, Lexi and Cole, were working with a group of campers at one table. It seemed every time she had a chance to work with him, she took it. Perhaps if love was not in the cards for me, they would find it with each other. I sat down with them at their table and asked, "How do you guys know how to make stained glass?"

Lexi replied, "Oh, Tucker comes here every year and does this craft with the kids. I've been making these since I first came here when I was twelve and I'm twenty now."

Cole added, "Even when Tucker was a counselor, he would always talk about making stained glass."

"And how old are you now, Cole?"

"Twenty-one."

When it came time for soldering, the counselors made sure everyone at the table was wearing safety glasses. The children drew lines with the liquid silver that fastened the pieces of glass to each other.

Since they had both been campers here, I asked them what activities they'd like to see more of. Cole was quick to answer,

"I'd like teach the kids some astronomy. I've always had an interest in the sky and the constellations. I've done a lot of studying about the stars and planets and I bet the kids would be interested in learning more. If we had a telescope, maybe we could find some cool stars."

Lexi remarked, "That's a great idea, Cole." She was trying so hard to make Cole see her. But he still seemed to have no idea that she was interested.

I asked, "What about you, Lexi, what would you like to do?"

It didn't take her long to think of something, "Do you think we could put on a play?"

I was floored, "Another great idea! Thank you. Let me see what I can do."

Lexi added, "By the way, I'm glad Brad is gone. None of us liked him."

Cole looked up then and glanced at Lexi with a questioning look. Finally, he asked her, "Did he do anything to you?"

She lowered her eyelashes, "Well, he always touched the girls whenever he could. He never passed by us without reaching out."

Cole's face turned red with anger, "You should have told me."

I put my hand on his arm, "It's all right Cole, he's gone now." It seemed I was wrong, evidently Cole was very aware of Lexi.

When craft time was over, the children all lined up and the counselors led them out to their next activity. I stayed behind to help Tucker put his materials away. I commented, "I think it's great that you come here to do this with the kids."

He shrugged, "This is where I got my start. I'm just 'giving back' as Oma always says."

I collected the small hand-held soldering guns that had been left on the tables and piled them all into a box. He seemed like he wanted to say something else but wasn't sure of how to say it. So, I started, "Have you heard that Brad was let go?"

"Yeah," his jaw stiffened, "and I heard what he did too."

"What did you hear?"

"Well, Haylie told me about Benny."

I nodded, "Yes. That was terrible."

"Then she told me you came back from a canoe trip with him and that you were crying."

"She said that?"

He replied, "Yeah, that kid doesn't miss a trick."

I agreed, "She's pretty special."

He wasn't going to let this go easily, "So what happened? What did he do to make you cry?"

I was surprised to find myself telling him what had happened. After all, I had just decided that men weren't worth my time. And yet here I was, telling Tucker about what had happened at the waterfall and then what Brad had called me in front of my grandmother.

He said, "I'm sorry Brad did that to you. You don't deserve that, but I can't say I'm surprised by the things he does and says."

"What do you mean?"

"It's just that I tried to warn Oma before she hired him this year. It was different when his father was around. He's always acted one way around his father and another whenever his father turned his back."

I was a little confused, "How well do you know Brad?"

"When I was a camper here, sometimes Brad would come for the day to spend time with his father. As soon as his father left the cabin, he'd start picking fights with kids. He's always had a bad temper. He'd get into fights and then tell his father some kind of story. Whoever fought him would end up getting sent back to the orphanage and banned from camp the following year. But all the time, it was Brad causing the trouble. His father never wanted to believe that, so he always took his son's side."

"That's interesting. He told me the campers never treated him right because they were jealous he had parents."

Tucker laughed, "Not even close to being the truth. But then again, he wouldn't know the truth if it hit him in his face. And believe me I've come close to wanting to hit him in the face." Then under his breath he said, "But never as close as I am right now." I could tell that Tucker was really seething, but then again, I felt the same way.

When we were done packing up his materials he said, "Do you think I could take you out some time?"

I shook my head, "I've got a lot on my plate right now. I'm sorry. It's just not a good time for me."

Tucker looked deflated, "Okay. Well, if you need any help . . . I mean with the camp, will you let me know?"

"Sure."

The next few days were spent acclimating myself to my new position. I arranged to have a therapist, Dennis Watson, join our staff at the camp. I realized that the children all had delicate issues to deal with and I certainly knew I wasn't prepared to help them on my own. Although I didn't know if counseling was available at the orphanage, I felt we could at least offer it to them while they were here.

I turned one room of Brad's cabin into my office, and another, into an office for Dennis. The living room became a cozy place for group sessions. Dennis's smiling face and upbeat attitude was like balm on an open wound. He was in his fifties and wore silver glasses and plaid flannel shirts over his jeans. Being the father of three teenagers himself, he appeared comfortable when dealing with the campers. It seemed there was nothing the kids could say that surprised him and I never saw him lose his cool.

Returning back to Oma's cabin one afternoon, I found her looking anxious while opening and closing various doors in the kitchen. "What's wrong, Oma?"

"I can't find my keys anywhere!"

"Well, when was the last time you used them?"

She looked at me with a blank stare and then replied, "I don't know."

I could see she was getting really upset with herself. "Oma, I have my keys, we'll just make a new set if yours don't show up."

"Ja, we can do that," she nodded her head. "Jace, I'm glad you are back early today. I was thinking about what I needed to tell you. I want you to write down more of the story."

"Okay, Oma. Let me get the pad and pen. I'll be right back."

As sorry as I was to have her dredge up all the difficult memories that surrounded the war, I noticed that when she focused on telling me her story, the anxiety she had been exhibiting more and more as of late, seemed to ease up a bit.

"I'm ready, Oma. So, the last time we spoke, you were telling me the war had ended and the Danes were now in control of your refugee camp."

"Ja, let me see now."

It took her a little longer than usual, but then the memories started to flood back in and she continued her story.

Oma explained, "Over the months that had passed, the borders of the countries in Eastern Europe had been renegotiated by the Allies and, as a result, much of Poland and East Prussia was given to the Soviet Union and the southern area of East Prussia was seized by Poland. We were told that any residents who remained in those areas were now officially exiled and forced to leave their homes forever. As for the rest of us refugees who had already left, we were banned from ever returning home."

CHAPTER TWENTY-SEVEN

1945

One day in late August, Rebekah and Issy took out the thread and needles they had taken from Helga's packed bag and began to alter their dresses to fit their emaciated bodies. Helga's bag had come in handy several times with its collection of first aid supplies and practical items. As they stitched, they noticed a girl sneaking out the back door of their cabin. "Where do you think she's going?" Rebekah asked. With a curious glance between them, they decided to follow her. They laid down their sewing and casually walked to the back door so as not to attract any attention. The women were busy talking to each other and watching over their own children who were playing in the center of the room. No one noticed as Issy and Rebekah slipped out the door.

It took them a moment to spot the girl near the fenced perimeter of the camp. The Danish guards were known to circle the camp routinely to make sure no one exited or entered. But, at the moment, there were no guards in sight. That's when they saw the girl carefully unhook a piece of the barbed wire from a post. She held some sort of cloth in her hand so the wire wouldn't rip at her skin. Apparently, she must have known the wire was not secured in that spot.

Rebekah whispered, "Let's follow her."

But before they could, they saw a guard turn the corner of their cabin. Issy and Rebekah dove behind bushes to hide as the girl disappeared from view on the other side of the fence. When they were sure the guard had passed and could no longer see them, they dashed for the fence. Carefully, Rebekah tried to lift the barbed wire, but it bit at her skin and her fingertips began to bleed. Issy looked around for something to use to protect them, and seeing nothing, decided to rip the hem off of her skirt. Issy was able to then lift the wire and quickly pass through the narrow opening. Rebekah followed while Issy held the wire fence open. Then Issy hooked the barbed wire back onto the post and put the piece of cloth into her pocket. They ran across the field until they reached the line of trees just beyond.

Together the girls followed along a path they found in the woods until they came to a clearing. "Look," Issy pointed to the girl they had been following. There was a farm field in front of them and the girl was on her knees digging around a plant with her bare hands. They saw her pick something off of the root and then hide it in her dress. Then the girl patted the dirt back around the plant and looking around to make sure no one had seen her, she dashed back toward the woods where Issy and Rebekah were waiting. When the girl saw them, she was startled and gave a tiny squeak.

Rebekah asked her, "What are you doing?" The girl looked

terrified for a moment, but then Issy said, "It's okay, we won't tell anyone. My name is Issy and this is my sister, Rebekah. What is your name?" Rebekah smiled at being called Issy's sister. During all the years that they had spent in the attic, they had imagined they were sisters. It was part of their game of make-believe. With no one at the camp knowing the truth, they had decided to keep the charade going.

The girl looked at Issy and Rebekah doubtfully. Truthfully, they looked as different as night and day, Issy, with her honey-blonde hair and blue eyes, and Rebekah, with her reddish-brown hair and brown eyes. But the girl understood the need for make-believe families, and so she let it go.

She answered, "My name is Ruth."

Issy pointed to the object under Ruth's dress, "What do you have there, Ruth?"

Hesitantly, Ruth reached into the bodice of her dress and pulled out a potato. The girls eyed it hungrily. Ruth explained, "I will show you how to do it, but you have to be careful. If you take too many from any one plant, then the farmer will know. Each plant has many potatoes attached to its roots, he will not miss one. But if you take more, the plant may wilt and then he will know someone has been stealing his potatoes."

Rebekah and Issy thanked Ruth and then ran toward the farm field. They dug with their hands on two separate plants and each took only one potato. They stuffed the potatoes in their dresses and then looked around to make sure they weren't being watched. Rebekah said, "Let's take two more." They moved to different plants and again took a potato each before patting the soil around the plants to hide the evidence of their theft.

When they made it back to the woods, Ruth was still waiting for them. She said, "Be careful when you go back to the camp. If anyone sees you with potatoes, they will want to know where you got them. Then, surely, we will all be caught."

Issy agreed, "All right, we won't let anyone know. We promise."

Cautiously, the girls waited for the guard to pass before making their way back into the camp. Ruth then held the wire open for them, as each girl slipped through. But in spite of what they told Ruth, as soon as it was safe to do so, Rebekah pulled Vera aside. "Vera, look what we found." She placed her finger up to her lips to indicate silence was needed. Then she handed Vera one of the potatoes. "This is for you and Markos. Issy has one she is going to try to bring to Hans and Friedrich."

Vera's eyes widened in surprise, "Where did you get these?"

"I'm sorry, Vera, I can't tell you. But don't let anyone else see you eating it."

"All right. I won't."

Issy waited until it was after midnight and then, under the shelter of darkness, she made her way toward the men's tent. Her heart was racing with fear as she inched her way across the camp and lifted the flap which covered the entrance. Soon her eyes adjusted to the darkness and she could make out silhouettes of cots and sleeping men inside. She was struck by the musty smell of mildew and decay that seemed much worse than in her cabin.

Cautiously, she searched each cot looking for her brother. When she found him asleep, she shook him gently and whispered, "Hans, I have something for you." Hans opened his eyes and saw his sister before him and quickly registering that this was a cause for concern, he asked, "What are you doing here, Issy? It is dangerous for you to be in here."

"Look at what I have Hans, for you and Friedrich." She handed him the potato. Hans sat up in alarm but tried to keep his voice to a whisper, "Where did you get this?" Issy spoke softly into Hans' ear, "There is a farm just beyond the woods."

Shaken, Hans asked, "You left the camp? How did you get out?"

Issy placed her finger on her lips to caution him against speaking. Hans realized that whatever she had done, she had made it back to camp safely and now she was offering him a potato. He took it from her, ate half of the potato, and then nudged Friedrich awake and handed the rest to him. As Issy snuck back out of the tent, she heard Friedrich say, "She's a risk taker, that girl. Your father always said he had a difficult time getting her to follow his rules. Issy's a wild one, she is." She almost turned back to defend herself when she heard Hans reply, "Ja, she is. But maybe that is what will save her."

Over the next few weeks, Issy and Rebekah retrieved more and more potatoes from the farm. Always careful to take just one from each plant.

"Rebekah, we should give some potatoes to the other children. They are so hungry."

"I know Issy, but look at the field, we've already taken so many. And what if the guards find out and then we can no longer get the potatoes at all?"

The following day, the problem was resolved on its own when

Ruth was caught digging for a potato. The farmer had indeed noticed the dirt around his potato plants being disturbed and his suspicions grew. He was waiting in the woods, watching, when he spied Ruth as she ran onto his field and started to dig.

Ruth was led through their cabin by the guards, the poor girl looked terrified. One of the guards announced, "It seems that we have a thief here who feels she can steal potatoes from the adjoining farm without consequence. For those of you who think there are no repercussions to your actions, let this be a lesson to you." After that, the barbed wire was mended and there was no way to leave the camp again. Ruth was placed in the prison barracks and the girls never saw her again. Over the next month, many refugees were moved to other camps and they hoped Ruth had been among them.

CHAPTER TWENTY-EIGHT

1945

Slowly, their life at camp settled into a new normal. A school was started up by the residents of the camp. The greatest difficulties came with the many languages that the residents spoke including German, Polish, Hungarian, and Czechoslovakian. But they did the best they could, often using English as the common language. Tradesman started up little businesses inside the camp and Friedrich became the shoemaker. Hans apprenticed with him and was learning the business in the hopes that when they made it to America, he would have a way to make some money and be able to care for his sister and Rebekah.

One September afternoon, Issy, Rebekah, and Hans were sitting in a field of clover, when Hans showed the girls the map he had carried all the way from their home in East Prussia.

Hans said, "Onkel Peter's address in New York is written on the cover. When we are able to send a letter out of camp, we should write to him to let him know what has happened to Mutter, Vater, and Oma."

Issy hung her head sadly, "Ja, he will want to know what happened to his bruder and mutter."

Hans nodded, "And we must ask him if we can join him in America."

Hesitantly, Issy's spirits started to lift at the thought of a brighter future after these dark times.

Rebekah added, "But I must try to find my parents first. I cannot leave for America until I know what has happened to them."

Hans' body suddenly convulsed in coughs. Issy jumped to her feet when she saw blood splatter across the clover. She scolded him, "Hans, you are not well! Why do you keep this from us? We can't help you if you're not honest with us." She felt his forehead but did not detect any fever. He brushed her hand away, "I am fine, Issy. Do not worry about me."

One day in early October, Hans handed the map to Issy while they ate the thin broth that had been stretched to serve the increased number of residents. It was so thin, it made Issy wish for the thick gruel that had once been served daily. As disgusting as it had tasted, at least it was able to satisfy her hunger for a few hours. This thin soup only helped to ease her thirst but did nothing to fill her belly. Handing Issy the map he said, "Take this Issy and hide it. Keep it with you at all times."

"All right, Hans. I will. But why give it to me?"

He said, "I just think it will be safer with you." Issy watched him carefully. She was sure there was something he wasn't telling her.

Over the following weeks, more and more refugees arrived, but the resources of the camp were already stretched to ten times its capacity. The deaths from disease and starvation were numerous, and yet there were more refugees taking their place every day. The stories which came along with these new refugees, some who had survived Hitler's concentration camps and hard labor camps, were heartbreaking. Loss had become the way of life for everyone. Fear and cruelty had been the constant companions to the homeless and motherless children who had survived a holocaust and now wandered around the camp in a daze waiting for whatever was to come next. The sound of babies wailing filled the cabins both day and night. Now at fourteen years old, Issy and Rebekah waited too. They waited for their lives to be given back to them. They waited for an end to this sentence in purgatory.

At night, Issy knelt beside her cot and said her prayers while holding the small cross that dangled from her neck and quietly asked, "Please Lord, haven't I paid enough? When will I be free?"

Hearing her, Rebekah pulled her own little cross out from under her dress, "Pray with me Issy. God will see that we have lost enough, and he will reward us for being faithful." So together, the girls recited the Catholic prayers they had learned. Rebekah thought, "Prayers were prayers; God was God. What did it matter which words you choose to use?"

In late October, everyone in the camp was tested for Tuberculosis. Hans' test proved positive. Those who tested positive were moved to a separate tent. A month later, he and many of the others were dead. Fresh graves dotted the ground as if bodies were being planted in the soil for the next harvest. Issy and Rebekah watched as Hans's body was rolled into his grave. Friedrich and several other men shoveled piles of hardened dirt on top of him until all that was left was one more mound among many.

Friedrich placed a hand on Issy's shoulder. "I am so sorry, Issy." She nodded in silence. Her heart felt heavy. She thought she should be sobbing, but the pain seemed to be trapped deep inside of her, too deep to be released. Instead she held onto her grief and it somehow became her companion. It was *her* grief and at least no one could take that away from her. But she lay awake at night wondering why she had been spared. Why was it that God had determined she should carry on while everyone else died? Was this extra time a gift or a curse? If it was a gift, she didn't feel worthy of it.

The cold November days were bleak and gray and foretold another harsh winter was on its way. But each day, Issy knelt beside Hans' grave and mourned for him without shedding a tear. Finally, Rebekah approached Issy and took her hand, "Issy, it's too cold and you will get sick if you stay outside. Come back to the cabin, if nothing else, it is warmer there."

"I don't care, Rebekah. What do I have now? My bruder is gone, my whole family is gone."

Rebekah was hurt, "But you have me."

The pain Issy felt was so overwhelming, she could not hold it in any longer. Rebekah held her as the sobs finally broke through. When Issy was able to take a ragged breath, Rebekah again urged her to come back inside. Once on her cot, all Issy felt was numb. Little Markos saw her and understood her loss, after all, he had lost his entire family less than a year ago. He knelt down beside her and laid his head on her lap. Absently, Issy stroked his brown head. The repetitive motion somehow calmed her aching heart. It reminded her of how she would stroke Hunter. She lowered her head to his and felt the softness of Markos' hair against her cheek. A little while later, Rebekah gently spoke to Markos. "It is time to sleep, little one. Go and put yourself to bed. I will take care of Issy now."

Markos did as he was told, and Rebekah urged Issy to lie down. Then she pulled the thin blanket over Issy's shoulders and left her to get some rest.

Issy woke in the middle of the night. Pulling her blanket around her, she left the cabin and sat on a bench. She imagined she was with her family again. They were watching their Christmas tree burn brightly against the dark night. She watched the ashes float up toward the sky and her eyes found the boundless stars above. She made a wish upon the brightest star of all. She wished her thoughts would reach her loved ones wherever they were. "I love you all and I will miss you forever. Help me to be strong enough to live without you." Then in the darkness her tears poured out once again. The release of her tears felt like a dam had broken within her and she cried until once again, there were no more tears left.

CHAPTER TWENTY-NINE

PRESENT DAY

Oma's face looked pale. The sadness that showed in the lines around her eyes and mouth made me ache for her. With her brother's death, she had been left alone. She had lost her entire family by the time she was fourteen years old. What could I possibly say to ease that kind of pain?

I asked, "How about some tea?"

She nodded, "Ja, that would be nice."

I filled the tea pot, turned on the stove, and reached into a cupboard for two tea cups. When the tea pot whistled, I opened a drawer and took out two spoons. Methodically, I took the sugar bowl from the counter and put it on the table and then poured the water into each cup. Each step prolonged my time to prepare what I should say to her. I knew I would have to address the horror that had taken place in her life, but I didn't have a clue as to how to do such a thing. Oma always drank her tea straight, but I liked to put milk in mine, so I opened the refrigerator and reached for the milk. As I lifted the carton, I was surprised to find Oma's keys on the shelf behind the milk.

Gratified for this gift of distraction, I exclaimed, "Oma! I found your keys!"

Shocked, she said, "What they are doing in there?"

"I don't know, but at least we found them."

She became agitated and it seemed that finding the keys in the refrigerator had only served to make her more upset than she already was. So, I said, "Don't worry, Oma, we found the keys, that's all that matters."

She nodded, "Ja." But she was visibly shaking, so I sat down next to her and took her hands in mine. "Oma, the past is the past. It's what has made you who you are today." I was about to continue when she took a deep breath and her entire countenance changed. She smiled, and pulling her hands out of my grasp, she then wrapped her hands around mine and said, "Ja, this is true for us both."

The next day, I was sitting in my office when Dennis knocked on my door, "Excuse me, Jace. I wondered if I could talk to you for a moment."

"Sure, Dennis, come on in. What's going on?"

"Well," he said, "you know Ginny and Olivia, the two sisters?"

"Sure, I know them."

Dennis said, "Well, some of the other girls have told me they think Ginny's bulimic and has been purging after every meal."

"Oh, no!"

He continued, "Yeah, so I had a session with Olivia and she told me there was a time when she and her sister were together in foster care and it seems Ginny may have been molested there."

"Did Olivia say that?"

"Well, not exactly, but there are indications. She said their foster father used to enter their bedroom at night and make Olivia leave and wait in the hall outside. He would lock the door behind her and Olivia would sit in the hall for hours until the door was opened again. When she went back into the bedroom, she would find her sister crying."

"What should we do?"

"Olivia told me that in the orphanage, some of the girls tease Ginny about her weight. In response, it seems she has completely alienated herself from everyone but her sister, even here at camp. Of course, I will start having some sessions with Ginny, but I was also thinking everyone could benefit by working on a project together, some big camp-wide activity to occupy their minds, build their self-esteem, and help them depend on each other and support each other."

"You know, Lexi suggested that we put on a play. What do you think about us doing something like that?"

"Sounds like a good idea. I think that might be the ticket to getting these kids to work together and maybe it will help them deal with some of their problems. When both mind and body are actively engaged in creating something, there is less time for self-destructive thoughts and behaviors. Some of the campers could work on the set. Others could be responsible for the props and costumes, while still others could be the actors. There'd be something for everyone and they would have to work together in order to make the play a success."

I offered, "It may even give me a chance to use some of what I learned in college. After all, one of my majors was Theater."

"Really?" Something in the way he smiled when he said that made me think he already knew what I had gone to school for. Dennis had a way of getting people to feel comfortable around him. Sometimes, I found myself telling him things I had never told anyone. One day when I was feeling overwhelmed, I had just started crying in my office. He heard me and asked what was wrong. A moment later, the whole story about losing Brian spilled out.

Dennis suggested, "You will need a carpenter to help with building the set. You know Tucker, the guy who comes to do the glass crafts with the kids?" I nodded.

"Well, he's also a good carpenter. Did you know he helped build his workshop?"

"No, I didn't."

He chuckled at the suspicious look I gave him, then continued, "Gatlinburg is a small town, and everyone knows everyone else's business here. Anyway, I could ask him if he'd be interested if you'd like."

"All right," I agreed, "I think this is a good idea. I like it." The more I thought about it, the more excited I got. Perhaps this play would be a good way for me to keep my own mind active and off of Brian. But thinking it through and realizing the limited time we had left at camp, I said, "Maybe, instead of doing an entire play, we should keep it to selected scenes. We could choose some scenes from *Oliver* and others from *Annie*. Both plays are about orphans and I think the kids will identify with the material. We need committees to make some plans. Let me call a meeting with the counselors and find out what kind of talents we have to work with." As I walked out of the cabin, I heard Dennis chuckle to himself.

At the meeting, it was determined that Cole should be in charge of props. Gavin's innate ability with music and musical instruments made him the best choice for music director. Shelby's artistic talents could be put to use as Tucker's assistant set director. Lexi was put in charge of scripts. Josie would handle costumes. After all, her quirky outfits were works of art in themselves. She was also good at rummaging through thrift stores to put together just the right combinations of colors and styles. Finally, I put myself in charge of choreography.

Tucker and Shelby turned the activities cabin into a theater and built a portable stage at one end of the large room. Everyone went to work and a week later, we held auditions for the individual parts. When I saw Ginny walk up onto the stage, I didn't know what to expect. But then she started singing, *"Let's Go to the Movies Annie"* and her beautiful voice filled the whole room. This shy thin girl who barely said a word, had a voice that was a gift from heaven above. She won the part as Grace Farrell, the love interest of Daddy Warbucks, played by Cliff. Ten-year-old Maggie with her glorious red hair was chosen to play the part of Annie. Haylie was given the part of Annie's best friend, Molly. Ginny's sister, Olivia, made an amazing Miss Hannigan, it seemed they both had inherited strong singing voices. For the scenes from *Oliver*, nine-year-old Dalton was chosen for the lead role. Thirteen-year-old Mack and his ever-changing voice made an interesting Fagin. Troublemaker Tanner was the perfect choice for

Jack Dawkins, the Artful Dodger, and eleven-year-old Benny got the part of one of the Workhouse Boys. Seventeen-year-old Wade was given the part of the terrifying Bill Sikes. Ella was chosen as Nancy, the only female member of Fagin's gang and the ill-fated love interest of Bill Sikes. And musical accompaniment was handled by Mazie on the piano along with Gavin on the guitar.

Everyone chipped in and worked together. Two weeks later, they were busy practicing their parts and putting the final touches on the set. Finally, the big night neared. I only worried that we would we have an audience. It wasn't like the children had families who would attend.

The night of the play, as I walked with Oma from her cabin to the new camp theatre, I was surprised to see so many cars coming up the road and parking in our lot. Townspeople took their seats and when there were no more chairs, they stood at the back and the sides of the room, waiting enthusiastically for the play to begin.

I asked in wonder, "Where did they all come from?"

Tucker was at my side, "Well, I posted signs everywhere and called my friends to spread the word."

"Thank you, Tucker! This is so great! The kids will never forget this!"

Backstage, the excitement was palpable. Haylie and Benny ran past me and I called out, "Slow down, I don't want anyone to get hurt."

Haylie smiled at me and said, "Ah, don't worry, Jace. Haven't you ever heard the saying, 'Break a leg'?"

"Yes, I have, Haylie. But that doesn't mean that you actually should." She and Benny started to giggle as they took their places on stage.

The show had a few glitches here and there, like when Dalton forgot to add the belt to his costume and in the middle of a scene, his pants fell down to his knees. He was quick to pick them up again and smile his charming smile at the audience and they erupted in laughter and applause. Glitches and all, the audience enjoyed it just the same. At the end of the night, each child individually came out on stage and the audience applauded in turn. Then once the entire cast was on stage, the children all linked hands as they bowed to the audience. In return, the audience gave the children a standing ovation. I could not have hoped for a better night. And to see Ginny smile with pride as the campers all hugged and congratulated each other after the show was just golden!

I turned to see Dennis standing there nodding his head with approval. I said, "This was a great idea, Dennis. I'm so glad Lexi thought of it! We will have to make this an annual event."

Oma overheard me and said, "Does that mean you will be here for us next year, Jace?"

I wrapped my arms around her and said, "Oma, I've got nowhere to go. Don't think you're getting rid of me now."

She clapped, "Oh, that's just grand!"

The last few days of camp went by in a whirlwind of activity. I hadn't realized how hard it would be to say goodbye to them all.

As the buses were loaded for the last time, Haylie hugged me, and tears filled my eyes. I had become especially fond of her and I knew I was going to miss her upbeat smiling face dearly, "Sweetheart, I will miss you."

"Oh, don't worry, Jace, I'll be back next year."

"All right, and I will be here waiting for you."

As the buses pulled away, I waved to them all and thought about how much joy this summer had given to me.

Later that night, Oma and I sat at her kitchen table once again. We had been too busy with the play to write down any more of her story. Now it was time to catch up. With pen and paper ready, I looked expectantly at my grandmother. But it took a little while before she spoke.

Oma said, "Sorry Jace, I guess it's just old age. It's getting harder to remember the details. Let's see. Where did we leave off?"

I reminded her, "It was after Hans' death."

With a deep breath she said, "Oh right, I, I remember now."

CHAPTER THIRTY

1946

The long months of winter were cruel to the refugees. So, when the warmth of spring returned, the residents rejoiced. Issy thought it was odd how life went on even in the midst of such sorrow. Seasons continued to come and go, children died, while others were born. It helped her to find joy in the small things. Issy walked around the camp and noticed the buds on the trees. Soon they would release the leaves and flowers that were harbored within. Spring would kiss the ground and the grass would turn green once again. She held onto renewed hope that maybe, like the flowers, she and Rebekah would be released from this Limbo. Perhaps they would finally be able to start their journey to America.

It was May 1st and a dance was being held in the cabin which was ordinarily used as the school. Not surprisingly, it was taking place under the watchful eyes of the Danish guards.

Issy and Rebekah helped move the chairs to line the walls. A group of refugees set up in the corner and played the instruments that they had carried with them from their homelands. The music echoed in the room and it reminded Issy of her father's violin. She felt saddened again for a moment. But then she shook herself out of it and allowed Rebekah to draw her out to the dance floor.

They danced about and grew silly with their movements. Markos came between them, they joined hands, and started to spin in a circle. They spun faster and faster as the music picked up tempo. When it reached a crescendo, they all fell to the floor in laughter. Every time they helped each other stand again, Markos begged for more dancing. It had been so long since they had laughed, that their giggles sounded strange even to their own ears.

Rebekah was the first to notice two young guards watching them. "Issy, those guards are smiling at us." Issy and Rebekah were nearly fifteen and had recently started to notice the guards taking an interest in them. One of the guards saw Issy glance at them, and he tipped his cap toward her. Feeling nervous, she quickly looked away and said to Rebekah, "I think we should go sit down for a while. I'm exhausted!" Rebekah responded, "Good idea."

Markos ran off to dance with the other children while Issy and Rebekah sat on a chair near Vera and Friedrich. It didn't take long for Friedrich to notice the interaction that was taking place from across the room between the girls and the young guards. He leaned down to speak into their ears and warned them, "Remember, girls, it is against the rules to fraternize with the guards."

Rebekah responded, "Ja, we know." But she smiled sideways at Issy, and they both stifled a giggle. They were young, and in spite of all they had been through, they had started to feel hopeful that the worst was over. Issy glanced at the young men. They were both blonde, but one had brown eyes while the other's eyes were green. The green-eyed guard was smiling at her and he nodded his head in her direction. Issy blushed and looked away, embarrassed that she had been caught looking at him again. Both guards were tall and slender and appeared to be only a few years older than they. She hadn't seen them before this night, so she guessed they were new and only recently appointed to their camp.

Later that night, as the girls lay on their cots, side by side, Issy took out her father's map and looked at the address. She decided she should memorize it just in case something happened to the map itself. She repeated over and over again, "2130 Fourth Street, Brighton Beach, New York." Markos heard her talking and came to sit on her cot with her. He gingerly touched Catrina's porcelain face and traced the cracks. Issy watched him and suddenly thought it would be best if Markos also remembered the address just in case they were separated. So Issy spoke to Markos. "We all need to memorize Onkel Peter's address. Here, say it with me, 2130 Fourth Street, Brighton Beach, New York." Both Markos and Rebekah repeated it.

A few weeks later, Issy was returning from the public outhouse late one night when she felt as if someone was watching her. The hair on the back of her neck stood up in alarm. She turned around quickly and tried to see in the darkness. Someone moved out of the shadows and she saw the floodlight flash over the young man and recognized him as one of the guards from the dance, the one with the green eyes.

He spoke to her in Danish, but she did not understand enough of the language. She asked him, "Es?" Although she had picked up some Danish words over her years at the camp, she still could not speak it fluently. Whatever he had just said, she didn't understand. Seeing she did not speak Danish, and not knowing German, he tried English, "You should not be out so late alone. It is dangerous for a young girl so late at night."

Issy felt an electric current run down her spine and goose-bumps appeared on her arms. She knew she should feel frightened, but instead, she felt a tingle of excitement. She replied, "You speak English?"

He walked closer to her and smiled, "Ja, and it appears you do too."

He kept a respectful distance and made a funny bow to her, "My name is Oliver. What is your name?" But still, she hesitated. He said, "I won't hurt you. Don't be afraid." Finally, she said, "My name is Isabela, but everyone calls me Issy."

Oliver smiled, "May I call you Isabela?"

He reached out his hand to hold hers. But as he took it in his, she thought of the dirt caked up under her fingernails and quickly withdrew her hand. In fact, there was a layer of dirt discoloring her skin all over, and she could only imagine what a fright she must look, even in the dark. Her other hand automatically reached for her hair. Her hair had grown in again after the time it had been shaved off. But without anything to tie up her braids, her hair fell in tangles around her shoulders. She lowered her eyes to the ground, embarrassed. She had never thought about how she looked before, it had never mattered. Not until now.

As if he could read her mind, Oliver said, "You are beautiful, Isabela."

Uncomfortable with the attention, Issy asked, "Where is your friend?"

He looked confused for a moment. "My friend?"

"Yes," Issy replied, "the other guard who was watching us at the dance."

He asked, "Ah, so you did see us watching you."

She blushed, "Ja, of course. We saw you both."

"He's not working tonight, but his name is Viktor. What is your friend's name?"

"She is Rebekah."

His eyes widened, "Rebekah? Is she a Jew?"

"Why? Does that matter to you?"

He blustered, "No, no, of course not. I was just asking."

"Then ja, she is a Jew. My family protected her and hid her from the Gestapo."

"Oh, I see. That was a very brave thing to do."

"Rebekah has become my sister. She is all I have left."

"What do you mean, she is all you have left? I see you with that man and woman and the boy."

"Vater and Oma were killed by the Soviets when they came to our farm. Mutti died along our journey here, and my bruder, Hans, died this past November in camp from Tuberculosis. Rebekah is my sister now. She is all the family I have left. The man and woman you see us with were our neighbors and the boy is Markos, we found him on our journey and took him with us."

He asked, "And Rebekah's family? Were they taken?"

"Ja. A long time ago."

Oliver said, "I'm sorry." After a long silence, Issy turned to leave. But he stopped her and asked, "Will you meet me here tomorrow night, at the same time?"

She felt the shiver run down her spine, the excitement and the fear of this unexpected request. Although it frightened her, she also welcomed the danger. It was better than the monotony that her life had become.

"All right."

He nodded, "Then until tomorrow."

And with that he left her. As she walked back to the cabin, she felt lighter. So much had been weighing her down for so long. Now there was a smile on her face. She lay on her cot and heard Rebekah rustle next to her. Rebekah whispered, "Where were you?"

For just a little while, she wanted to keep her meeting with Oliver a secret. For now, it was hers to hold and treasure. So, she answered, "I was in the latrine."

It wasn't a lie; it just wasn't the whole truth.

CHAPTER THIRTY-ONE

1946

The next night when Issy met Oliver again, he was carrying something wrapped in a towel, "This is for you."

Issy opened the towel and peeked inside. Too loudly, she exclaimed, "Apples!" Then quickly placed her hand over her mouth as if to stop any other sound from coming out. They both looked around in the darkness but saw nothing. She lifted them to her nose and breathed in the smell of them. It reminded her of the apple orchard by her parents' farm. She whispered, "Danke."

"There is one for you, and the other is for Rebekah."

She lifted one to her lips and immediately took a bite. The juice felt glorious in her mouth and she closed her eyes as she tried to let the sensation linger on her tongue.

He urged, "Come. Sit over here. No one will see us here." She sat next to him on a bench in the shadows just outside one of the cabins.

Oliver asked, "How old are you, Isabela?"

"I will be fifteen next week."

She asked, "And how old are you?"

"I'm eighteen," he replied. "I have to admit that I thought you were older."

She looked at him with regret, "Am I too young then?"

"No," Oliver smiled at her, "You are just right, just the way you are."

They talked for hours and he wouldn't let her go until she agreed to meet him again the following night.

Rebekah awoke when Issy returned to her cot. "Here Rebekah, I have a present for you." Wiping the sleep out of her eyes Rebekah asked, "What is it?" Issy placed the apple in Rebekah's hand. "Where did you get it?" Issy replied, "It's a secret."

For the moment, Rebekah didn't care what the secret was, all she cared about was that she had an apple.

Soon, Issy was meeting Oliver every night. This went on for almost a month. Each time, he brought her a treasure, like apples, strawberries, carrots, or potatoes.

One night Issy asked, "Oliver, tell me about your family."

He moved her hair away from her shoulder so he could see her face better in the dim moonlight and said, "My parents were killed when the Germans came. All I have left is my grandmother."

Issy was surprised by his answer. It was her turn now to say, "I'm sorry."

"It is not your fault. You didn't kill my parents. Death is a part of war. Violence is a part of war. That's just the way things are."

She nodded, only too aware of the truth in his statement. She said, "Ja, the superiors plan, the soldiers kill, and the innocent suffer. That is war."

Oliver regretted the sadness in her voice, "We do not have to speak of it anymore, if that's what you prefer."

But she answered, "Why not speak of it? It is what I live every day. Talking is easy; living is hard." The weight that had been lifted so briefly by his visits, now returned in full force. Her shoulders slumped as if the weight was physical instead of metaphorical.

For Oliver, this was an awakening. He had not considered the situation fully before deciding to pursue Issy. Now that he knew her better, he genuinely cared for her; and as his feeling grew, so did his concern. A moment later, both of their heads turned at the sound of a branch breaking beneath a footstep. Rebekah appeared out of the darkness. She bravely took the final steps and joined Issy and Oliver. Having overheard a bit of their conversation, Rebekah spoke in the English that Issy had taught her. Addressing Oliver, Rebekah asked, "Is there a problem, sir?"

Issy turned to face her, "Rebekah, this is my friend, Oliver. He is the one who has been bringing me the fruits I shared with you."

Rebekah looked at the guard warily, "Friend?" Rebekah was

alarmed. When she had pressed Issy as to where the treats were coming from, Issy told her it was from a friend. But she would not tell her anything more than that. Now she knew why.

Oliver spoke, "Ja Rebekah, we are friends." But Rebekah didn't like the looks of this friendship; she wanted to protect Issy from being hurt. She said, "Issy, you should come back to the cabin before you get into trouble."

Seeing how worried Rebekah was, Issy said, "All right, Rebekah. I'll come with you." Then Issy turned to Oliver, "Danke, for everything. But perhaps Rebekah is right. It is probably best if we do not meet again."

Oliver looked deflated, but he said, "If that is what you want. Goodnight Isabela, goodnight Rebekah." He bowed and took his leave.

Back in the cabin, Rebekah asked Issy, "Why didn't you tell me, Issy?"

Issy thought for a moment and then said, "I guess I knew you would tell me not to meet him anymore."

"Well, you are right. That is what I would have told you." Rebekah saw the look on Issy's face and asked, "Do you love him?"

Issy replied, "I don't know."

"Does he love you?"

In a small voice Issy said, "I think so."

"Well, let's get some sleep. We can talk about this in the morning."

Rebekah's questions spun in Issy's head. She had never been in love before. She wasn't entirely sure that she was now. She only knew that she enjoyed talking to him and would miss him if she never spoke to him again.

The following day the sun was shining brightly in the sky. Summer was finally here, and she lifted her face to the sun to feel its warmth.

Rebekah suggested, "Let's take a walk, Issy."

Rebekah put her arm through Issy's as their feet kicked up the dust from the well-worn path. "So, tell me about him."

"Oh Rebekah, he's very kind. And this war has been hard on him too. He lost both of his parents when Germany invaded."

Rebekah softened her tone a bit, "I'm sorry for that. But Issy, it is forbidden for us to talk to them."

"I know."

Rebekah asked, "So what will you do about it?"

"You heard me, Rebekah; I told him we couldn't meet each other anymore."

Rebekah nodded, "Ja, I heard you. But I don't believe you. I know you too well, Issy. Knowing you shouldn't do something has never stopped you before."

Issy hung her head, Rebekah was right. Her mind wandered back to the time when she told Rebekah about the secret of Hans still being in the house. She realized she couldn't hide anything from her best friend, she never could. And it wasn't long before Issy was meeting Oliver again at night.

CHAPTER THIRTY-TWO

1946

One night, Oliver asked her, "Isabela, I've told my grandmother about you. What if you and Rebekah came with me to our house?"

"What do you mean? We can't leave here."

"What if I could sneak you both out and you could stay with us?"

"Oliver, as much as I would like to, I couldn't do that."

"Why?"

"Because then I would feel like I owed you something." She blushed having to say the words, "I'm not that kind of girl."

He sounded hurt when he responded, "I know that, and that's not what I am asking."

Issy explained, "Oliver, when this is all over, Rebekah and I have to see if her family has survived. Then we are going to go to America, together. So, you see, it wouldn't be right of me to impose on you and your grandmother. Besides, it might put you all in danger."

Oliver shook his head, "I won't deny the fact that I have feelings for you. But I also wouldn't want you to feel like you owed me anything. I just want to help you, and if I can do that, I'd feel a whole lot better." He could see that his words were having some effect on her so he continued, "You don't have to stay forever, but if I can help you get on with your life, that would mean everything to me. I've spoken to my grandmother about you, many times, and it was her idea that I come up with a plan to sneak you out."

"Oliver, I don't understand that. I don't see why you would do this for me without getting something in return."

"But you are wrong, Isabela. I would be getting something in return. It would bring me much happiness to help you get out of this place. I guess the best way to explain it is a lot of terrible things have come out of this war. If I can turn one of those terrible things into a good thing, then maybe I'm not powerless. Maybe it's a chance for a regular guy like me to make a difference."

Issy considered his offer again and then explained, "Rebekah would have to agree to come too. I won't leave her behind."

"I know. Tell her there is room for you both."

"Well then, I will talk to her and I'll let you know what we decide."

Issy told Rebekah that Oliver had offered to help them escape, and that they could stay at his grandmother's house. Rebekah responded, "It would give me a chance to get back to

Germany and start the search for my family." So, it was decided, but the girls had only one regret, they would have to leave Friedrich, Vera, and Markos behind.

They couldn't just leave without any explanation, so they decided to tell Vera about their plans. After hearing the whole story, Vera said, "I think you should go with him. We don't know how long it will be before we are separated anyway. They may decide to send us to different camps. Friedrich and I will take care of Markos. Go with your Oliver. After all you have told me about him, I trust him."

Issy replied, "We will miss you all."

When Issy informed Oliver that they would take him up on his offer, he said, "Don't worry, I will take care of everything. Just meet me here tomorrow night."

The girls packed their belongings in their satchels. Of course, they made sure Catrina was hidden among their clothes, along with the blood-stained map with Onkel Peter's New York address.

The following night, Oliver met them and guided them through the darkness to where his friend, Viktor, was waiting with a car. Handing a blanket to the girls, Oliver said, "Take this and lie down in the back seat. Cover yourselves and don't say a word. No one will question us."

Their hearts were beating wildly as they hid together beneath the blanket on the floor of Viktor's car. As soon as they had cleared the gates, Oliver said, "You can sit up now." The girls were both thrilled and terrified as they watched the camp disappear from view, but at least they were together on this adventure.

As they rode through the unfamiliar dark streets of Copen-hagen, the girls began to question their decision to go with these young men. They didn't say a word, but the looks that passed between them, told what they were thinking. Finally, the car was parked in front of a stone house and Oliver opened the car door. Hesitantly, they climbed out, unwilling to let go of each other for even a moment.

Oliver understood, and with a gentle smile he said, "It is all right. My grandmother is here. Please don't be afraid."

Inside the house, a small fire was set in the hearth to take the chill out of the summer night. The aroma of roasted chicken filled the room and a plump old woman sat at the kitchen table. She stood to greet the girls and seeing their unkempt appearance, immediately took over the situation and spoke to them in English. "Ah, I am Oliver's grandmother, but you can call me Johanna. Put your suitcases down, I will clean the clothes for you. Now, come with me."

The girls followed the old woman up the stairs to the bath-room. She turned on the water and filled the large claw foot tub with hot water before handing them a bar of brown soap. Johanna explained, "I will get some of Oliver's mother's old clothes for you to wear while I wash your dresses. Take a bath, and when you are ready, come back downstairs for supper." When she left them, the girls looked at each other trying to comprehend the kindness which was being bestowed upon them. Steam rose from the white porcelain bathtub as Rebekah dipped her hand in to test the water. A moment later, Johanna returned with clothes and draped them over a rack while she instructed, "Leave your soiled clothes on the floor and I will take them." Then, as she left, she closed the bath-room door behind her.

They discarded their dirty dresses and stepped into the large tub. Sharing the bar of soap, they scrubbed away the dirt and grime. They became giddy as they helped each other wash their hair in the warm water. When they were finished, they wrapped large towels around their bodies and vigorously dried themselves. Dressing quickly in the simple dresses, they looked each other over with approval.

Johanna knocked on the door, "It is only me, girls." Hearing Johanna's voice, Issy said, "It's all right, you can come in." Johanna picked up the pile of discarded clothes and handed them a large comb before leaving them again, "When you are ready, come downstairs. Supper is ready."

The tangles in their hair took quite a lot of effort to tame. But when they finally entered the kitchen, they couldn't believe their eyes. A feast had been set on the table. Plates full of roasted chicken, cabbage, and beets along with a basket filled with homemade bread and butter.

Both Oliver and Viktor were already seated and waiting for them. As the dishes were passed around, the girls were amazed at the delectable bounty. Johanna warned them, "Eat, but be careful not to take too much, your stomachs are not used to eating."

However, in spite of the warning and not able to stop themselves, the girls ate generously. But it wasn't long afterwards, that they felt their stomachs churn and cramp in response. They felt like their insides were twisted in knots and they spent all night taking turns running between their bedroom and the toilet. After that night, they were more careful about how much they ate until they had regained the ability to digest the food properly.

Notwithstanding the care they were given, a few weeks later, Rebekah fell ill. Her joints were inflamed, and a rash developed on her back. Although she tried to hide the pain in her knees and ankles, a fever overtook her and soon she was unable to walk. Johanna examined Rebekah and asked her, "Have you had a sore throat lately?"

"Ja, before I left the camp. It was the worst sore throat I've ever had in my life."

Johanna nodded, "I see. Oliver, go fetch the doctor."

Rebekah protested weakly, "No, if the doctor tells anyone we are here, they will put us back in the camp!"

"Don't worry, child. Dr. Jenson has been a good friend to me for all of my life. He won't tell a soul." When the doctor arrived, he took charge quickly. It wasn't long before he announced, "It's rheumatic fever." Issy asked, "Is she going to be all right?" He nodded and took out a needle and a vial of medicine. "Penicillin will take care of it, but it's a long road to recovery."

Joanna thanked the doctor and then comforted Issy, "We will take good care of her until she is well again. Don't worry."

"Danke, Johanna. It is good that we are here. There would not have been any penicillin for Rebekah at camp." Johanna nodded, aware that the Danish government had refused to allow medical care to many of the refugees.

Slowly over the next two years, Rebekah regained her strength. During this time, Oliver continued to work at the camp. One night he came home to tell Issy, "Vera, Friedrich, and Markos have been transferred to another camp." Issy bowed her head upon hearing this and then said, "Perhaps it is getting close to the time when we should move on as well." Seeing his face drop, she laid her hand on his arm and continued, "Oliver, if you had not saved us when you did, Rebekah would surely have died. I will forever be grateful to you and your grandmother for your kindness."

Oliver placed his hand over hers, and said, "Isabela, I know you have your plans, but I cannot let you go without at least asking. Would you consider staying here and becoming my wife?"

Issy's heart constricted; she wished she could change her feelings for him. But as much as she loved him, it was not in the way of a wife for her husband. Her only response was, "I'm sorry, Oliver." He nodded as his hand fell away from hers, it was what he had expected, even if he had hoped she'd answer differently.

CHAPTER THIRTY-THREE

PRESENT DAY

As Tucker and I walked around the camp, it seemed strangely quiet. Everyone was gone now and I wondered how I would fill my days.

"Jace, there's something I'd like to show you. Would you take a ride with me?" Tucker had a mischievous grin on his face.

Cautiously, I responded, "What is it?"

"It's a surprise. We can take a picnic lunch with us because it will take all day."

He looked so hopeful, so I said, "Oh, well, I guess it's okay. When do you want to go?"

"Now is as good a time as any. It's a beautiful day, not too hot, not too cold, clear sky, it's perfect!"

I laughed, "Okay, okay, let's go tell Oma and make some sandwiches then."

Oma watched us with a broad smile on her face as we spread some of her special honey chicken salad onto sesame seed rolls. It only took us a few minutes to fill the cooler and then we were off. I saw Oma waving happily from the screened-in porch as we drove away.

The mountains were beautiful! Along the way, I was able to take some beautiful pictures from breathtaking overlooks. Then we drove past a sign, welcoming us to North Carolina. We saw some picnic tables at another overlook and stopped to have our lunch.

"So, are you going to tell me where we are going yet?"

"Nope, you'll just have to wait until we get there."

"How much farther is it?"

"Not much."

Back in the car, I opened my window and let the warm wind blow against my hand. I wiggled my fingers in the breeze and felt content. Tucker had an easygoing way about him that put me at ease. I looked over at him and admired his handsome profile.

Jokingly, I asked him, "So tell me Tucker, why hasn't some Southern girl caught you yet?"

He shrugged, "There was a girl, her name was Ellie. We grew up together in the orphanage. We used to go to your grand-mother's camp each summer."

"What happened?"

"After she turned 18, she stayed on as a counselor during the summers. Of course, I was living with Oma by then and worked as a counselor at camp too. We were planning on getting married. But one day, she found a lump on her breast. She was so young; we didn't think it would turn out to be anything, but it was cancer."

"Oh, I'm so sorry! I didn't know!"

He continued, "She fought really hard and she made it into remission. A year later, it came back again. She fought it again and made it into another remission. I wanted to marry her then, but she said no. She wanted to wait, to make sure she was cured before getting married. Two years later, it was back. Of course, she fought it again, but this time, it didn't work. After fighting for five years, she lost the fight."

"How long ago was that?"

"Two years ago."

I was silent for a while and then I knew it was time for me to tell my story, "I lost my fiancé too. We were at a party and he had too much to drink. On the way home, he complained that his seat belt was bothering him and he undid it. The seatbelt alarm was beeping at him to put the belt back on and I was trying to reach over and buckle it in place. But then we were hit from behind by a pickup truck and pushed off the road and down a ravine. When I came too, Brian wasn't in the car anymore. Since the airbag had inflated, it took me a while to open the door. I found him about ten feet away. He had been thrown from the car. His body hit a tree. He was still alive, but it was terrible. He kept calling my name."

Tucker said, "I'm sorry."

Then I blurted out, "The thing is, I was driving. I knew he had had too much to drink, so I took the keys from him. It was my fault. The accident was my fault. He died because of me." I looked out at the beautiful scenery which was passing by, but all I could see was Brian's broken body.

Tucker tried to reassure me, "It wasn't your fault. You did the right thing. It was just an accident and he should have been wearing his seat belt. What about the guy driving the pick-up truck? What happened to him?"

"I don't know, he left. It was a hit-and-run."

He stared ahead as he drove on, "How did you get help?"

"I couldn't find my phone. It must have been thrown into the woods somewhere. I made it up to the road by the guard rail and a little while later someone stopped. They called an ambulance. I had two broken ribs and a fractured arm."

Tucker took a deep breath but still didn't say a word.

I continued, "When they put us in the ambulance, Brian was still alive. But the tree had broken his back and he died on the way to the hospital."

Tucker reached his hand out to me and I took it. He said, "I'm really sorry you had to go through that."

"Thank you."

We were quiet after that, neither of us knowing what to say, each of us lost in our own thoughts. As we drove on for miles in silence, slowly the scenes of the accident in my mind faded and I was able to take in the beauty of the landscape once again. We left the mountains and came to some flat grassy land and I noticed brown dots in the fields in the distance. As we got closer, the brown dots grew. My eyes widened in surprise as I realized what they were. I cried in disbelief, "Elk!"

The mood in the car lightened immediately and Tucker chuckled at my response. I looked at the beautiful regal animals as they lifted their antlered heads to gaze in our direction. I exclaimed in wonder, "I didn't know there were elk in the Smoky Mountains! I thought they were only out west, like in Wyoming or Montana."

"Do you like it? This is the surprise."

"Yes, it's beautiful." I lifted my camera and started clicking the shutter and adjusting the lens to get the optimum settings.

We sat there for a long time, just watching the elk graze and walk. The peaceful pasture had plenty of tall grass for them to enjoy. Their tails continuously swatted at the pesky flies as they walked on their long graceful legs. It was mesmerizing to watch, and the scene helped bring me back to my earlier peaceful frame of mind.

When the sun started to go down over the mountains, Tucker said, "Let's drive a little farther, there's a nice restaurant a few miles up along this road."

We stopped for some down-home Southern fried chicken with gravy and grits. The restaurant had a big porch with rocking chairs set on it. The meals were delicious, and we enjoyed the costumed waitresses who looked like they were out of a storybook with their old-fashioned country dresses and frilly aprons. After filling our bellies, we headed back home. "Home," this place had become home to me, but then again, hadn't it always been. I no longer felt like I was drifting without an anchor. This was where I belonged.

Back at the camp, we walked up to the porch door together. But before we entered the cabin, he put his hand on my upper arm to stop me. I turned to look at him. "Jace, I had a great time today. I hope you did too."

"I did, thank you, Tucker. It was really wonderful."

Then, with his other hand, he lifted my chin and lowered his lips to mine. The kiss was sweet and I welcomed it. I opened my mouth to his and his hand moved from my arm to my back. He held me close and I knew one thing for sure, I didn't want the kiss to end.

CHAPTER THIRTY-FOUR

"Oma, would you prefer a small dog or a larger one?" I could tell from her face that the idea of taking home a dog was growing on her.

She glanced over the cages and said, "I suppose I'm more inclined to larger dogs. I don't like the little dogs that yip all day and pee as soon as a someone pets them."

I asked the salesgirl to let me hold a pure-bred Labrador puppy. He was cute and soft and I showed him to Oma; she smoothed his fur and then glanced away. Finally, she said, "Jace, I'd rather go to an animal shelter. I think an older dog would be better for me."

Of course, she was right. We left the pet store and headed for the animal shelter. At the end of the aisle, away from the other dogs, was a large cage and inside was a full-grown female golden retriever and collie mix. The dog was lying down and shaking, she was obviously frightened of strangers. Oma stared at the dog for a long time and finally put her fingers in between the bars of the cage. She said, "Hello old girl. What do you think? Do you want to come home with me?" The dog's demeanor instantly changed, she raised her head and licked Oma's fingers as if she already knew my grandmother. The dog had a very sad look to her and so I asked the attendant, "What do you know about this dog?"

The young woman said, "Her name is Bonnie and she was rescued from a puppy mill a few years ago. At the time, all the other dogs that were rescued with her were in such bad condition, they had to be put to sleep. She is the only dog from that rescue who survived. She spent a few months recovering in an animal hospital when an elderly man adopted her. He named her Bonnie. As you can see, her name is embroidered on her collar. Unfortunately, about a year later, the old man passed in his sleep. His son found Bonnie guarding his father's body and the police had to called to drag her away. She wouldn't let anyone near him. The man's son said he couldn't care for her because he had a small apartment. They brought her to us after that, but she can't be kept near the other dogs. They frighten her. So, you see, she's had a very traumatic life and we have to be careful about who adopts her." The attendant continued, "But I can see she's taken a liking to you ma'am. I've never seen her lick anyone before."

I asked, "How old is she?"

"We believe she's about four or five." Then the attendant asked, "Ma'am, do you have any other dogs?"

Oma answered, "No, I don't."

"Well, that's good, because she probably wouldn't do well with other dogs in the house."

Oma made up her mind, "All right, then. Let's take her."

But I wasn't sure if this dog was more than Oma could handle, so I asked, "Oma, don't you think we should talk about it first?"

"No, this is my dog." And with that she walked up to the counter to fill out the paperwork.

We brought her home and she ran right into the house and lay down on the carpet in front of the fireplace. Oma sat down in her rocking chair while Bonnie watched us cautiously, her huge eyes taking in any movements that we made.

"How did you know that she was the right dog?"

"She has Hunter's eyes."

"Your horse?"

"Ja, my horse, Hunter. Bonnie has the same eyes. I'll never forget Hunter watching me as the ship pulled away."

I could see that even now after all these years this memory was one of the most painful for her.

"Oma, I was hoping that a dog would cheer you up. Are you sure you want this dog if she brings back sad memories for you?"

"Jace, I had years of happy memories with Hunter before the sad ones came. Besides, Bonnie and I are both survivors. And if I can bring some peace and comfort to her, I feel as if I'm righting the wrong I did to Hunter by deserting him."

Watching Bonnie rest her head and instantly fall to sleep, I said, "Well, I guess if nothing else, at least she's not going to run away. I think we'll be lucky if she moves from that spot."

"She will be fine. Now tell me, how was your date with Tucker?"

I was about to protest and say it wasn't a date, but then I thought it over and said, "It was really nice."

"Good. That is good."

I explained, "Tucker is a great guy, but I'm not sure if I'm ready for another relationship yet."

Oma advised, "You don't need to rush into anything. Time will tell. You will know when you are ready."

"Oma, I don't remember Opa. What was he like?"

"Ah, he was a good man and a patient man. I think he didn't know what he was getting himself into when he decided to pursue me," she laughed.

"Where did you meet him?"

"It was at Coney Island."

"Really?"

She raised a hand in caution, "Ah, but that is getting ahead in the story. I still have more to tell you."

"Oma, I'm glad Oliver helped you and Rebekah escape that terrible refugee camp. I think he was in love with you."

"That is true. He was. He told me as much. But I did not have anything left inside of me at that time to offer him." She shrugged, "Or maybe he just wasn't the right one. I was grateful for all he and his grandmother did for us. As I told you, we stayed at their house for over two years. By 1948, people were returning home. But Rebekah and I couldn't return home. The land we had lived on was now occupied by The Soviet Union. Anyhow, after her long recovery from her illness, Rebekah was anxious to get to Hamburg."

"What did she think she'd find there?"

"Hamburg was under British rule and we heard the British had set up a system to help reunite families. The office helped people searching for those who had been separated during the war. There were many people looking for relatives who had been sent to refugee camps, work camps, and concentration camps."

"Did you go?"

"Ja. We did."

"How did you get there?"

She nodded, "With a bit of luck and a lot of prayer."

"Did she find her family when she got there?"

"All right, all right, get your pen and we will continue with the story."

In my bedroom, I saw Catrina sitting on the dresser. It was amazing that Oma was able to keep the doll with her all of this time, especially with the cracks. I decided to bring Catrina with me into the living room and I sat her on the coffee table as I prepared myself to listen to the next part of Oma's story. The more I heard, the more I realized her significance to my grandmother. She was so fragile, and yet she had survived all the traveling and difficulties that Issy and Rebekah had faced.

Before Oma resumed her story, I asked, "Why have you never had Catrina repaired?"

Oma opened her hands wide in a gesture and said, "I always thought I would find a way, but I never did."

CHAPTER THIRTY-FIVE

1948

In September of 1948, Oliver put Issy and Rebekah on a train heading for Hamburg, Germany. Issy watched him wave with a heavy heart. She knew she would miss him, but she also knew that her future lay somewhere else in a land she had always dreamed of, America. As the train left the station, she saw Oliver turn and walk away. She wished him well and hoped he could forgive her for not loving him the way he had wanted her to.

As the train rambled on, Issy clutched the satchel that still held Catrina. When they neared the border, the girls shook with fear, afraid the conductor would not let them enter Germany. They were thankfully surprised when no one questioned them as the train crossed the border. Out of habit, they each made the sign of the cross and thanked the Blessed Mother for watching over them once again.

The buildings in Hamburg were crumbling on the sides of the streets, but people walked passed the hollowed-out structures without taking notice. Although those who had lived in Hamburg through the war were numb to the destruction, Issy and Rebekah were shocked by the devastation that still existed three long years after the war had ended.

They walked directly to the Office of Missing People and took their place in the long line that filed out of the building. Issy's stomach rumbled and Rebekah pulled two apples out of her coat. "Where did you get those?"

Rebekah replied, "Oliver gave them to me before we left."

Feeling guilty about this last bit of thoughtfulness that he had shown for them, Issy replied, "That was kind of him."

The girls munched on the apples as they waited patiently in line. It was two more hours before they were able to ask after Rebekah's family. Without even looking up at them, the stern woman at the desk mumbled with indifference, "Who are you looking for?" Rebekah replied, "My parents, Samuel and Helga Fränckel, and my Opa, Günter Aranburg."

The woman seemed annoyed to have to search the names on the long alphabetical list. She sighed, "All right, let's see what we have here." She ran her fingers down the page and then turned to the next page. Issy looked around, there was still a long line of people standing behind them, waiting to have their turn. Others were sitting on benches in the next room. It appeared to be some sort of waiting room. Finally, she heard the woman clear her throat and say, "Ja, Samuel Fränckel. He is searching for his daughter, Rebekah. Is that you?" The woman looked at Rebekah suspiciously as she focused on the cross around Rebekah's neck.

"Ja! That's me!"

The woman wrote an address on a piece of paper and handed it to Rebekah. "You'll find him there."

The girls could not believe their ears. Rebekah grabbed the paper from the sour-faced woman and held it against her heart as they ran out to the street. The girls looked around for someone to help them with directions. They finally saw a woman who was dressed well in a gray suit and low sensible heels. Issy asked the woman, "Can you help us find this address?"

The woman looked from Issy to Rebekah and then back at Issy again. She had seen the building the girls had come out of and understood what was happening. She smiled at them before taking the piece of paper and giving it her full attention. She pointed, "Take this street to the end, until you have to turn either right or left, make a left and go down three blocks. Then make a right. That is the street, but I can't tell you exactly where this address is." Rebekah took the piece of paper back, "Danke. You have been a great help." The woman wiped at her own eyes in spite of her smile and said, "Good luck, girls. I hope you will have better luck than I." Then the woman turned away and the girls headed in the direction she had suggested.

Finally, the girls stood across the street from the address and watched the building as the minutes ticked away. They checked the house number several times to make sure they had the right house. But still they hesitated. Rebekah said, "The last time I saw my parents I was just turning nine years old. I'm seventeen now."

Issy was worried for her friend, so she tried to reassure her, "Whatever happens, whatever we find, we are together. I'm right here next to you."

"Thank you, Issy. I don't know why I'm feeling this way, I've come so far and now I can't make myself move across this street."

"Why are you frightened?"

"I'm frightened that they won't be there. That maybe the woman was mistaken."

Issy locked arms with Rebekah and nudged her to cross the street. But as they approached the concrete steps in front of the building, the door opened.

A man appeared in the doorway. He was bent over and much older, but there was no doubt that it was Samuel. Still, Issy was shocked by his appearance. She remembered the large strong man from her childhood. And seeing him now, she had a difficult time accepting in her mind what her heart already knew. He glanced directly at them and then back down at the steps, continuing his descent. He started to shuffle away when Rebekah finally found her voice, "Papa!"

He turned then to look at her, but he didn't move toward her. There was no recognition in his eyes, only confusion.

"Papa, it's me, Rebekah."

Samuel took in a shaky breath and tears welled up in his eyes. He repeated her name in disbelief, "Rebekah?"

"Ja, Papa. Rebekah and Issy. We found you!"

Samuel couldn't move. His heart was beating so fast. He could only open his arms as his daughter ran into them.

She was as tall as he now, but she buried her face in his shoulder and cried. Issy watched the reunion from a short distance away and was brought to tears of her own. She was happy for her friend, but it also reminded her that there would be no reunion for her family; she knew they were gone forever. Samuel looked up to see Issy standing there. He took one hand off of his daughter and opened his arm wider. "Issy, come here." Issy ran to him too, and he held onto both girls with all of his might.

He said, "Come, come inside. I was just going to the refugee office to ask again if there was any word from you. I go there every day and wait in their waiting room, hoping you will walk through the door." The disbelief in his voice was unmistakable, "And now, here you are!"

They turned back toward the building which Samuel had just exited. He ushered them into a small apartment. It held one bedroom, a kitchen, a tiny living room and a bathroom. Rebekah looked around the living room and then walked to the doorway to peek into the bedroom. "Papa, where is Mutter and Opa?"

He shook his head and holding his hand against his heart he said, "They are gone, Rebekah. It is only me."

Rebekah looked at him desperately, "Then we must search for them. They may still be looking for us."

"Nein mein liebling, they are not looking for us."

Not wanting to accept what he was trying to tell her, Rebekah said, "Nein. We must Papa."

"Come, take and sit girls. I'll put on some tea and we will talk and tell each other where we have been."

"Nein Vater!"

Even though Rebekah knew what he was telling her was the

truth, she didn't want to believe him. Issy felt helpless and unable to prevent the pain that she knew was coming for her friend. She took Rebekah's hand and led her to the small table in the kitchen.

Samuel filled the teapot with water and turned on the small stove. He cleared his throat and began telling his story, "We were taken by train to Dachau, a camp in southern Germany. When we got off of the train, we were separated. They took the old people to the side of the road and shot them." He spoke in a detached way, as if he were telling someone else's story. "I watched Opa as he fell, he was gone immediately; he did not suffer. Mutti was taken with the other women. I saw her once again, a few weeks later, across the barbed wire. But soon they moved me to work camp. They saw that I was strong enough. There I worked all day and night with little food or water. We cut large tree trunks and loaded them onto trucks. The work was endless. Boys and men who were much stronger than me died of exhaustion and starvation. Somehow, I lived."

His voice broke now as the memories accosted him, "I did some things I am not proud of. I turned on my own people in order to survive. God forgive me." He continued on, "I saw two boys trying to escape. I wanted to go with them, but they told me I was too old and pushed me to the ground. So, when they ran, I called out. The guards shot them dead. After that, the guards wanted me to keep my ears open and let them know if I heard of any plans for escape. They gave me food and water in exchange for my treachery. I was disgusted with myself, but I would not have survived without that food." Shame shadowed his face.

"When the war was over, I went directly back to Dachau.

They told me your mutter was chosen for one of their horrible medical experiments. She did not survive. I'm sorry, Rebekah. It is only me who is left."

Rebekah saw that the pain her father was in was even greater than her own, and so she went to him. She circled her arms around him while he cried. Finally, he was able to go on with his story, "I traveled from there back to our house. It was burned to the ground. I had hoped I would find you at the Brummel house, but what I found there were the remains of Issy's Vater and Oma and some Soviet soldiers. Issy, I buried Rolf and Oma near the apple orchard. There was nothing else I could do."

The teapot screamed on the stove. Issy removed it from the flame and poured tea into three cups and brought them to the table. She said, "Come, have some tea."

Rebekah obeyed, and Samuel followed.

After taking a sip, he asked, "Where have you girls been? I searched for you. They said you were registered at a camp in Copenhagen, but the camp said you had both disappeared. I didn't know how to find you then."

Rebekah answered, "After the soldiers came to the Brummel house, Hans took us to the Herr Schultz. Issy's mutter was there to help Frau Schultz deliver her baby. It was a boy. The Soviets found us there and they tried to hurt us, but Hans and Herr Schultz saved us. I had to kill one myself. We had to leave then and we walked in the bitter cold for many days. Issy's mutter froze to death along the way. We kept going. Frau Schultz's baby died too. Hans arranged for passage on a ship across the Baltic Sea to Denmark where we were assigned to a refugee camp in Copenhagen. It was not such a good place to be. Hans died there from Tuberculosis. There was a Danish guard there who was kind to Issy and he gave us food. He helped us escape. His name is Oliver. Oliver's grandmother took care of me when I became ill. I had rheumatic fever and it took me a while to be able to walk again. We lived there for two years until I was well enough to travel. When we heard that people where finding their lost relatives in Hamburg, we decided to come here."

Samuel nodded.

"I am sorry you both had to suffer too. But God has answered my prayers and now Issy must stay with us."

"Ja, of course, Papa."

He said, "I have a job, working in a men's clothing shop. I can take care of you both. You girls can have my bed. I will sleep on the couch."

"Vater, we can help too. We will get jobs as well."

He nodded, "We will be all right now. Everything will be all right now." But he still looked like a broken man and only a shadow of his former self.

CHAPTER THIRTY-SIX

I n October, the mountains blazed as the trees turned orange and red. The view from the back deck of the cabin was awe inspiring. "Oma, I think I'd like to get some paints. Do you want to come into town with me?"

"That would be lovely, Jace."

The road that led into Gatlinburg reminded me of Woodstock in upstate New York. It had been a favorite place of mine to spend summer and fall weekends with Brian. Both had streets lined with art galleries, gift shops and antique stores. As always, the memory of time spent with Brian was painful. I missed him terribly and I missed exploring the tiny shops and quaint restaurants with him. I remembered the time we went to the Mower's Flea Market in Woodstock and he insisted that I have my fortune read. Brian had walked away so I would have privacy while the woman told me my future. He wasn't there when she said, "This is not the man you will marry. There is another." I recalled how I had discounted her words as silly and chalked it up to her being a charlatan. When Brian asked me what she said, I told him, "It seems like I'm going to be stuck with you." We had both laughed after that. But now I knew she had been right. Brian was gone and what was worse, I was to blame. The words played over and over inside of my head and the heaviness weighed me down.

Oma and I continued our drive and we passed one of the beautiful wooden chapels set against the mountainous skyline. Oma broke the silence, "Tucker would make a good husband for you, Jace."

I brushed away my tears, not wanting my grandmother to see them. I replied to her lightheartedly, "Oh do you think so? Are you arranging a marriage for me now, Oma? Is that the way they did it in the old country?

"Well now, there's nothing wrong with family having some input into the situation. After all, whoever you marry will inherit me too."

"Oma, what are you saying?"

"Well, with your parents so far away, it's just the two of us. I'm glad you've decided to stay, Jace. I don't think I could have kept the camp going on my own much longer. But it would be nice to know that you wouldn't have to do that alone after I'm gone."

I pulled into the parking lot of the arts and craft store. As I helped my grandmother out of the car, I chastised her, "I don't want to hear you talking like that."

"Well, mein liebling, there's no sense in avoiding the inevitable."

I grabbed Oma's cane from the back seat and handed it to her.

Then attempted to distract us both from morbid thoughts. Pointing to the array of art supplies in the window, I said, "Watercolors are my favorite." Oma placed her cane in the shopping cart as we walked through the store and I examined various paint brushes and tubes of paint.

She said, "You know, I used to paint too, Jace."

"You did?"

"Ja, in fact I was painting when I met your grandfather."

Remembering our previous conversation about how she met my grandfather, I added, "You said you met him on Coney Island."

"Ja, I did. I was painting on the boardwalk. You could do that in those days. I don't know if they would allow it now."

"I'm sure they do, Oma. Did you paint the ocean?"

"Sometimes, and then at other times I would paint the people. The boardwalks and beach were crowded with people from so many different places! The scenes were ripe with color and emotion. Have you ever had a Nathan's hot dog? I don't mean one you buy in the grocery store. I mean one from *the* Nathan's on the Coney Island boardwalk. I can smell them cooking right now. The air surrounding that store smelled like hot dogs for a quarter of a mile in either direction, mmm-mmm!"

I admitted, "No, actually, I've never been to Coney Island. From what I hear, for a long time it was falling into disrepair. But I understand there are now efforts to bring it back to its former glory."

"Well, you should have seen it in the 50s. It was a sight to behold." And with an enthusiasm I had rarely seen in her, she explained, "So many umbrellas and blankets! Children playing with their toys in the sand! Ah! And the boardwalk, it was alive with music, entertainment and restaurants. Even the sideshow! Now that was an experience! There were bearded ladies, sword-swallowing gentlemen, and girls being sawed in half!"

We paid for my supplies and loaded them into the car. I suggested, "Maybe you should paint again. I bought plenty of supplies, we could paint together."

Oma seemed to weigh the suggestion, "Maybe. We will see." She sat in the car like a queen, her back straight and regal. I could imagine a crown upon her braided silver hair, diamond earrings hanging from her ears, and a scepter instead of a cane. But Oma wasn't much for jewelry; all she wore was a simple cross around her neck like the one she'd given to me.

She suggested, "Let's stop in and visit Tucker for a moment. We're right here. He will be hurt if he finds out we were so close and we didn't stop by."

"All right, Oma. Are you sure you aren't a Yenta?"

She looked at me with surprise, "You know that word?"

"Of course I do. It means a matchmaker."

She furrowed her brow, "Actually the word for matchmaker is *shadchanit*. A Yenta is really a gossipy old woman. I was Jewish for a while you know."

I opened my eyes wide in shock, "You were? How did that happen?"

"I will tell you when I tell you more of my story. You wait till

241

we get back to the cabin. You can write, 'My Oma was Jewish when she arrived in America.'"

"Okay, Oma. Whatever you wish." But I was thinking that maybe she was losing her mind.

Tucker looked up as we entered his shop. "Well, hello! It's so nice to see you ladies! What brings you down here?"

I said, "Paint supplies."

"Are you going to paint the cabin?"

I laughed, "No, not that kind of paint supplies, we're going to paint the trees and the mountains."

"Oh, very nice."

Being in Tucker's shop was like being in a wonderland of color. I looked through the shelves until I came upon a glass menagerie of animals. I picked up the elk and admired it. It reminded me of the drive Tucker had taken me on. It had been pleasant, and I even enjoyed his kiss, but I had made excuses since then to keep him at arm's length. It was a struggle to allow myself the luxury of his company when the guilt always had a way of seeping in and destroying my attempts at happiness.

Tucker came up behind me, his breath tickled my neck as he spoke, "It's yours if you like it."

"Thank you, I would like it, but I insist on paying for it."

"Well, I'll tell you what, you can pay for it by taking me out to dinner."

"Oh really?" I smiled.

"Yes, I think that is the price." He took the glass elk from me and turned it over to see the sticker on the bottom. "See, it says it right here. Special price for Jace Johnson, 'one dinner'."

I smiled, "All right than, I'll take it."

Oma was looking at the menagerie when she said wistfully, "Rebekah's Opa used to carve tiny animals out of wood. You would have liked him, Tucker. For Hanukkah, he carved animals and tiny spinning tops he called dreidels, and gave them to Rebekah. He was such a kind man and so gentle." Oma was soon lost in her memories again.

I was curious, and I asked Tucker, "Has my grandmother told you about Rebekah?"

"Oh, she not only told me about her, I met her."

"You met Rebekah?"

"Yes, she came to visit your grandmother one summer. Actually, I think it was the first summer I came to the camp."

I was curious, "What was she like?"

"Well, I remember she had some health problems. But other than that, she was like an extension of your grandmother. It was hard to see where one ended and the other began. I remember they even talked at the same time and finished each other's sentences." He smiled at the memory and then said, "You know, I thought about her a lot after that summer. She was a sweet lady, but there was something really sad about her. When I came back the next summer, she wasn't here. Your grandmother told me she had died. I was just a kid at the time." He shook his head and shrugged, "A few years after that, Oma took me in."

I was curious, "So when, exactly, did you come to live with Oma?"

"It was the September after the summer when I first saw you. I was sixteen by then."

"Really? I want to hear more."

Oma silenced him, "No! You have to wait till I tell you my story, myself."

Taken aback by her reaction, I said, "Okay, well then let's get back to the cabin so you can tell me some more."

Tucker asked, "Dinner? Tomorrow?"

I agreed, "Sure, and as long as I'm buying, I'll pick you up on the way."

He asked, "Where are we going?"

I smiled, "You will find out when we get there."

At home, Bonnie greeted us and sniffed our feet to see where we had been while we were away from her. Oma took her usual seat in her rocking chair as Bonnie settled by her and rested her muzzle on my grandmother's foot. Oma bent down to pet her and started to sing, *My Bonnie lies over the ocean, my Bonnie lies over the sea. My Bonnie lies over the ocean, oh bring back my Bonnie to me.* From the first time Oma sang that song to Bonnie, we realized the dog recognized it. The song had calmed her anxiety and we realized that her last owner must have sung the same song to her. Bonnie sighed in contentment and closed her eyes.

When I finished setting up the paints and easels on the deck, Oma joined me, and we painted the sunset together. I was surprised by the extent of my grandmother's artistic talent.

Although her hands had a habit of shaking, when she painted, they remained steady.

After we were finished, we stood back to examine our work. Both paintings had turned out beautifully.

She said, "See that Jace, you take after me in more than just your looks."

There was a knock at the door. When I answered it, I was surprised to see Murray standing there. I hadn't seen him since camp had ended. My grandmother became like a little school girl at the sight of him.

"Come in, Murray."

He said, "I've brought you some strudel, Issy. I made it just for you."

Oma beamed, "Delightful! Jace, put up a pot of coffee, please."

I nodded, "Will do."

As I measured the coffee and filled the pot with water, I watched how sweet the two of them were together. They sat at the kitchen table as Murray brought her up-to-date on some of their common friends whom she hadn't seen in a while.

His strudel was delicious and after we had our coffee, Oma took out a set of dominoes and insisted on teaching me how to play. Murray apologized profusely when he won by a landslide.

It was dark out when he took his leave, "It's getting late and I better head home. But I hope you enjoy the strudel!"

Oma smiled at him and her blue eyes sparkled as she said, "Of course we will, it's delicious and thank you so much for stopping by for a visit."

After he left, I chided her, "Oma, is Murray your beau?"

"Well, Jace, like I said, it's always good to have a diversion."

I laughed, "Yes, it is."

We settled in the living room then and Oma continued her story.

CHAPTER THIRTY-SEVEN

1950

Issy and Rebekah stood at the stern of the ship as it pulled out of port. Two great smokestacks belched as it made its way out to sea. Issy's emotions were varied as she waved good-bye to Germany. On one hand, this was the only real home she had ever known, on the other, it was no longer the home she knew. East Prussia no longer existed. Her parents' farm was now on Soviet land. Issy watched as the people on the dock waved farewell to their family and friends. She imagined that Papa, Mutti, Hans, and Oma, were standing among the crowd, wishing her a safe voyage across the great Atlantic Ocean.

Rebekah said, "Remember the times we dreamed of this? From the attic of your farmhouse, to the refugee camp, to Oliver's house. For all of these years, we have imagined setting off for America."

"Ja, I remember. But Hans should be with us. He was supposed to marry you so we could be real sisters."

Rebekah answered, "Well, being cousins isn't so bad."

"True." Issy squeezed Rebekah's hand. She was traveling to America as Rebekah's cousin.

Rebekah and Issy had worked as waitresses for two years. Their salaries paying for the rent on their apartment, while Samuel worked hard as a tailor to save money to pay for their tickets. He knew about the restrictions on immigration but was not about to leave Issy behind. Rolf and Helga had taken care of his child and offered her their protection. Now it was his turn to repay the debt. He had papers forged for Issy that identified her as his niece, his sister's child, and he applied for visas for all three of them as soon as he could.

The newly passed Internal Security Act of 1950, was meant to exclude arriving immigrants with previous links to communist and fascist organizations. But it had made it difficult for all Germans to travel to America, unless they were Jewish refugees, and even they had no guarantee of admittance. The quota system, which was already in place in America, limited the number of refugees who could enter in one year. The sheer number of those seeking asylum, was causing The United States to turn ships away, and redirect them to South America.

So, the process had slowed them down, but now they were finally on their way. Although she was nineteen years old, she still held onto her old satchel with her broken doll inside. Issy had written to her Onkel Peter at the address her father had left on the old map. She explained that Samuel and Rebekah were traveling with her and that, without them, she would not have been able to make the journey at all. He had answered her letter and assured her he would be at the dock waiting for them and that there was enough room at his house for all of them.

The people on the shore were far away now, and in a little while, she would be too far from land to see it at all. Issy's heart beat wildly with excitement, fear, wonder, and trepidation. She had no idea what lay ahead of her, but she hoped that somewhere she would find a place to call home again.

The rest of the passengers left the stern to mill about the ship, but Issy and Rebekah remained. Soon Samuel found them and said, "There is no more looking back girls, we must look forward now. Come, let's get you both settled."

The cabin was small with two cramped bunk beds in a claustrophobic space. It was without a window and on a lower level of the ship, but at least it was private. Samuel had a bed in a dormitory on the level below them.

One night Rebekah asked Issy, "What do you think America will be like?"

"I think it will be friendly, after all, they are opening their arms to us."

"I hope we will be allowed to disembark there. What will we do if we are sent to South America?"

Rebekah replied, "Both are strange places to us, but we are together. We will find a way to survive. We always do."

"True, but at least we can speak English and our English improved so much when we were living with Oliver and Johanna. If we go to South America, how will we communicate with anyone? We don't know how to speak Spanish."

It took twelve days to cross the ocean. While the ship heaved to and fro over the stormy sea, in their small cabin, Rebekah called out, "Gott uns retten!" And Issy corrected her in English as she lost the contents of her stomach over the side of her own cot and cried, "Speak English, Rebekah, God save us!" That brought Rebekah to giggles at the thought of how pathetically comical the two of them were. The laughter did not help abate the sourness of their stomachs, but it did help to improve their moods.

The day they approached the New York harbor, there was a shroud of fog covering the land. Suddenly, out of the fog, the statue of the grand lady standing in the sea appeared in a clearing before them. As they approached the Statue of Liberty, Rebekah was proud that she was able to read the English words carved into the base:

"Give me your tired, your poor, Your huddled masses yearning to breathe free, The wretched refuse of your teeming shore. Send these, the homeless, tempest-tossed to me, I lift my lamp beside the golden door!"

After living in fear for so many years, after losing so much, they had finally made it to America. It was difficult to believe.

Rebekah said, "You should pinch me, Issy, I must still be in your attic dreaming."

Issy laughed and pinched Rebekah's arm.

"Ouch!"

The girls cried tears of joy as they hugged each other with wide smiles on their faces. The men on the ship threw their hats in the air as everyone cheered! Issy was aware that others on the ship had suffered worse fates than she and Rebekah had. She looked around at them and saw the ghosts who had surely traveled with them to this new land. Issy and

Rebekah had ghosts of their own though, the ghosts of Rebekah's mother and grandfather, and the ghosts of Issy's entire family.

Their worst fears were appeased when they were allowed to dock in Manhattan Harbor. It took time to be processed through Ellis Island and many of the passengers were whisked away for interrogation. The detainees that numbered well over a thousand, would have to prove upon entry that they had no connections to the Communist Party or they would be sent back on the return journey. Issy held onto Samuel's hand as he explained that she was his Jewish niece. They were all relieved when the man behind the counter told them to move on.

Thousands were ferried from Ellis Island to the New York pier. When Issy, Rebekah, and Samuel finally stepped off of the ferry, they were overrun by desperate family members searching for their loved ones.

Issy searched the faces until she saw a man holding a sign that had her name written on it, "Isabela Brummel." He looked so much like her father, for a brief moment she thought it was Rolf. But realizing quickly the impossibility of it, she looked more closely. This man was grayer, and he had a bristly, but neatly trimmed, beard. The smile was the same though, as were his kind eyes.

She took her hat off with one hand and raised it as high as she could above the crowd as she shouted, "Onkel Peter!"

Onkel Peter made his way toward his niece who he hadn't seen since she was a baby. She was all that remained of the family he had left behind in East Prussia. When he reached her, his great arms lifted her into the air with joy. Above the noise of the crowd, Issy said in English, "This is my friend Rebekah and her vater, Samuel."

After shaking hands with Samuel and nodding to Rebekah, he said, "Quickly, follow me." The four of them walked away from the pier and into the streets of lower Manhattan. A woman was there waiting for them. Onkel Peter introduced her, "This is your Tante Bridget." Bridget was a short stocky woman with a kind face. She immediately opened her arms to enfold Issy within them. Onkel Peter ushered the group toward the subway. "Stay close," he warned.

Although there was much to see on the streets of Manhattan, Issy kept her eyes locked on her uncle. The crowds on the sidewalk pushed and shoved her as she tried to keep up. She was glad when they left the street level and entered the subway. It was quieter underground, but the subway soon showed itself to be a maze of stairs, gates and platforms. Afraid that she would somehow be lost in the confusion, she tried desperately to stay close to him. When the doors of one subway car almost closed on her, she screamed, "Onkel!" But the doors immediately opened again like magic, and the rest of the group was able to board. The subway train made its way through the dark underground tunnels and, eventually, into the open air on the elevated track. Finally, the train came to a stop and the group exited at a station called Brighton Beach, Brooklyn.

CHAPTER THIRTY-EIGHT

1950

When Issy, Rebekah and Samuel first set foot off of the elevated train and walked down the concrete steps to the street, they observed their surroundings with childlike fascination. The streets were lined with bakeries, cigar shops, drug stores, butcher shops, and open-air groceries. In the middle of the road there were boys hitting a ball with a stick and running around in a circle. Radios were blasting music from open windows as they passed houses stacked close together. Two girls sped by on roller skates and laughed at Issy and Rebekah who were still dressed in their cumbersome traveling clothes. Issy looked around at the high-heeled young women whose dresses clung to them, revealing the form of their bodies. They wore red lipstick and rouge on their cheeks. Then she saw a group of men on a stoop gathered around an open window. The men were intent on watching moving images that came from a box just inside the window.

Issy asked, "Onkel Peter, what is that in the window?"

"That's a television set. The men are watching the Yankees play the Cubs."

Issy was still confused, "The Yankees? You mean the American soldiers?"

Onkel Peter explained, "It's baseball."

Issy still didn't understand so Onkel Peter said, "Yogi Berra? Phil Rizzuto? Joe DiMaggio? You've never heard these names before?"

"No, who are they?"

"They're the Bronx Bombers."

Alarmed, she looked up at the sky for an areoplane, "Do they drop bombs?"

Onkel Peter laughed, "No, no, don't worry, Issy, it's just a game. Like the boys you saw hitting the ball with the stick. You are safe here. Soon you will understand."

The newcomers were amazed by the diversity of the people who lived here and the lack of post-war rubble that had become part of the landscape of Hamburg. It was as if crossing the ocean had brought them to a different reality. This was a place which seemed untouched by war. It was incomprehensible to them that while there had been so much change and suffering in Europe, life appeared to have remained unaffected here. They had dreamed about America, but they could never have imagined a place like Brooklyn.

When Samuel saw some older men sitting around a table on the street openly wearing yarmulkes and speaking in Yiddish as they played checkers, he pointed at them in amazement. He couldn't get over the fact that they were free to be Jewish out in public and his heart felt lighter than it had in years. Although the men were Russian Jews, they had the Yiddish language in common with the German Jews who were now flooding into their neighborhoods. Even though Samuel could not speak English yet, he could converse with them in Yiddish and bade them a good evening in their common ancient language.

Issy's Onkel Peter and Tante Bridget had a three-bedroom brick house in Brighton Beach. The houses on the street were so close together you could almost shake hands with your neighbor through the windows. Inside the house, the kitchen was filled with gadgets they had never seen before. In Germany there were ice boxes, but here there were refrigerators. Rather than hand-cranked devices, here there were electric mixers and electric can openers; everything seemed to be run by electricity. The girls were led up to the bedroom they would share. In it, there were twin beds with matching mustard-yellow, chenille popcorn-stitch bedspreads and a desk in one corner. White wallpaper with delicate blue and yellow flowers covered the walls. Above the desk was a set of encyclopedias which, on further inspection, were filled with colorful pictures of exotic animals and places which Issy had never known existed. Issy and Rebekah were overwhelmed by it all!

Rebekah bounced on one bed and said, "Issy, we made it! We are safe in America." But in spite of the wide smile that spread across her face, tears began to fill her eyes. Issy didn't need to ask her what she was thinking, as the same thoughts were going through her own mind. As happy as she was, it hurt so deeply to have made it to Onkel Peter's house without the rest of her family. But, she knew how happy her family would be to know that she had indeed reached safety and the loving arms of her Onkel.

Issy opened her bag on the other bed and looked through her meager collection of clothes until she found what she was looking for. She lifted Catrina out of the satchel and placed her gently on a shelf above her bed. The doll was still wearing the ribbon that Rebekah had wrapped around its head to keep the crack from splitting further. "Do you think we will be able to get Catrina's head fixed here in America?"

Rebekah replied, "I think after all that we have seen today, it seems anything is possible in America."

That night, the girls were awakened by the sound of a man yelling, "Nein!" They looked at each other through startled eyes until they heard the agonized sound again, "Nein!"

Rebekah said, "It's Papa."

Issy nodded her head and Rebekah quickly jumped out of her bed and sped to the next room where Samuel was asleep, deep in one of his frequent nightmares. Issy could hear Rebekah's soothing voice as Samuel woke and found he was in a different place than he had expected. Through the wall, Issy heard Rebekah say, "Papa, we are in America. You are safe." Still, the muffled sound of a tortured man crying filled the darkness. It was a sound she had heard often over the past two years.

Although Samuel could converse with Onkel Peter in German, it was different with Tante Bridget. So, she took time each day to teach him English. Before long, Samuel's English improved, and he was able to get a job in a men's shop. One warm autumn day, Samuel took Rebekah and Issy to Mrs. Stahl's Knishes for a special treat. The shop was on the corner of Brighton Beach Avenue and Coney Island Avenue. Mrs. Stahl's Knishes had been a neighborhood favorite since it first opened in 1935. They sat together and enjoyed the best potato knishes in Brooklyn. Samuel observed the Jewish clientele and said to his daughter, "Rebekah, you were away from me for a very long time and there are things I should have taught you, but I wasn't there to do so."

"That's all right, Papa. It wasn't your fault. We are together now, that's all that matters."

He reached across the tiny table and lifted the cross necklace she still wore around her neck and said, "Ja, but it seems you have forgotten you are Jewish while I was away."

Issy's eyes widened with guilt.

Rebekah answered, "Nein Papa, I haven't forgotten! I know that I am Jewish."

"It is one thing to know that you are Jewish, and it is another to know what it means to be Jewish. I think it is best if we start to go to temple, so you can learn what I should have been able to teach you."

Rebekah saw how much this meant to her father but was afraid that this would mean adding restrictions to her life. She had seen how the Orthodox women in Brighton Beach wore wigs and drab cumbersome clothing. She wanted to be an American girl like the ones she saw who took the elevated train to work in Manhattan. She explained this to her father and he nodded his head. "I understand, Rebekah, and that is how your mutter would have wanted it. She was a very progressive woman. But there are Jews in America who have formed what they call *Reform Temples* where the traditions of our people can be kept while also allowing for adjustments to

257

life in the modern world. I have found one I think will be a good fit for both of us."

Samuel went on to explain that the Reform Temple was a split from the Orthodox Jews in that it taught tolerance and acceptance of Christians and their beliefs. It was a nice compromise, especially for those "hidden children," European Jewish children who had come to America after living much of their young lives, secretly, in convents and Christian homes. These children lacked the conventional knowledge of the customs that had been part of their families for generations.

After that, every Saturday, Samuel and Rebekah walked to temple together and she took classes to learn about her religion and the traditions the Nazis had tried to obliterate. She took off her cross and put it back around Catrina's neck as she explained, "I can't wear this anymore, Issy. Like you said, it protected me when I was in Germany, but now I am in America, and I am free to be who I was born to be."

"I understand, Rebekah. I am glad for you. And perhaps you and Samuel can teach me more about Jewish traditions and I can share in them while you are living here in Onkel Peter's house."

Rebekah agreed, "Ja, that would be good. After all, Jews and Christians share the same history in the Old Testament. The more I learn, the more I realize that there is not much that is different between us. We are more alike than I thought."

Issy enjoyed learning about the rich history of the Jewish people. And in the spring, Samuel helped Tante Bridget prepare for Passover and the Seder plate. As they sat together around the table, Samuel explained, "There are six items on the plate, the first and second are Maror and Chazeret, they are bitter herbs that symbolize the bitterness of slavery. The third is Charoset, a sweet brown mixture made from apples, nuts, wine and cinnamon representing the mortar the Israelites used to build Pharaoh's cities. The fourth is Karpas, it reminds us of the taste of our ancestors' salty tears. The fifth is Zeroa, it is a roasted lamb or goat shank that represents a sacrifice. And the sixth is Beitzah which is an egg to symbolize rebirth and renewal. However, the roasted shank and egg are not to be eaten. We also include a stack of three matzahs to represent the unleavened bread. Now we will add a fourth matzah to our plate to remember the Jews in Europe who were unable to celebrate Passover. Then we add four cups of wine which are consumed during the Seder, and a fifth cup which we leave untouched for Elijah."

Samuel also told the others the story of Moses and the ten plagues and how when God brought the last plague to the people of Egypt, He passed over the houses with lamb's blood above their doors indicating that they were Hebrews. Issy was fascinated by the stories and thankful Onkel Peter and Tante Bridget respected Samuel and Rebekah enough to allow them to celebrate Passover in their house.

Over the year that followed, they all slowly acclimated to their new home. Samuel became indispensable to Onkel Peter's good friend, Efraim Fleishman, who had hired Samuel to work as a tailor at his men's clothing store in Lower Manhattan. And Issy and Rebekah began working on the Coney Island boardwalk at a soda fountain that was owned by another friend of Onkel Peter's, Al D'Agostino.

CHAPTER THIRTY-NINE

SUMMER 1951

Issy was working at D'Agostino's Soda Fountain, when three towheaded young men walked into the shop. They sat on the stools which lined the counter and one of them said, "We'll take three chocolate egg creams." The three of them were obviously brothers; they looked quite a bit alike except that one was taller than the other two.

She was busy blending the frosty treats when the tallest one slipped some coins into the jukebox. Frank Sinatra's voice filled the room, and the young men slipped off their stools and went to talk to a group of girls who were sitting at a table by the window. Soon they led the girls to the center of the room and began to dance on the black and white checkered tile floor, their chocolate egg creams forgotten. Issy enjoyed watching them dance as she wiped down the Formica counter; she admired that they seemed so carefree. When the song ended, two of the young men grabbed their egg creams and joined the girls who were sipping soda pop from large red and white striped straws. Issy noticed that the girls had rouge on their cheeks and dark red lipstick highlighting their lips. Their long eye lashes batted as the boys tried to charm them. Issy hadn't taken to wearing the fashionable makeup yet, instead her face was bare of artificial enhancements.

The tallest young man remained on his stool, watching Issy with an amused smile.

He asked, "Don't you like to dance?"

"I am working. Besides, I cannot dance."

He shrugged, "If you can stand on two feet, you can dance. It doesn't matter if you are behind the counter or in front of it."

"Well, I don't think my boss would appreciate my dancing on the job."

He shrugged, "Can I tell you something?"

"Sure."

"My brothers and I were passing by and I saw you standing behind the counter. Suddenly, I had the urge to have a chocolate egg cream."

Issy remarked, "Well then, you came to the right place. We make the best egg creams on the boardwalk."

"Good, I like a woman with confidence."

She smiled sweetly back at him and when he finished his egg cream; he placed an extra dollar bill on the counter before rejoining the other young men. A few minutes later, the group of young people left the shop together. But before he walked out, the tall one turned back toward Issy as if he expected her to leave with him. He shrugged his shoulders and with his hands placed over his heart, he spun around and walked away.

Issy had become used to this kind of flirting. Coney Island was filled with young people enjoying their summer vacation, and it seemed to her that being behind the counter made it safe for her to flirt back. She also found that flirting a bit ended up with more tip money for her. But flirting is where it always ended; she was not interested in dating these young carefree American men. She took the dollar bill off the counter and slipped it into her apron pocket.

The following day was Issy's day off. She was facing the ocean when he came up behind her; he let out a sigh as he watched her paint. At the sound, Issy quickly turned around to see him standing there. She recognized him immediately; he was the tallest of the towheaded boys she had seen the day before. But without the counter standing between them, she felt vulnerable. So, she turned back to her painting and ignored him, hoping he would go away and leave her in peace.

He said, "I stopped in at D'Agostino's, but you weren't there. The girl behind the counter told me I could find you painting on the boardwalk."

Issy didn't say a word; she just continued painting, adding blues and grays to the sky on her canvas. But the young man was not about to give up. He cleared his throat and said, "Well, let me introduce myself, my name is Andrei Ruskin and I live in Brighton Beach. I am a senior at Columbia University in Manhattan where I'm studying Biology. I expect to be attending their medical school next year."

He must have thought that his accomplishments and goals would impress her, but to Issy it sounded more like he was on a job interview. Besides, when she heard his name, she could only think of one thing. So, she turned to him and asked, "Are you Russian?"

He hadn't expected that, so he faltered when he replied, "Well, uh, yes, my family is Russian. My parents came to America before I was born. My brothers and I were born here in Brooklyn."

She turned her back to him again and said, bluntly, "The Russians killed my family."

Andrei wasn't usually at a loss for words, but Issy's declaration silenced him. When he didn't reply, she finally turned again to look at him. He looked devastated, so she took pity on him and apologized, "I'm sorry. I shouldn't judge you just because you are Russian; after all, I don't like it when people judge me because I'm German. But I prefer to paint alone, if you please." She turned away from him once again.

Andrei did not move from the spot, but instead, continued to watch as she painted. Issy was very aware that he was standing behind her and this distracted her from her work. The longer he stood there, the more annoyed she became. Finally, she closed up her paints and was folding her easel when he spoke again, "Here, let me help you."

She didn't acknowledge his help, but she didn't stop him either. He picked up the easel and followed her to the train platform. Issy was glad to see Rebekah standing there waiting for her. But then she heard Rebekah call out to Andrei, "Oh, I see you found your wife!"

Issy looked at Rebekah as if she had lost her mind and wondered what would make her say such a thing.

Rebekah explained with a shrug, "He came looking for you at D'Agostino's and he told me he was looking for the girl with 'the bluest eyes he had ever seen' because she was going to be his wife. So, I told him where to find you."

Issy narrowed her eyes in Rebekah's direction and replied sarcastically, "Danke schön." Then she turned to Andrei and reached for the easel, "I've got it from here. Rebekah will help me."

He shrugged, "There's no need; remember I said I live in Brighton Beach too, we're going the same way."

They boarded the train and he squeezed in next to Issy on the crowded subway car. Although she was tall for a girl, he was much taller than she was. Issy turned her head to the side so as not to look directly into his chest. Knowing she was feeling uncomfortable, but unable to move away from her, Andrei tried to distract her, "So, you girls work together."

Rebekah laughed, "Ja, we work together."

"Do you live near each other?"

Rebekah said, "You could say that. We live on 4th Street near Brightwater."

"You're neighbors?"

"No," Rebekah explained, "we're family."

Andrei looked at both girls and asked, "Sisters? Cousins?"

Rebekah laughed, "Sort of both."

The train came to a stop and he followed them off the train, still carrying the easel.

Issy said, "Look, I can carry the easel myself, you really don't have to follow us all the way home."

"Oh, but it's no bother, really, I don't mind. Besides, like I said, it's on my way. I live on 2nd, not far from you." He continued to smile with the hope that Issy might smile back.

They walked in silence the rest of the way to Onkel Peter's house. Rebekah stopped on the sidewalk and said, "Well, this is it! See you inside Issy." And with that, she quickly climbed the steps and ducked into the house.

Andrei handed the easel to Issy, "May I call on you sometime?"

With obvious annoyance, Issy replied, "Listen, I have to work a lot and when I'm not working, I'm painting. I really don't have time to go out on a date."

Andrei looked deflated, he asked, "Is it because I'm Russian?"

She really didn't want to discuss it any further. "I'm sorry. I need to go inside." Leaving him standing alone on the sidewalk, she turned away from him and walked into the house.

She glared at Rebekah and demanded, "What was that?"

Rebekah shrugged, "I don't know, like I said, he thinks you're going to be his wife."

Issy shook her head, "You're both crazy."

She carried her easel and paints up to their bedroom and put them away in her closet. Tante Bridget called to them, "Time to set the table for supper girls."

That night, Rebekah told the others about Andrei. Onkel Peter asked, "Is he a Russian boy?"

Issy nodded, "Ja."

Tante Bridget said, "Better to stay away from him."

Issy replied, "Don't worry Tante Bridget, that's exactly what I intend to do."

Rebekah defended him, "But Issy, he's a nice guy."

Issy said, "I agree he's nice, but no matter how nice he is, it wouldn't work. I even told him that. I know it's not right to hold it against him that he is Russian, but at the same time, I can't just ignore the fact. Don't you remember Rebekah? Don't you remember what the Russians did to my Vater and Oma? Don't you remember at Friedrich's house, when the Russian soldiers assaulted us?" Issy shuddered.

Rebekah quietly replied, "Ja, I remember."

"Then please, let's forget this."

But Andrei continued to pursue her. He came often to D'Agostino's and tried to draw her into conversation. Sometimes he would just find her on the boardwalk and he would compliment her and draw the attention of passersby to observe her talent. Gradually she became used to having him around, and eventually, there were days when she would turn around looking for him, feeling disappointed if he wasn't there. Still, no matter what he tried, she never gave him any indication that she was slowly becoming fond of him.

Then late one night, Issy was locking the door to the soda fountain after work. Usually, Mr. D'Agostino closed up at night, but it was his wife's birthday and he had asked Issy to close up for him. Most of the lights on the boardwalk had been shut down and there was only a sliver of a moon in the sky. Issy had barely turned away from the door, when a large man grabbed her by the hair and put a knife to her throat. In a thick Irish brogue, he ordered, "Open the door again lassie. Let's see what's in that cash register, shall we?" She tried to struggle against him, but then he yanked her hair and forced her to her knees. "Give me those keys lassie." Tears stung her eyes as the pain seared through her scalp. She opened her hand and the keys fell to the ground. But a moment later, her attacker collapsed next to her. Andrei had surprised him from behind and hit him hard on the head with a large wooden board. The man fell down unconscious on the boardwalk.

Andrei voice was filled with terror as he asked, "Are you all right?" But she couldn't answer. Her face had gone white and her mind blank. He picked up the keys, opened the door, and helped her inside before locking it behind them. Then Andrei sat her in a booth and then dropped a coin in the pay phone to call the police.

Coming to America and living in peace for the past year had not wiped away the memories of all that Issy had been through. There were times when she still woke at night, terrified, as if she were still in the middle of the war. Andrei saw her sitting, huddled in the booth, shaking violently. He sat next to her and wrapped his jacket around her and then pulled her into his arms. He held her until her trembling stopped. Andrei tried to reassure her as he whispered, "No one is going to hurt you, I'm here." Finally, she started to relax, and leaned against his chest like a small child in her father's arms. When she looked up at him, he could see the pain of her memories evident in her eyes. Quietly she spoke to him, "Danke."

He nodded and brushed her hair out of her eyes. He wanted to kiss her, but instead he said, "Let me get you some water." He went over to the counter and filled a glass and brought it to her. She sipped quietly and then asked in a shaky voice, "Is he still out there?"

Andrei saw the man lying in a heap outside the door, "Yes, but the police will be here soon, and he can't get in, the door is locked."

When the police arrived, the man was still unconscious. They called Mr. D'Agostino and Onkel Peter to inform them of what had happened at the shop. By the time they both arrived, Issy had regained her composure. As her attacker groggily came to his senses, he found himself in handcuffs. Issy tried to reassure her distraught Onkel and employer that she was all right, "I'm fine Onkel. Really, Mr. D'Agostino, I'm not hurt."

Mr. D'Agostino asked, "Who is this young man who saved you?"

Issy replied, "That is Andrei, he is one of your customers. He must have been on the boardwalk when he saw what was happening."

When Andrei joined them, Onkel Peter said, "Thank you, young man. Issy was lucky you happened to be walking by."

Andrei kept his head down not to give away the fact that he had been waiting for her to come out of the shop. He had been hoping to have another chance to talk to her. But he kept that to himself. After all, he didn't want to further alarm her Onkel and employer.

Mr. D'Agostino said, "Son, that man could have hurt Issy and could have taken all the money in my cash register. Please, let me give you a little reward for your efforts."

But Andrei refused, "No sir, I can't take anything for this. I am just glad I was here, and that she is all right."

So Onkel Peter said, "Well, at least let me have you over for dinner one night to thank you. I'm sure Issy would like that. What do you think, Issy?"

She looked from her Onkel to Mr. D'Agostino and then to Andrei and said, "Ja, that would be nice."

CHAPTER FORTY

PRESENT DAY

A diversion . . . a way to take my mind off of what consumed it. Is that what I was looking for? As I drove down the quiet country road, I wondered what was next for me. Putting the past behind and leaving the regrets that tortured me, sometimes seemed an impossible task. And yet, here I was, driving toward Tucker's shop and hoping that being with him would be the respite I so longed for. I thought to myself, "In the midst of despair, a light shines. Dim as it may be at first, it is the hope within us which drives us forward."

I was early for our date. After being restless all day and without thinking it through, I decided I just needed to get outside to clear my head. I told myself, just keep moving, get out of your head. I lowered the car window and felt the breeze blow through my hair. I said to the breeze, "Please, blow the cobwebs away." Once again tears threatened to fall. When would this end? When would I start living again? My chest felt heavy and my breathing labored. For a moment I wondered if I was about to have a heart attack. I pressed my open palm against my breast to feel my heartbeat. It was fluttering quickly. I told it to slow down; it was just the anxiety. I tried to breathe more evenly, my heart responded, and it slowed down its beating.

The parking lot in front of Tucker's shop was empty and the sign in the window said, "Closed." I knocked on the front door, but no one answered. Trying the knob, I found that it turned and opened. The late afternoon sun shone brilliantly through all the stained glass. My senses became alert at a sound that came from the workshop behind the store. As I approached the back room, I could feel the heat that emanated from within. The kiln had been fired and the sound of crackling flames met my ears.

Tucker stood shirtless holding a long pole; the mouth of the kiln engulfed it within its depths. Tucker's skin was shiny with sweat and his muscles tensed as he maneuvered the pole. I realized that it was actually a tube when Tucker blew air through it and the bulbous piece of clear liquid glass at the end began to take shape. I didn't want to disturb him, so I watched silently as he withdrew the tube from the kiln and then dipped the molten glass into a dish. Soon colored shards adhered to the glass. Then he placed it back into the kiln and rolled it above the flames. Once again, he withdrew the pipe from the heat and blew into the pipe. This time when the glass cooled, it turned blue.

I took a step back and inadvertently knocked into a table. The sound made Tucker turn toward me.

He smiled, "Hey. You're early."

"Yes, I know. Sorry."

"Don't be. Come closer. Let me show you how it's done."

As he blew into the pipe again, the glass at the end grew into a cobalt blue vase. Taking the vase out of the kiln, he lit a blow torch and applied the heat to the glass as he rolled the pipe creating the details of its shape. Then with a tool, he formed a flat bottom. He placed it in the kiln once again and twirled the pipe as he blew into it. Finally, he let the glass cool and then gently tapped the vase where it was connected to the pipe and it gently slid off and onto the table.

I said in wonder, "It's beautiful! I had no idea what it took to make a simple vase."

He chuckled, "I've been at this for years, and believe me, there have been many disasters along the way. But I've learned from them, and with a little creativity, the possibilities are endless."

The workshop was full of glass objects, some a mosaic of colors cut into angles to make amazing pieces of art, others were simple and understated, but beautiful just the same.

He wiped his hands on a towel, "I've got to clean up. Do you mind waiting for a bit?"

"No, not at all. I'm enchanted by this garden of glass."

He placed both of his hands over his heart, "Thank you. I'm glad you like it."

"Oh, I do!"

He smiled again, "Okay, I'll be back. Don't go anywhere."

I waited in the workshop as he went upstairs to his apartment for a shower and to get dressed for the evening. A half hour later, he directed me as I drove to a complex of restaurants, bars, rides, and shops in Pigeon Forge called "The Island". It was teeming with families who had come to vacation at Dollywood. After we ate dinner, we walked around and peeked into the various shops before deciding to take a ride on the giant Ferris wheel.

Once locked into the small carriage, and in close proximity to Tucker, I felt self-conscious. I couldn't meet his eyes; so instead, I looked down on the crowd far below. Tucker asked, "Jace, where is this going with you and me? Sometimes you give me mixed signals and I'm not sure if you want me around or not."

The wheel stopped and the carriage we were in rocked back and forth. I really didn't want to get into categorizing our relationship just yet, but I said, "I know and I'm sorry. I think I'm just afraid of taking chances right now. It's easier to just cut myself off from feelings so that I don't get hurt. After what happened to Brian, it's taken me this long just to date again."

He was silent for a while, we watched the ground get closer and then further away again. Then he broke the silence and asked, "Do I have a chance? Will you let yourself open enough to fall in love?"

Tucker looked at me with such earnest eyes. I couldn't just avoid this, I had to give him an answer. "Tucker, if I were to give anyone a chance, it would be you."

He asked, "But *can* you give me that chance?"

I wanted to say yes. I knew what the answer was in my heart, but I was still too afraid to say so. Instead, I said, "Can't we just be friends for a while longer?"

He looked hurt by my answer as he pulled himself away, as far as our confined quarters would allow, and said, "No, Jace. We can't be just friends."

Frustrated, I asked, "Why not? I don't understand. What's the rush?"

Now it was his turn to look away from me, "Because, I'm already in love with you."

My heart lifted and deflated as if it were on a tiny Ferris wheel of its own. I was happy to hear him say he loved me, but sad to think I wasn't ready to say it back to him, and I knew how much that had hurt him.

Our ride ended and soon we were back on solid ground. I noticed a familiar face in the crowd. Brad was watching us with what appeared to be intense hatred. My body shook involuntarily, as if his hatred physically passed through the air and hit me. Tucker, looking down at the ground the whole time, was walking ahead of me and hadn't noticed. He couldn't walk fast enough to get back to my car. I had to run at times, just to keep up with him.

When we got to the parking lot, I turned back to see Brad was following us. I called out, "Tucker." But Tucker just kept walking ahead of me. The longer Brad followed us, the more nervous I became. When we finally reached my car, Tucker opened the door and turned to look at me. By then, Brad was standing just behind me.

Brad said, "So I see the two of you have become good friends."

Tucker asked warily, "What do you want Brad?"

Brad responded with menace in his voice, "You know me. We

274

go way back. I don't like it when people try to stop me from getting what I want. I was fired because this little girl over here ran back to her grandmother with some stories about me."

Tucker put out his hand and pushed me behind him and behind the opened car door. He stood between us as he tried to calm the situation, "Look Brad, I don't want any trouble."

Brad laughed at him, "Tucker, you were always a coward."

"No Brad, I just wasn't always looking for a fight like you were."

"Then why were you always running behind Issy's skirts to get away from me when we were kids? Come to think of it, you and Jace seem to have that in common."

Tucker shook his head and warned, "You can think what you want Brad, but leave Jace alone."

"Yeah, the two of you are perfect for each other, a whore and coward." I felt my heart beating wildly again as both the anger and fear pumped through my veins.

Before I could say a word, Brad pushed Tucker to the ground. I screamed, "Tucker!" Brad laughed as he stood there, confident in his control over us.

Tucker picked himself up again and said, "Jace, get in the car."

I was really scared of what Brad could do to Tucker; he was so much bigger, and he was full of hatred. I protested, "But Tucker!"

He replied emphasizing each word slowly, "Please . . . Jace . . . get . . . in . . . the car." I think Tucker knew what was coming and was afraid that after he was beaten, Brad would come after me. I did what he asked and got into the car. I had just locked the door when Brad punched Tucker in the face. I fumbled through my handbag, looking for my cell phone. Tears hindered my search.

Brad was a head taller than Tucker and the force of the punch sent him back down to the ground. A moment later, I heard a big thump and saw that Brad had tumbled onto the pavement. Tucker must have tripped him. They were wrestling around when a man yelled, "You boys better stop this horsing around, there are kids here. Someone's gonna get hurt." He warned, "I'll call the cops if you don't stop this right now." The man's wife and children watched in horror as he approached. The woman lifted her phone to her ear.

Brad stood up and warned Tucker, "We'll finish this later." Then looking toward the man, he lifted his arms above him in surrender and walked away. The man reached a hand down to Tucker and helped him to stand. Tucker was pretty banged up. "Are you all right, son?"

"Thank you, sir. I'll be fine."

I jumped out of the car to have a better look at him. Blood was pouring down the side of his face and I said, "Maybe we should go to the hospital."

His reply was curt, "No, I'm fine."

Tucker got into the passenger seat and I started the car. Looking around again, there was no sign of Brad. At first we drove in silence, then I asked, "Is there more between you two then this?"

Looking out into the darkness, Tucker responded, "He used to come by the camp with his father and act like he owned the place. He picked fights with kids who were smaller than him. He's a year older than me and was always bigger. Others backed down from him, but I never did. He didn't like that. Of course, he beat me, but still, I never feared him and that was what he wanted. He wanted me to fear him. He wanted every kid in that camp to fear him."

"If that's what he was like when he was a kid, then why did Oma let him take over running the camp after his father's death?"

"I guess she believed he had grown up and that he would respect his father's reputation and follow in his footsteps. After all, Brad's a teacher in a school. Other people trust him with their kids. But as we have all seen now, he hasn't changed, and he shouldn't be trusted."

When I dropped him off at his apartment, he just said, "See you around, Jace." His eye was already swollen from where Brad punched him, but I knew that his eye wasn't what was hurting him the most.

At home, Oma had turned the gas fireplace on and was sitting in the dark watching the flames with Bonnie curled up on the floor by her feet. I joined her on the sofa and leaned my head on her shoulder. "Oh Oma, I don't know what to do."

"What's wrong, Jace?"

I didn't want to upset her by telling her about our encounter with Brad. So, I left that part out. Instead I just said, "Tucker told me tonight that he's in love with me and I couldn't say it back to him."

She rubbed my arm in a comforting sort of way. I remembered

her doing the same when I was a little girl crying over a lost toy. "And *do* you love him, Jace?"

"I think so. But I'm afraid."

"Jace, I remember when I would come to visit you. Your father was overseas a lot with the Air Force and your mother was busy working. You spent a lot of time alone, too much time. You didn't have many friends because you moved so often. The first person you took a chance on was your Brian."

I answered, "Yes, and look how that ended."

"There are no guarantees in life. But that doesn't mean you shouldn't take chances when your heart tells you it's the right thing to do."

"I'm not so sure of that. Sometimes I think it's better to just stay alone and not have to be waiting for the day when something happens."

She kissed my head, "Jace, have I left you?"

"No, Oma, you are the one exception."

"That's not true, Jace. Perhaps your parents made their share of mistakes, but they have always loved you and they never left you. Life isn't predictable, and it isn't forever; don't miss out on the good things because you are fearful of the bad. I think it is time for me to tell you more about the love of my life. Why don't you go get your writing pad?"

"All right, Oma."

CHAPTER FORTY-ONE

1951

The night Andrei came to dinner at Onkel Peter's house everyone was on their best behavior. Onkel Peter, Tante Bridget, and Samuel were embarrassingly aware of how they had prejudged him based on his ethnicity.

Tante Bridget made her famous pot roast with potatoes and carrots. "Tante Bridget, you have to show me how to make this! Really it's so tender, it just melts in my mouth."

"Certainly dear, I will write the recipe down for you."

Andrei spoke up nervously, "Thank you, ma'am for this delicious meal. With my brothers at home, I don't always get to enjoy a full plate of anything."

Tante Bridget beamed and as she spooned more pot roast onto his plate, she asked, "How many brothers do you have, Andrei?"

"Well, at home there is Stephan and my youngest brother, Sasha." He turned to face Issy, "You met them, Issy. Remember, when we ordered the egg creams the day I met you. Those fellows with me, they were my brothers."

He looked back at Tante Bridget and said, "But my oldest brother, Daniel, was killed during the Battle of the Bulge."

Onkel Peter cleared his throat, "Your brother fought in the war?"

With a mixture of pride and sadness, Andrei replied, "Sure did, he got awarded the Medal of Honor, posthumously, for his sacrifice. He saved his whole platoon."

Samuel asked, "Would you mind telling me what the circumstances were?"

Andrei continued, "Daniel was able to wipe out a mess of Jerries . . . Uh." He stopped himself for a minute, realizing he had just used a derogatory nickname for Germans. "He, he was able to wipe out the enemy so that his platoon could safely enter the city. That's all they told us, there weren't many details in the telegram." Andrei hung his head down thinking he had just made a terrible mistake by using the word Jerries.

Onkel Peter was sitting next to Andrei and understood why his guest was feeling uncomfortable, so he placed his hand on Andrei's back and said, "Please, thank your parents for their sacrifice. Your brother saved many lives by his actions, including the lives of the people at this table. Without young American soldiers like your brother fighting to liberate Germany, Samuel and many others would not have survived. We can never thank the men enough who liberated our Fatherland."

With his head low over his plate Andrei said, "Thank you."

The war was a raw wound for so many. And the connections that the people sitting around the table had to the men who lived and died in that war, were complicated.

After dinner, the men adjourned to the living room and Onkel Peter turned on the radio. They sat together discussing the war in Korea while the women cleared the table. At the end of the evening, Issy walked outside with Andrei.

"Thank you for inviting me to dinner."

A cool breeze caused a chill and Issy buttoned her sweater as she stood on the stoop in front of the house. The porch light was on, shadows played on her face as the moths fluttered to the light. "I'm glad you came, Andrei."

Those few words bolstered his confidence, "You have a good family, Issy. I'm glad for you and I'm thankful you all made it out of Germany." As soon as the words were out of his mouth, she once again felt the weight of all she had lost. She took a deep breath and sat on the stoop. Seeing the immediate change, he coaxed her, "Tell me more about your family, Issy. What happened to them in Germany? What did you see? What did you live through? Help me to understand."

She sat down on the stoop and looked out toward the street. She could see families inside their homes having dinner, watching television, and reading newspapers. Ordinary scenes of everyday life, but in her mind, she traveled back to East Prussia, back through the years to her childhood. She said, "I saw children, my friends, executed for being Jewish. I saw terrifying soldiers, both German and Russian, terrorize my family. I saw my Vater and Oma after they were shot dead by

Russian soldiers. I saw my mutter freeze to death in a ditch at the side of a road while we were fleeing for our lives. I saw a small boy trying to get comfort from his dead mother in an abandoned warehouse. I saw bombs dropped and I ran from airborne artillery. I saw those who weren't so lucky, blown to pieces. I saw children board a great ship only to find out that most of them drowned after it was torpedoed by a Soviet submarine. I saw my neighbor's dead baby torn from her arms as she sobbed. And I saw my brother and many others die from illnesses that could easily have been cured with the proper medicine." Then, she closed her eyes as if the images in her mind could be blocked out.

Andrei sat down next to her and asked, "May I put my arm around you, Issy?"

She nodded her head in silence. He reached his arm around her and leaned the side of his head against hers. The rays of light from the streetlamps became blurred through her tears. He said, "I am so sorry you had to see all of that." Then thinking about the man who had just attacked her outside of D'Agostino's, he said, "I'd like to say that you are safe now, but I suppose anything can happen anywhere. That is something you know even better than I. But as long as you will let me, I will be here to do whatever I can to protect you."

She spoke softly, "Thank you, Andrei. Thank you for everything."

The sleeves of her sweater didn't reach all the way to her wrists and she shivered when a chilly breeze caused goosebumps to appear on her arm. He stood then and reached his hand down to help her rise.

"I don't want you to get sick, you should go back inside. But before you do, perhaps you will agree to see me again?"

She nodded, "I think that would be very nice."

He did not try to kiss her; he simply brushed away a tear from her cheek before turning toward his own home, just a few blocks away.

CHAPTER FORTY-TWO

PRESENT DAY

The house phone woke me early the next morning. I heard Oma answer it and then a moment later she called to me in a panic, "Jace! Jace! Something's happened to Tucker!"

"What is it?" I struggled to escape from the tangled bedsheets and quickly ran to open the bedroom door. I found her clutching the phone with terror etched on her face as Bonnie watched her warily. She said, "There's been a fire."

"What? Where?"

"Tucker's workshop."

Startled, I asked, "Oh my God! Is he all right?"

She explained, "That was the hospital on the line. He's suffered some burns and he's been admitted. I'm not sure how bad it is. They told me to come right down."

Oma was beside herself and it took quite a while to calm her down. After a chaotic half-hour, I was finally able to get her and myself dressed and into the car. We arrived at the hospital in record time. The nurse told us that although Tucker's injuries from the fire were non-life-threatening, he had some second degree burns on his arms and hands that he had suffered while trying to put out the fire. "We want to keep him here for a while to make sure that the burns heal and don't become infected. Thankfully, he had realized he couldn't save the building and instead made his way outside in time."

Oma leaned on me as we entered his hospital room. But seeing his hands and arms wrapped in bandages almost caused me to lose the use of my own legs. I could also see that his eye and the right side of his face were purple and swollen from where Brad had hit him and there were stitches on his forehead.

Oma took the seat beside his bed. She caressed his head as if he were a child. I stood back against the wall feeling awkward. I wasn't sure if he even wanted me there. Perhaps he only wanted Oma. After all, she was evidently the only mother he had ever known.

Oma stood up on shaky legs to have a better look at him. She fussed over him as he tried to smile through the pain. He told her, "Don't worry. I will heal, Oma."

Oma fretted, "But your business? Your home?"

He shook his head, "It's all gone. But I've got insurance, I'll rebuild."

My grandmother insisted, "Well, until you do, when you are released from this hospital, you are coming home with me."

He looked toward me then and said, "Is that all right with you, Jace? I don't want to impose."

I felt awful that I had hurt him to the point where he thought I wouldn't welcome him into Oma's home. I said, "Of course you will come to stay with us." I walked closer to his bed and looked down on him. He looked like a little boy and I could see in this man the orphan whom Oma had taken in. She must have cared very deeply for him to decide to raise him. Out of all the orphans who came to her camp, he was the one she had chosen.

Tucker smiled broadly at me, showing his dimples, "Well then, that almost makes this all worthwhile." Then he winced as he tried to move his arms.

It took three weeks for Tucker to be released from the hospital. I picked him up while Oma put finishing touches on the third bedroom in her cabin and made it comfortable for him to stay while he recovered. Before he was released, the nurse gave me instructions on how to clean the wounds and change his bandages and then we were off. On the drive home, he said, "Thank you, Jace. I really appreciate this."

Looking straight ahead at the road, I said, "It's no bother, really. I'm glad you're coming to stay with us." Then I quickly followed that up with, "Uh, not that I'm glad you were injured or anything." I felt flustered and it didn't help that as I glanced sideways, I could see him watching me intently.

When we parked in front of Oma's cabin, she came out of the porch and greeted us. I could see her body was visibly shaking with anxiety as I ran around to the passenger side of the car and opened the door for Tucker. Oma called out, "Be careful, Jace!"

I called back to her across the front yard, "Don't worry, Oma, I won't hurt him."

He smiled at me again and asked, "Is that a promise?" It was evident that he was going to milk this for all it was worth. I had to smile back at him, after all, he was so endearing and vulnerable. So, I said, "I promise, as long as you are a good boy and do as Oma and I say; I won't hurt you. We want you to be able to go back to making your beautiful art."

"Oh, so you just want me to mend so you can get rid of me."

"No Tucker. That is the furthest thing from my mind right now."

As hard as it was for me to admit, I had no doubts anymore. After watching him deal so gracefully with this terrible setback, I knew I was in love with him.

The first time I changed his bandages, I saw that it was clearly a painful experience. I tried to remove them as carefully as possible, but there were still raw places where his skin had not yet regrown. Through the pain, he managed to somehow continue to smile at me and joked, "I should start calling you Florence Nightingale."

I just shook my head and said, "What am I going to do with you?"

And to that, he said, "Marry me."

I looked up from the bandages to see if I could tell from his expression if he was serious. There was no longer a hint of a smile. Instead, he was looking directly at me when he continued, "Marry me, Jace. Make me the happiest man on this Earth."

I was speechless. I had only just realized that I loved this man, but I wasn't ready to make a lifetime commitment yet. This was all too new for me. Just then, Oma walked into the room.

She opened her mouth to say something and then shut it again. She looked distressed. I asked, "What's wrong, Oma?"

In a voice full of panic, she said, "I can't find my Catrina!"

Bonnie's watchful eyes picked up on my grandmother's agitation. Oma was distraught, as if she had just lost a real child and I was confused and at a loss to understand her outburst. I tried to explain, "Oma, you gave her to me. I have Catrina. She's in my bedroom."

I hurried to my room to retrieve the doll so I could show it to her. I held Catrina carefully, the old ribbon was still wrapped around her head in an effort to prevent the cracks from spreading. Although the sight of Catrina, calmed her, I also saw the blood drain from her face in shock.

She muttered, "Oh, dear. All right then." She still looked confused and now she also seemed embarrassed. She walked unsteadily over to the kitchen table and sat down. Bonnie immediately stood up and followed her into the kitchen, settling once again next to Oma as she licked my grandmother's feet.

Although I was distracted and continued to glance over to see if Oma was okay, I finished dressing Tucker's arm and then said to him, "We will continue this conversation later."

He responded, "I look forward to that." But the smile had disappeared from his face. He was obviously just as concerned about Oma as I was.

Oma called to me in a shaky voice, "Jace, g-go get that pad and pen, I want to tell you more of my story."

I was stunned for a moment by her quick change in mood. But not wanting to upset her further, I retrieved the items from my bedroom. Still I asked, "Are you sure, Oma? We have plenty of time for this."

But she snapped at me, "No, we don't!" My initial reaction was to feel hurt by her sharp tone. She had never spoken to me like that before. Bonnie felt it too and she yelped as she jumped backward away from Oma as if she had been slapped on the nose. The dog slunk into Oma's bedroom and wandered around looking for a safe place to lie down. Finally, she cautiously approached my grandmother again, and after turning in additional circles, settled once again by Oma's feet. I wondered if Bonnie had already sensed a difference in Oma before this. Animals tended to notice subtle changes before people did. For me, this was the first time I realized that there was something very wrong with my grandmother.

Oma looked intently at Tucker. "Young man, I want you to listen to this too."

"Of course, Oma."

CHAPTER FORTY-THREE

1951

Issy and Andrei planned a double date with Rebekah and Andrei's brother, Stephan. When the boys came to pick up the girls, Onkel Peter warned them to be careful of pickpockets on the boardwalk, "Boys, keep one hand on your wallets at all times."

"Yes, sir. We will."

Then Onkel Peter added, "And bring my girls home safe."

Issy remarked, "Oh Onkel, we will be fine." Ever since the night that Issy was accosted by the would-be thief, her Onkel and Samuel continued to accompany them to and from work each day.

Just a year younger than Andrei, Stephan was almost an exact replica of his older brother, but a head shorter. They both had light blonde hair and warm hazel eyes. Trying to impress Samuel, Stephan explained, "Like Andrei, I want to attend medical school soon." Samuel smiled broadly; he liked the idea of his daughter dating a future doctor.

The young couples went to Steeplechase Park in Coney Island. Andrei held tightly onto Issy, and Stephan onto Rebekah, as they raced down a roller-coaster-ride on the backs of wooden horses. At the end of the ride, Issy and Rebekah tried desperately to hold down their skirts as they exited through the narrow gateway. An intentional burst of air was blown up from the ground beneath them, raising the girls' skirts to the amusement of all who were gathered to watch.

Later, Andrei stole a kiss for the first time in the darkened tunnel on a slow boat through Luna Park's Tunnel of Love. Having never been kissed before, Issy worried her kiss was awkward, and quickly turned away from him. Alarmed, Andrei apologized, "I'm sorry, Issy." But then she leaned her head against his shoulder in the dark and heard him heave a sigh of relief.

The gay sounds of organs piping carnival music throughout Coney Island rose above the screams and laughter of all who partook in the rides. The girls screamed as they hung precariously from the Wheel of Wonder in cars that were suspended on wheels which caused them to roll back and forth as the giant wheel turned. They tumbled and spun through fun houses and marveled at the extraordinary creatures they saw in "The Sideshow by The Seashore". Although Issy and Rebekah had been working on the boardwalk, they had never spent their hard-earned money on the rides. It was an extravagance that neither could have afforded.

When they finally found a shaded bench, the four sat down to enjoy some lemon ices. It was obvious to Izzy that Stephan was completely smitten with Rebekah and that the feeling was reciprocated.

Rebekah said, "In all of my dreams, I've never imagined a place like this. I always wanted to come to America, but I had no idea such wonders existed."

Andrei replied, "I haven't ever been outside of this country. I was born here and raised here, so I have nothing to compare it with."

Stephan nodded, "But that is going to change soon. Andrei and I haven't told our parents yet, but we have both been drafted."

The mood quickly changed as Rebekah asked, "Will you be going to Korea?"

"No, I don't think so. They say we'll be sent to Austria. We'll be with a medical unit and will get some valuable experience along the way."

Rebekah looked down at her shoes and tried not to show how this news affected her. Also shocked by this revelation, Issy asked, "When do you leave?"

Stephan said, "Probably in January. We've still got some time. But we should tell our parents soon."

Issy said, "I guess that's a hard conversation to have with what happened to your brother and all."

Stephan said, "Yeah, well losing Daniel left a big hole in our family. I know they'll be upset but it's not like we enlisted, we don't have a choice."

The rest of the afternoon, Andrei was silent. Issy felt a distance growing between them and this concerned her. After all, her feelings for him had grown considerably since they first met.

Later in the evening, as they made their way back home, Andrei asked Issy, "I hope you won't let my leaving in a few months stop us from getting to know each other better."

Issy had a hollow feeling in the pit of her stomach, but in spite of it she said, "I had a really nice time today and I'd like to see you again."

"Good, then we'll do that."

That night, Samuel asked how the day had gone. Rebekah announced, "It was fine until the boys told us they have been drafted."

Samuel and Peter exchanged a look of concern. Samuel remarked, "Well, they are fine young men and I'm sure they will be an asset to this great country." Then, perhaps as a distraction, he added, "Girls, I had an eventful day myself. I bought a little shop in Brighton Beach. I'm going to open my own men's clothing store. I could use some help in the shop if you would both like a job."

Rebekah was astonished, "Of course, Papa. Whatever you need, you know Issy and I will be there for you."

He continued, "There's more, I've also bought that house." Samuel pointed outside the window. "It is time that we planted our own roots here, Rebekah. Peter and Bridget have been more than generous in all they have done for us since our arrival." At the look on the girls' faces he said, "Now don't worry, it's not as if we are moving to another country. We will be right across the street."

Over the following months, Issy and Andrei spent as much

time together as her new job and his classes would allow. One autumn afternoon, they were sitting on the deserted beach and she became self-conscious as he stared at her. Finally, she said, "What do you see when you look at me like that, Andrei?" He said, "Your skin is as smooth as porcelain, like that doll of yours, you are perfect. Sometimes I feel I don't deserve you. I can't believe how lucky I am."

She blinked as she looked at him and said, "My doll is not perfect, Andrei, and neither am I. She has deep cracks that have nearly split her face in two."

He leaned in close to her and she could smell his aftershave. Having him so near gave her a tingling sensation up and down her arms. She examined his face and attempted a bit of wit when she said, "You have a few creases of your own!" She reached up and traced the lines around his mouth. Finally, the words he had longed to say made their way past his lips, "When this war is over, when I come back, will you marry me, Issy?"

She had lived through a war and its aftermath, she had lost her entire family and so many friends, and yet she had survived. She didn't know why she had been spared, but she knew there must be some greater purpose to her life. Issy was determined to look for those moments when she could repay fate for bringing her to safety and into Andrei's life. She took Andrei's hand in hers and said, "Ja, Andrei, I will be happy to marry you."

The boardwalk was deserted as they walked back toward the train. The rides at Coney Island were silenced and Issy thought they seemed like metal giants looking down on the fragile couple who passed below. She shivered, and Andrei took off his jacket and put it around her shoulders. She told him, "I'd like to be married in June when the roses are in full bloom." He replied, "Then let's do that. I want to make all of your dreams come true, Issy."

Issy smiled at him, "You already have, Andrei."

The following week, Issy and Rebekah had dinner at the Ruskin family home. Mr. and Mrs. Ruskin were delighted to meet the girls their sons could not stop talking about. A thick stew was served that they called Borscht. Issy was a bit self-conscious that the family she was eating with was Russian, but she tried to hide her feelings of trepidation. After dinner, Issy and Rebekah helped to clear the table. As Issy placed the dishes in the kitchen sink, Andrei's mother asked her, "Are you comfortable, Issy? You seem nervous." Rebekah over-heard and answered for her, "Not at all, she's fine." Mrs. Ruskin looked from Rebekah to Issy and asked, "Does she always answer for you?" Issy stammered, "Nein, no. I am a little nervous, ma'am." Mrs. Ruskin asked, "And why are you so nervous? We don't bite."

Issy gathered her courage, "Ma'am, we ran from the Russians in Europe. You know there is a long history between the Russians and Germans. Well, Russian soldiers killed my vater and my Oma."

"I am sorry for that Issy, but that was not us."

"I know."

Rebekah joined it, "Ma'am, Russian soldiers accosted us as well."

The older woman looked again at these two girls whom her sons had brought home, "You must put that all behind you if you are going to be part of our family. You are in America now. We are all one, here."

Issy responded, "Ja, this is true. I am trying." Rebekah started to wash the dishes and Issy began to dry them.

"Good. I want my sons to be happy."

Sasha entered then, "Hey, what's going on in here? Where's dessert?"

His mother answered, "It's coming; it's coming my boy."

He kissed the top of his mother's head. Then turned to Issy, "Hey, Andrei was telling me you have this porcelain doll that looks just as pretty as you."

Issy blushed, "Oh." She snapped a hand towel at him. "You are a trouble maker, aren't you, Shasha?"

"No, but I'm disappointed that there isn't another one of you for me. Andrei and Stephan told me they could set me up with a real doll. They said she was as pretty as you, Issy. I thought they were talking about a girl when they said her name was Catrina. But then they started to laugh and told me who Catrina is, or should I say, what she is. There's no girl left for me, Andrei and Stephan have all the luck!"

Mrs. Ruskin shooed him away, "Inside with you. We will be there in a moment."

Afterward, Andrei and Stephan walked the girls home. Andrei said, "My mother likes you, Issy. She says you speak the truth to her."

"Well, I told her what the Russian soldiers did to us."

"Is that still bothering you? Is it still worrying you that I am Russian?"

"Nein. Not anymore. I was concerned about meeting your parents, but they are both very kind. I don't want to think about the past anymore. I want to think about our future." Then she teased him, "Sasha says you tried to set him up on a date with my doll and told him that she was as pretty as me."

Andrei smiled and put his arm around her as they walked, "Catrina is the image of you and she is pretty little thing. But she is the image of a child and you are a woman. The most beautiful woman I have ever met."

CHAPTER FORTY-FOUR

1952-1956

In January, Issy and Rebekah waved good-bye to Andrei and Stephan as their ship pulled away from the harbor. Issy turned to Rebekah, "Now it is our turn to stand on the shore and watch as the ship disappears from view." Rebekah had tears in her eyes, "I'm going to miss him so much, Issy." Issy nodded in understanding. She linked her arm with Rebekah's, "Here we are again, just the two of us. We'll have to be strong once again, for ourselves and for each other."

Rebekah leaned her head against Issy's, "Stephan and I made plans. When he comes home we want to be married."

Issy smiled and whispered, "Andrei and I did the same."

Rebekah brightened up, "We should have a double wedding!"

Issy nodded, "Ja, a double wedding in June; even if we have to wait a year or so."

Although Stephan and Andrei were both sent to Austria where they practiced drills and prepared for war, in April, Andrei was then sent to Korea.

Issy received a letter dated June 27th, 1952. In it, Andrei wrote,

"My dearest, Issy,

We spend much time in trenches and there are those who say this war is fought more like the Great War than World War II. Yard to yard, we advance and retreat over and over again. Communist China and the Soviet Union arm and fight alongside the North Koreans and push us back. On and on it goes without an end in sight.

I tend to the men as best as I can, but often, there is nothing I can do for them. For those whose injuries are too severe, we strap them to platforms outside of helicopters that lift them into the air and take them further behind the lines to Seoul or on to Austria where Stephan takes care of them. This war is God awful!

I carry your photograph with me wherever I go. It gives me the strength to keep going. Soldiers fall around me every day. I know now what you must have seen in Germany when you were fleeing from the Soviets.

Please keep writing, your letters sustain me. I enjoy hearing all about what is happening at home. It gives me a reprieve from this hellish place.

Each day that passes, brings me closer to seeing you again. I imagine seeing the roses braided into your hair on our wedding day. Perhaps next June? Please keep me in your prayers and send my regards to Rebekah, Samuel, Onkel Peter and Tante Bridget.

Your devoted, Andrei."

It was the last letter she ever received from him. When

Andrei's letters stopped coming, Rebekah tried to reassure her. "It must be harder to get letters out from the war zone. I'm sure he's fine, Issy."

But then, in August, a letter arrived from Stephan saying he had received word that Andrei had been killed in action. Issy and Rebekah sat on Issy's bed as they read the words. Issy didn't want to believe it, she cried, "It can't be! Not again, Rebekah! I can't keep living while all the people I love die. I can't keep waking up each morning knowing I am alone again."

Rebekah held onto her friend who she had consoled after losses so many times before. She whispered into Issy's ear, "I'm so sorry, Issy. I'm so sorry." Of all the people in the world, there was no one who understood Issy's sorrow more than she.

After spending the entire year in Austria, Stephan returned home in February of 1953. Finally, the war ended when an armistice was signed on July 27th, 1953 with an agreement to divide the country along the 38th parallel. By the end of the Korean War, 40,000 U.S. soldiers were dead and over 100,000 were wounded in action. Sadly, over 4 million lives were lost from both sides during this war, including both military and civilian.

Stephan started medical school in September at Columbia University and then he and Rebekah were married on June 5th, 1954. Issy stood next to Rebekah on her wedding day and attended to her best friend as her maid-of-honor. Sasha was Stephan's best man and it twisted Issy's heart to see Sasha had grown taller than Stephan and was now the spitting image of Andrei.

Although Issy's heart was broken, it gave her solace to know Stephan had made it back safely, and that he and Rebekah would have the chance for a happy life together.

As the years passed, Issy kept Andrei in her heart. At first, she only stumbled blindly through her life as the days ebbed and flowed. But time healed her enough to be able to appreciate life once again. She marveled at how the devastation of loss could linger, and yet, time allowed her eventually to move on. But the young men she met never seemed to quite live up to her memory of Andrei.

Then one afternoon as a storm approached, she was painting on the boardwalk when she heard someone behind her. Issy turned, half expecting it to be Andrei. But there was a young man standing there whom she had never met before. He admired her painting and said, "You paint beautifully, your paintings should be in an art gallery."

She felt disconcerted by the intrusion, but managed to say, "Danke, I-I mean thank you."

"Let me introduce myself, I'm Paul, um, Paul Colton."

"Hi Paul, my name is Issy. Do you paint too?"

"I used to, but now I work at an ad agency in Manhattan. There's not much time for painting these days. Now television commercials pay the bills for me instead of my paintings."

Issy looked him over; he had dusty brown hair and hazel eyes. It was the eyes that reminded her of Andrei. She smiled at him and returned her attention to her painting. She could feel a tingling up her spine. Ordinarily, she didn't like it when people watched her paint. It often made her feel self-conscious. But somehow, she didn't mind his watching. He was quiet and patient as she worked on the canvas. When she was done, he exclaimed, "Both beautiful and haunting at the same time."

Then the first rain drops from the approaching storm spotted the ground. Quickly she grabbed the tablecloth she carried with her and he helped her to cover the fresh painting.

He suggested, "We'd better get that painting somewhere safe before the downpour begins. Do you need a ride?"

"I was just going to take the train."

"Nonsense, I'm parked just over there. Let me take you home."

She hesitated; after all, she didn't know this man. He lifted his hands in defense, "I'm harmless, I promise."

She laughed, "Somehow, I doubt that."

"No, no, really. I just want to help."

"All right. That *would* be a great help. She packed up her easel and, together, they carried her belongings to his car. "Oh, my!" She exclaimed as she saw a sporty Jaguar parked on the narrow street. He skillfully maneuvered her painting and easel into the back seat and then held the door open for her. She ducked into the luxurious seat and sat back astonished at the rich upholstery.

On the drive home they exchanged pleasantries but kept things casual. Then once at her house, he jumped out of the car and sped around to her side to open the door for her. As he held her hand in his, he asked, "May I see you again?" Surprising herself, she agreed and then carrying her easel and painting, she hurried into her Onkel's house. Immediately, she telephoned Rebekah and told her about the man she had just met. "He sounds dreamy and rich too!"

Issy replied, "Oh, I'm not sure if I'm ready for this."

"Come on, Issy. Don't let this pass you by. At least have some fun, please."

Issy took a deep breath, "Okay, I'll try."

The next weekend, Paul brought her to Manhattan and they dined at Delmonico's. She had never before experienced such luxury and extravagance. He spent the evening watching her with admiration in his eyes. By the time the evening was over he asked, "I know this is quick, but I'd love to introduce you to my family and to meet yours as well. What do you think?"

Their conversation was so easy and her level of comfort around him was astonishing to her. "Ja, that would be nice." She agreed.

When he came for dinner at Onkel Peter's house, she saw how he charmed her Tante and Onkel and Samuel as well. Rebekah and Stephan were there too, and the two young couples got along amazingly well.

After Paul left that night, Rebekah and Issy sat for a while on the stoop. Rebekah asked, "Do you love him?"

Issy wasn't sure how to answer that. In agony she said, "How can I love him? I feel like I am being unfaithful to Andrei. I know that's ridiculous, but I can't help feeling torn between them."

Rebekah thought about it, "Maybe, Andrei sent him to you? Perhaps it wasn't a coincidence that he noticed you while you were painting on the boardwalk. Andrei would want you to be happy, Issy. And I know if it is at all possible, he would send the best man he could find to you. And I have to say, Paul is a really great catch."

Rebekah's words lifted a weight off of Issy's chest, "Maybe you're right, Rebekah."

CHAPTER FORTY-FIVE

1959-2002

Issy and Rebekah pushed their sleeping babies in carriages along the Coney Island boardwalk. Rebekah's daughter, Cindy, had her father's light blonde hair and hazel eyes. Issy's daughter, Lily, was a tiny replica of herself. There was a quiet satisfaction for them to be able to share this milestone together. They had become mothers within months of each other and it felt as if all of their dreams had finally come true.

Issy raised her face to the sun and felt the warmth it offered. She listened to the waves as they crashed against the beach and the laughter of the children who played on the sand below her. It all seemed worthwhile now. If all the struggles and all the loss had brought her to this place, then she couldn't wish to change a thing. She sighed as the guilt for feeling this way edged into her mind.

"What's wrong?" Rebekah asked.

"Nothing. Just thinking."

Rebekah looked intently at Issy, "Now, tell me the truth."

"I was thinking about all we have been through. If things hadn't worked out the way they did, I wouldn't have Lily. I wouldn't trade her for anything, and yet, I can't help but feel guilty for feeling this way. Of course, I wish my parents and bruder were here to see her. And if Andrei had lived . . ." The pain of that thought was too much for her to finish.

Rebekah reasoned, "You can't think that way, Issy. Things are the way they are. Accept and appreciate what we have. There should be no place for guilt in your heart; you did all you could do to save them. Life doesn't always go as we plan, but it goes as it is meant to."

Issy smiled, "And when did you become a philosopher?"

Rebekah chuckled, then said seriously, "When I decided to let go of my own guilt. The guilt only stops you from enjoying what you have, it doesn't change the past."

Issy nodded, "This is true."

Rebekah stopped walking and reached for Issy's hand, "I wish you still lived across the street. We could have walks like this every day if you did."

Although Rebekah and Stephan had moved into Samuel's house, Issy and Paul had moved into an apartment on the Upper East Side of Manhattan.

Issy said, "Just because we moved, doesn't mean that we won't raise the girls together."

Rebekah looked into Issy's bright blue eyes, "Promise me,

Issy. Promise, we will never grow apart, and our children will grow up together."

"Of course. I'll only be a train ride away. We will continue to visit Onkel Peter often. Don't worry."

Over the following years, Issy and Rebekah brought their young daughters to Coney Island to enjoy the carousel and other rides until Steeplechase closed on September 20, 1964. By then, the children had become as inseparable as their mothers.

For the girls' eighth birthdays, their parents took them to the circus at Madison Square Gardens. As Issy watched the girls share cotton candy and point in astonishment at the man who put his head in the lion's mouth, she leaned close to Rebekah and whispered, "Remember when we were eight years old?"

Rebekah smiled, "Remember the time you brought Catrina over to my house to show me her new dress? Remember the dreidel my Opa made for me?"

Issy hugged her friend as more memories flooded their minds. "Remember how he made a coin spin on the table?" There was no need for Rebekah to answer. They linked arms and watched their daughters enjoy the wonders that unfolded in the rings below.

After the circus, Lily and Cindy begged to have a sleepover at Issy's house. "All right," Rebekah agreed, "As long as you get some sleep." In unison the girls replied, "We will! We promise!" as they dramatically crossed their hearts, and each held two fingers in the air as they said, "Cross my heart and hope to die."

Later that night, Issy listened at the door as the girls shared

Lily's bed. She heard Lily ask, "What do you want to be when you grow up?"

Cindy replied wondrously, "I want to be one of those girls in the circus who spins on a rope while holding on by her teeth."

Issy smiled to herself as she peeked into the darkened room and heard Lily reply, "I'd like to be a lion tamer."

Then the girls were quiet for a while, perhaps each was caught up in their own imaginations until Lily said, "We can run away together and join the circus! That way no one can ever separate us again."

Cindy squealed, "Oh, and we can travel everywhere and see the mountains and the deserts and even the redwood forest!"

As the girls continued to make plans, Issy quietly closed the door. Lily and Cindy were all the evidence needed to convince herself that her life had been worth living.

Over the following years, the girls spent as much time as they could together, but as they became teenagers, Lily and Cindy started to develop other friendships and different dreams for their futures.

Issy answered the phone one day and heard Rebekah's shattered voice on the other end, "Issy, papa is gone. His heart gave out in his sleep." Issy's reply was immediate, "I'll be right there." Rebekah and Stephan had taken care of Samuel until his death in 1969. Rebekah made sure Samuel had a proper Jewish wake and Issy, Paul, Onkel Peter, Tante Bridget and the girls joined Stephan's family as they all sat Shiva for him.

Within the years that followed, both Onkel Peter and Tante Bridget also passed away. As Rebekah's and Issy's lives became busier and as the demands on their husbands' jobs increased, the women saw less and less of each other. But regardless, what bonded them was deep in their hearts and no amount of time apart could change that.

In 1976, the two families decided to go on a ski vacation together in upstate New York. At eighteen, Lily and Cindy took beginner lessons and soon Cindy was swooning over their young instructor, Woody. He said, "I think you girls are ready to leave this bunny hill and go up the lift." Rebekah wanted to object, but when Cindy rolled her eyes at her mother, Rebekah stepped back. All day long the girls skied with their instructor. When they came down from one run, they met their mothers in the lodge and shared cups of cocoa. Lily complained to Issy and Rebekah, "Cindy keeps falling so that Woody will have to stay with her." Cindy laughed, "Come on Lily, you have to admit, it worked, didn't it?" Cindy gently poked at Lily's cheek until her friend was smiling too.

Both girls were laughing as they left their mothers. But an hour later, Lily's face was full of tears when she found the adults again.

She screamed, "Mom, Cindy's hurt!" Issy grabbed Rebekah's arm as concern quickly took over and Rebekah asked, "What happened?"

"She skied into a tree. They're taking her down from the mountain now."

Rebekah, Stephan, Issy, and Paul ran out of the lodge and toward the bottom of the hill where they saw Cindy being brought down on a stretcher. They followed the ambulance to the hospital and Stephan consulted with the doctors. "Your daughter has broken her collar bone and four ribs. She also hit her head hard and is suffering from a concussion. But we expect her to make a full recovery."

Rebekah collapsed in her chair, exhausted from the stress and fear of the last few hours. A look passed between her and Issy. There was no need for words, they both knew what the other had been thinking.

After one weeks' stay in the hospital, Rebekah and Stephan brought their daughter home. When the pain medication ran out, Cindy complained, "Daddy, it still hurts so much!" As a doctor, Stephan continued to prescribe the drugs for his daughter. He couldn't stand to see her in such pain. But long after she was healed, she still came to him begging for more pills. Finally, Stephen refused, "No more Cindy, you don't need them anymore."

A year after the accident, Cindy's left home without even so much as a note for her parents. Over the years, once in a while, Rebekah would hear from Cindy, but it was always only to ask for money. Money Rebekah knew would be used for drugs no matter how much Cindy denied it. Once, Stephan was able to find his daughter and he brought her back home and placed her in a rehab facility. For a few weeks, they had their daughter back, but then she relapsed and disappeared again.

Meanwhile, Lily grew up and married a man named Carl Johnson. He was a sergeant in the Air Force when they were married in 1990. Lily left New York to follow him from base to base.

In 1992, Lily and Carl had a daughter of her own, and they named her Jacelyn. But right from the start, everyone called her Jace. She was a tiny replica of both her mother, Lily, and her Oma, Issy.

Rebekah and Stephan didn't hear from Cindy again until 1993. Cindy sent a photograph from Nashville to her parents of her little boy. On the back of the photo all that was written was the words, four years old. He had Stephan's light blonde hair and hazel eyes. The note that accompanied the photo said,

"Dear Mom and Dad,

This is my son. I've left him in an orphanage. I can't do this anymore and I know he'll be better off without me. So, will you. I'm so sorry.

Cindy"

The envelope had a Nashville address scrawled on it. Stephan and Rebekah flew to Tennessee to try to find their daughter and grandson. They found Cindy in a hospital morgue. She had died of an overdose in a flea-infested motel room. When they approached the orphanages, they were told all records were sealed and they had no right to any child given up for adoption by his mother. Rebekah was devastated.

When Issy heard that Cindy had died, she dropped everything and ran to be by her friend's side. Rebekah's heart was completely broken, "Issy, I cannot face life without my daughter. With all the loss I have known, none I have ever experienced has been as severe as this."

Issy held onto her friend as they had done for each other so often through the years. Issy promised her, "Somehow we will make it through this too."

But only a year later, Stephan took his own life. He had never gotten over feeling guilty for having supplied his daughter with barbiturates in the first place. After that, Rebekah refused to leave her house. She shut herself away from the world.

Those years that were spent without her daughter and her husband were difficult for Rebekah. As much as Issy wanted to console her, she knew there were no words for this loss. When they did spend time together to commemorate Lily and Jace's milestones, it only served to increase Rebekah's pain.

And It seemed like almost every year there was more grief. Issy mourned when Paul passed away from a heart attack in 1996. The following year, Rebekah was diagnosed with complications resulting from the Rheumatic Fever she had suffered as a child. Her aortic valve was defective, and the condition only seemed to be mildly responsive to medications.

Issy decided there was only one thing she needed to do, she needed to try to find Cindy's son before her friend died. In order to do so, she bought some land in eastern Tennessee and planned to open a summer camp for orphans. She begged Rebekah, "Come with me, I'll take care of you and we will find him together." But Rebekah didn't have the strength to do so, "No Issy. I can't start over again somewhere new. This is where I will die." Issy coaxed her friend, "If I need to meet every orphan in Nashville, I promise, I will find him for you."

"If you do find him, no matter how sick I am, I will come. If anyone can do it, Issy, you can."

Stephan's younger brother, Sasha, moved his own wife and children into Rebekah's house to take care of her.

Issy opened her summer camp specifically for children who lived in orphanages in Nashville. Every summer, when the children came off the buses, she searched their faces, looking for someone who looked like Rebekah's Stephan, someone who was the right age and who looked like her Andrei.

In the summer of 2002, a thirteen-year-old boy named Tucker came to Issy's camp. Just like in the picture Cindy had sent to her parents, he had the same familiar light blonde hair and warm hazel eyes. He was the image of his grandfather, Stephan. Issy went to the orphanage the following week and asked about the boy. Mrs. Carmel, who ran the orphanage, told Issy, "Those records are sealed." But since the two women had a friendship that had grown over the years, Mrs. Carmel casually left the room with Tucker's records open on her desk. Issy quickly glanced through the papers and saw Cindy's name, clearly written as his biological mother. His biological father was listed as "unknown".

After returning to camp, Issy called Rebekah on the phone, "I found him!"

Rebekah was stunned, "Are you sure?"

"Ja, Rebekah, he is your grandson."

"How?"

With tears in her eyes and a catch in her throat Issy responded, "He's at my camp right now and he looks just like Stephan, just like Andrei."

"But how do you know for sure that it's him, Issy?"

"I went to the orphanage. The woman there has known me for years. She was kind and left the room with the boy's records open and on her desk. Cindy's name was listed on them as his birth mother."

There was such a long silent pause on Rebekah's end, "Rebekah, are you all right?"

"Issy, I'm not well but I am coming down there. I have to."

Issy replied, "I'll be waiting."

"Danke, Issy. I will be there as soon as I can get a flight. I'll let you know by tomorrow."

Two days later, Rebekah arrived at the airport in Knoxville and Hank went to pick her up. When Issy saw her old friend, she was more worried about her then ever. Rebekah had wasted away to almost nothing. Her clothes hung on her as if they were hanging on a pole. At 71 years old, her once bountiful reddish-brown hair was thin and gray, and her face had hollows sunken into her cheeks. But her eyes were still as clear and brown as always. Issy hugged her friend carefully; afraid she would cause her more pain.

Rebekah asked Issy, "Have you told him anything? Does he know who I am?"

"Nein. I thought I would leave that to you."

"I've been thinking about this Issy. I think it would be cruel to tell him I was his grandmother only to have him lose me so soon afterward."

Issy started to argue, "Nonsense!" But then one look at the resolution in Rebekah's face made Issy realize the truth of what her friend was saying. So instead, Issy said, "Whatever you decide, Rebekah. It's up to you."

Later, at supper, Issy introduced Rebekah to the campers as her dearest and oldest friend. Issy didn't have to point out Tucker to her, Rebekah noticed him instantly. The resemblance was undeniable. Tears filled her eyes as she looked at her grandchild for the first time. All the memories and worries over the years for Cindy came flooding back to her. There was nothing more she could do for her daughter. And the fear that there was nothing more she could do for her grandson filled her heart with regret. It was too late.

While they ate their supper, Rebekah took a seat next to Tucker. "How are you doing young man?"

Tucker replied politely, "I'm well, ma'am. Thank you."

"Do you like it here at the camp?"

"Yes, so far it's pretty good."

"How about at the orphanage? Do you like it there?"

"I do all right. I have my friends." He shrugged, "They're all I got." Rebekah's heart ached for him.

When he saw her frown he said, "But we're like a family. You don't have to worry about me, ma'am."

Rebekah spent the rest of the month at the camp. Tucker grew attached to this strange old woman who seemed so frail but also so intent on spending time with him. When the last day of camp came and he was about to climb onto the bus and out of her life, Rebekah pulled him aside. "Tucker, never forget that you are very special. Make the most out of your life. Sometimes, it may seem like you have nothing, but you have all you need within you." She kissed his head, ruffled his hair with her hand, and then took him in her arms and hugged him.

As he looked at her, he felt sorry for her. It seemed to him, she was just as alone in the world as he was. Rebekah called out to him as he boarded the bus, "Have a good life, Tucker!" He looked at her, still a bit confused by all the attention she had given him, but wanting her to feel better he said, "I will. Maybe I'll see you next summer when I come back to camp." And then he waved as he disappeared onto the bus.

Issy cared for Rebekah until she needed to be hospitalized. They spent Rebekah's last days together. On Rebekah's deathbed, Issy promised to do all she could to adopt Tucker and take care of him for the rest of her life. But Issy soon found out that because of her advanced age that was easier said than done. The orphanage would not allow it. She began a battle which lasted for years as she tried against the odds to adopt him. But in the end, she finally settled for being his foster mother.

CHAPTER FORTY-SIX

PRESENT DAY

Both Tucker and I were stunned by the revelation that he was Rebekah's grandson.

Tucker implored her, "Oma, why didn't you ever tell me?"

Oma said, "I was afraid you would think I felt obliged to take you in because you were Rebekah's grandson. I didn't want you ever to question my love for you. Maybe I made a mistake, but I thought it was best not to bring up the past."

I said, "But Oma, didn't you think he would want to know? That he had a right to know that he was part of Rebekah's family?"

Oma's eyes filled with tears and I felt bad that I had pressed her further on this sensitive topic. Then she said to us, "Rebekah was my sister, but she wasn't my flesh and blood. Family might be who you are born to, it might be who you end up with, or it may be those you meet along the way.

There's only one way to know for sure who your family is; they are the people you carry in your heart; the ones you think of when you think of the word home. I hope this is home for you, Tucker. I hope that you know Rebekah and I are both your family. She couldn't be here to raise you, so I did. And I did the best I could."

I asked, "Oma, why now? Why are you telling us all of this now?"

As my grandmother gently petted Bonnie's soft fur, she looked at me in earnest, "Jace, I'm getting forgetful. I know you've seen it, and don't think I haven't noticed it as well. Sometimes I struggle to remember the simplest things, like if I ate lunch or if I took a shower. I don't remember recipes I've been cooking all my life. I tried to make Tante Bridget's pot roast last night, but I couldn't remember how to make it anymore. Did I ever give that recipe to you?"

I shook my head, feeling regretful. She continued, "I have to write myself little notes and I find the same note written in different places because I didn't know I had already written the note five times before. I've seen this happen to my friends and I know what's happening to me. I'm afraid I will forget my childhood soon." Her voice cracked as she continued, "I'm afraid I will forget my Vater and Mutti, I'm afraid I will forget Hans and Andrei and Rebekah. And I'm most afraid that I will even forget the two of you."

I felt a lump in my throat and I didn't know what to say. Of course, I had been noticing her getting forgetful, but I just told myself it was normal for her age.

Tucker suggested, "Maybe we need to make an appointment with a neurologist. Someone who can determine if this is something that will progress or if maybe you've had a minor stroke or something else is affecting your thinking process. We don't know for sure until a doctor has checked you out."

I clung to Tucker's words of hope; maybe this was not what Oma feared. My grandmother looked at Tucker directly and said, "Well mein liebling, this I have already done. I have had the CT scans and blood tests and we know it is dementia. The doctor said it was 'dementia of the Alzheimer's sort.'"

I repeated the word out loud, "Alzheimer's." The word felt heavy on my lips and I was having difficulty breathing. I sat down as my head began to spin, but a moment later I told myself I couldn't afford to feel ill now. Not with Tucker and Oma both needing my help at the same time. I took a shaky breath and said, "I would like to meet your doctor. Maybe he can explain it all to me."

Oma said, "That is a good idea, Jace. His phone number is in my book by the telephone. His name is Dr. Schlesinger."

A week later we were sitting in Dr. Schlesinger's office. He was a man in his late sixties with thick glasses and a kind smile. He told us, "I have studied her CT scans and although there are signs of old minor strokes, there are none that would explain memory loss. All the tests suggest it is Alzheimer's. I can't determine exactly if it is Alzheimer's without further invasive testing, but I am sure it is a progressive form of dementia. There is a wide range of how this affects an individual, but in time, it will most certainly advance. What we have here is the early stage where independence is still possible. As it progresses, it will enter a middle stage where it will be best if she is supervised. There is no saying how long the early stage will last and when the middle stage will begin."

I asked, "Well is there any medication to help her?"

"Yes, there is, and we have already started her on it, but as I said, there is no way of knowing how much it will help or for how long it will prolong the early stage. As of now there is no medication or procedure that will reverse this disease. There is much we still don't know about Alzheimer's and we are only now receiving data on patients who have been treated for a substantial length of time with medication. In the next few years, we hope to have a better understanding of how effective the medication is." He said, "Let's make another appointment for three months from now and we will see how she is doing."

In a surprisingly steady voice, Oma said, "Thank you, doctor."

Dr. Schlesinger said, "I'm sorry I didn't have better news for you, but don't give up hope. Your best medicine is a healthy attitude and a loving family. And I can tell that's exactly what you have here."

I shook Dr. Schlesinger's hand. "Thank you, doctor."

As we drove home I was still in shock and also somewhat in denial. Of course, I had heard about Alzheimer's, but it was something that happened to other people, it wasn't something that happened to my own grandmother. Perhaps it would be different for her, perhaps she wouldn't progress further. Grasping for straws, I held onto this hope.

Oma said, "Jace, I know you don't want to talk about this, but I made an appointment with my lawyer. I want to make sure if anything happens to me, you have the authority to make decisions for both my health and my finances."

Although I wished it hadn't come to this, I knew she was being practical, and so I said, "All right, Oma."

The investigation into the fire that had burned down Tucker's shop and apartment was finally completed, and they concluded the cause was arson. I couldn't help thinking Brad had something to do with it, so I told the police about the scuffle between Brad and Tucker. They said they would investigate him. I wasn't sure if I wanted them to find him guilty or not. But either way, the truth had to be found out. Throughout the fall, construction progressed on the rebuilding of Tucker's workshop. Meanwhile Tucker continued to recover and live with us in Oma's cabin. But neither of us spoke of marriage again, instead we both focused on taking care of Oma.

CHAPTER FORTY-SEVEN

PRESENT DAY

I had to admit, I was really enjoying having Tucker at the cabin. It was nice to have late night talks and also quiet times. Since he was still unable to turn pages with his bandaged hands, I searched for a book to read to him. But the only one I could find in Oma's house was an old copy of Franz Kafka's *Metamorphosis* and it was in German.

We grew closer simply by spending ordinary days together. One night in early January, Tucker spoke softly after Oma had gone to bed and asked, "So tell me what you know about Oma and my grandmother, Rebekah. Oma has told me some of the story, but I think she's left some things out."

I brought him up to date on all that Oma had told me about her life, and when I had finished, he asked me, "And the doll she calls Catrina, it has been with her all this time?"

"Yes."

He marveled, "And she was never able to get it fixed?"

"Never."

He shook his head in amazement and said, "I can't imagine two young girls going through all that they did and the courage it took for them to survive."

The last light in the cabin shut off as its timer hit 2 a.m. and we sat in the dark with the only light coming from the gas fireplace. I looked at him and saw the desire in his eyes. I moved closer to him on the sofa and leaned my head on his shoulder. His bandaged arms were lying stiffly on his legs and I tenderly touched them. "Tucker, I'm sorry about all of this, about the fire and about finding out Oma has always known who your biological family was. This is a lot to handle all at once. And now, knowing she is struggling with dementia, it seems like it's just too much."

"Don't be sorry, Jace. Somehow, all that has happened has brought you to me. That just can't be a bad thing."

It felt good to be this close to him. He moved and turned his head toward me and kissed me. It was a long kiss, full of desire. I pulled away from him and tried to put some distance between us so that I could collect my thoughts. I said, "Oma is going to need us both. We're in for some difficult times ahead."

He nodded, "Yes, I know."

As much as I wanted him in that moment, the time still wasn't right. So, I kissed him on his cheek and said goodnight. I left him by the fireplace as I went to my bedroom alone.

The months that followed showed the disease continuing to progress even with the medication that was attempting to slow it down. Along with the progression, Oma's frustration also grew. So, we took her checkbook, her wallet, her keys and her medications and put them in a locked cabinet.

One day, Oma was with me in a grocery store and she stood in the aisle, blankly staring at the cans of soup which were stacked on the shelves. I asked her, "Do you want to buy some soup?"

She simply repeated the word, "Soup?" as if it were a question, all on its own.

I felt a lump in my throat and then I hugged her. "Don't worry, Oma. I'm here, I'll help you," and I piled some cans into her cart. She pushed the cart along, following me like an obedient child. As we approached the cashier, she reached into her handbag and found only tissues. I opened my own bag and she pushed my hand away. She said, "Let me pay for it." But no matter how much she searched, there was no wallet, no money in her bag.

Her eyes told of her confusion. She said in alarm, "Oh no, I must have lost my wallet! I-I don't have my card!"

I said, "I've got the money, I'll pay for it."

She still looked distressed and said, "Nein, nein, nein! I don't want you to pay for it, I have my own money."

To calm her I said, "I have your wallet in my bag. It's okay. I've got your credit card." And I handed my own card to the cashier who was looking at my grandmother as if she were afraid of her.

Oma was relieved, "Oh good. Danke, Jace. I don't want you spending your own money on me." I looked at this woman who had been so strong through so much of her life and I ached for her.

Later, while I was driving her home, she rummaged through her empty bag once again. This time she shouted, "My keys! I don't have my keys!"

I reassured her, "Don't worry, Oma, I have your keys." I pointed to my car keys in the ignition, "See, they're on the same key chain as my keys."

This time she only said, "That is good," and then she turned her head away from me. I felt like crying, but I didn't want her to see my tears. She was so used to being independent and now she was as helpless as a baby.

Tucker finally recovered from his burn wounds and had to spend a lot of time overseeing the rebuilding of his shop. He agreed to continue to live with us until the construction was finished. I was glad he was there. His strength helped me to be stronger and I couldn't have accomplished all that needed to be done for Oma alone.

There came a time when we couldn't leave her at home by herself. On the rare occasion when we both went out at the same time, we would call Murray and he would come and sit with her. She still liked to play dominoes, and so he would entertain her for hours playing the game. He teased her, "Issy, I can never win against you." She would smile and confess, "I don't know what I'm doing." And he would say, "But it doesn't stop you from beating me." That would always make her laugh.

Tucker and I didn't have a lot of time to spend together alone anymore, but somehow it didn't matter. Just caring for Oma had brought us closer than ever. But there were times when I doubted his affection for me. I started to think it was only our shared love for Oma that we had in common. Since that night on the couch, he had not tried to kiss me again. As I lay alone in my bed one night, I thought of Brian and whispered into the darkness, "I'm sorry Brian that you had to leave. I will always miss you. But it is time for me to get on with my life. I hope you understand." And with that, the ceiling fan above my bed started to spin all on its own accord. I felt the breeze swirl around me and felt Brian's presence as if his fingertips were touching my arms. Goosebumps appeared where he had left his touch. As I closed my eyes I whispered to him, "Thank you, Brian."

And as quickly as the fan had started to spin, it stopped.

CHAPTER FORTY-EIGHT

PRESENT DAY

In March, there was a knock on the door. When I answered, it was a police officer, "Ma'am, I wanted to inform you that there has been an arrest in the arson case." A few months later, we sat in the courtroom and watched as Brad was sentenced to seven years in prison for attempted manslaughter and arson. His mother sat in a seat behind him crying. She had lost her husband, and now she had all but lost her only son. I felt sorry for her, but not for him. After all, he had almost killed Tucker out of anger and selfishness.

The construction on Tucker's store, workshop, and apartment was finally finished, so in June, he moved back into his apartment. I was sorry to see him go, after all, I had gotten used to having him around. But having some space from him, also allowed me to regroup and focus on myself a little. I began preparing for the upcoming camping season. And thinking of Cole's suggestion from last summer, I ordered a telescope and hired a local Astronomy Professor to oversee a few nighttime stargazing activities.

The counselors moved in earlier than usual, by mid-June. I had a lot planned for the summer, and I wanted to make sure that all were trained and ready before the campers arrived. At our first meeting together, I was glad to see so many familiar faces. I noticed that Wade had joined the staff as a counselor. Thinking of the other campers who must have turned eighteen over the winter, I asked him, "How is Ginny doing? Didn't she want to become a counselor this year?"

He shook his head, "She's in the hospital. She's not much more than a skeleton these days. Actually, to tell you the truth, we were told she may not make it."

I was stunned, "What? Really? Oh, my God! How is Olivia doing?"

"Not good, I don't think she's coming either this summer. She doesn't want to be that far away from her sister in case something happens."

"Oh my, I'm so sorry to hear this."

Wade continued, "Yeah, it's hitting everyone pretty hard at the orphanage. You just don't think about death at our age, you know what I mean? Even as an orphan, I just haven't thought of it. I guess many of us have lost our parents when we were young, but you still don't think of a kid possibly dying. It's messed up." I could see that Dennis' expertise as a psychologist was going to be needed more than ever this summer.

"Well, thank you for telling me, Wade. Please, let me know if you hear anything else."

"Sure thing, Jace."

Cole and Lexi were back again as counselors and, it seemed, they had become inseparable. "Cole, I wanted you to know that we have a telescope this year. And I've hired someone to come by to give us Astronomy sessions. I thought you could be his assistant if you'd like."

"Sounds awesome!"

"And Lexi, I've got plans to put on an entire musical this summer."

"Which one?"

"*The Sound of Music*"

"Cool! I love that movie!"

It was a good group of counselors and I felt like we were prepared for anything this summer. But I was wrong.

A few weeks later, I helped my grandmother get dressed in the morning and told her, "Oma, the campers are coming today!"

Oma smiled and said, "Oh, that will be good, Jace."

I intended to have her participate as much as possible in the activities of the campers, but I also knew she couldn't be with me at all times. Both Murray and Tucker would also be busy, so I hired an aide, Maria, to be her caregiver.

You could feel the excitement among the counselors and staff as we waited for the buses to arrive. Oma and Maria sat on a picnic bench and watched the flurry of activity around them. When the campers disembarked from the buses, I was excited to see Haylie among them. I had missed her. I waved and called out, "Hi Haylie, good to see you back!" But she looked at me with wounded eyes and just turned away. Without a word, she walked straight toward her cabin.

When I saw Maggie walking with Dalton, I caught up with them. I rustled Dalton's hair and his big blue eyes smiled up at me. I asked them, "Hey guys, what's up with Haylie? She seems upset."

Maggie tossed her red curls with a jerk of her head and said, "Well Jace, a lady and man came to the orphanage and they wanted to, you know, like, meet some of the kids. So, you see, they were looking for a kid to, like, adopt. So, they picked Haylie and Benny to spend the day with." Maggie lifted her shoulders and frowned. Dalton finished the story, "But then the couple decided, you know, that they only wanted to take Benny."

"Oh, no. When did this happen?"

Maggie put her arm around Dalton protectively and said, "Last week. We all miss him, but like, he and Haylie were really close. Like, they were almost brother and sister. You know what I mean?"

"Yeah, I know what you mean. All right, well, thanks for telling me. I'll see what I can do about this."

I knocked on Dennis' office door. "It seems we have a problem with Haylie."

Dennis was as surprised, "What's wrong? She's always the cheerleader, encouraging everyone else to smile."

"Well, it seems last week some couple almost adopted her, but then they decided they only wanted Benny."

"Ah, that's a tough one. I'll schedule an appointment for her tomorrow, but I'd like you to be there with us. Let's give her a day to adjust to camp before we meet with her. We'll help her through this, don't you worry, Jace."

"Sounds good and thanks so much for all you do for these kids."

Dennis said, "It's nothing compared to what you and your grandmother do for them. If this camp wasn't here, I don't know what these kids would do. They tell me they look forward to coming here all year long."

"Thank you, that's nice to know." I thought about how important the camp was to the children and I decided it was time to speak with Oma's lawyer to ensure that the camp would continue in the event something happened to her.

The children were excited to see my grandmother and even more excited to meet Bonnie. As they filed into the mess hall, each one petted Bonnie and then hugged Oma. Some of them didn't want to leave Bonnie to take their seats, so they sat on the floor and nuzzled with the dog. Oma enjoyed the attention and said hello to each child even though she wasn't able to recall all of their names. Bonnie sat tall and stood guard as she licked each child to make sure they passed her test before she would allow them near Oma. Bonnie had become more and more protective of Oma as the months passed and as the memory loss increased. She was never more than a foot away, always ready to calm Oma when she sensed her confusion or frustration.

I called out to the campers above all the talking, "Hello everyone! As most of you know, I am Jace, Oma's granddaughter. I saw you all had a chance to meet Bonnie too." The crowd of children cheered.

"Well, I'm going to be running things this summer at camp. I thought since the scenes from both *Annie* and *Oliver* went over so well last year, that this year we might attempt an entire musical, *The Sound of Music*. What do you all think about that?"

The children cheered again.

"Do any of you know the story behind *The Sound of Music*?"

Some of the older ones raised their hands. One girl shouted out, "It's based on a true story about a family during World War II. They escaped from Nazi-held Austria and climbed over the mountains to freedom."

The chatter among the campers increased as they talked to their friends about what part they would like to take on in either producing or starring in the play. I continued, "Well, let's not waste any more time. Camp has started and there are hot dogs and hamburgers cooking on the outdoor grills. Everyone follow your counselors to the picnic tables."

I found Haylie in her cabin lying on a bed. I said, "Hey girl, what's going on?"

She turned her head away from me and buried it in her pillow. I tried again, "Aren't you hungry? Everyone's getting a bite to eat by the picnic tables."

She mumbled, "No thank you."

My heart broke for her. I could see how deeply she was hurting. She had just lost her best friend, and most likely, would never see him again. And in the process, she had been over-looked and discarded as unworthy.

I kissed the back of her head. For a moment she looked at me with sorrow filling her brown eyes. She said, "I'll be all right, Jace. I just need a little time to get used to things."

"Okay, honey. You got it. You take as much time as you need."

The next day, it took quite a while for Dennis to get Haylie to open up about how hurt she was. But when she finally did, it poured out of her like a waterfall. Between sobs, she told us, "He left me. He was my best friend, and he left me."

Dennis said, "You know it wasn't his decision to leave you, Haylie. It wasn't up to him."

She hung her head, "Yeah, I know." Then in a small voice she said, "They didn't want me, and he-he was my f-family."

She was still so young. And, as alone as she was before; without Benny, she was even more alone. I reached out to her and took her small hand in mine. "You know, it's very expensive to adopt and raise a child. They may not have had enough money to adopt both of you."

Through hiccups and tears she continued, "Yes, but they chose him."

Dennis handed her a tissue and asked, "Are you happy for him, Haylie? Would you really rather he wasn't adopted?"

She sniffed, "I guess not. They seemed like nice people."

Dennis nodded his head, "Haylie, they were the right parents for him. The people who are right for you are still looking for you. You wouldn't want to be with someone else when the right parents came along? Would you?"

She shook her head and wiped her fingers across her face to dry the tears, "But what if, hic, no one e-ever wants me?"

I gave her a hug and she held on to me with surprising fierceness. There were no words that could ease her pain, so instead, I smoothed her hair and kissed the top of her head. Finally, she let go of her grip on my shirt and sat up tall.

Dennis said, "Don't let this ruin the rest of your life, or even the rest of your summer, Haylie. If you don't look up, you won't see all the people who love you and who are still here for you."

She tried a weak smile and wiped at her nose with her sleeve. Putting on a brave face that broke my heart even more, she said, "Yeah, maybe if I keep looking, I'll find those right parents you were talking about."

I continued to run my fingers gently through her hair to straighten out the wet mess that resulted from all of her tears.

Dennis smiled at us as he watched carefully, "Yes, I think you might just do that."

I wished he could comfort me too, I felt overwhelmed and helpless. These children needed so much from me, and for a moment, I wasn't sure if I was up to this job. But then I could hear Oma's words mulling around in my head, "Family might be those who you are born to, it might be those who you end up with, or it may be those you meet along the way. There's only one way to know for sure who your family is; they are the people you carry in your heart. The ones you think of when you think of the word home." I looked from Dennis to Hailey and realized what Dennis was hinting at. A small light ignited deep within me, and I decided then and there, to learn all I could about the adoption process.

A week later, the cast of our musical was set. Cliff, who had played Daddy Warbucks the summer before, was now cast as Baron von Trapp, and Ella was cast as Maria. Vicky would play the role of the mother superior and Tanner would be Max Detweiler. Mazie made a great Liesl, the oldest von Trapp daughter, and Haylie would be the youngest of the children, Gretl.

Travis was cast to play Rolf Gruber, the love interest of Liesl. Although Travis had been overweight the year before, he had experienced a huge growth spurt during the winter and had slimmed down in the process. He had a beautiful voice and had grown into a very handsome young man. I teased Mazie, "He's turned into quite a charmer." But she responded, "I don't think I am of any interest to him, he prefers Cliff over me, if you know what I mean."

Finally, Mack took on the role of Friedrich, the eldest son in the family, and Dalton, who had been Oliver the past summer, was now chosen for Kurt, the younger of the two von Trapp brothers.

In mid-July, we received terrible news. I gathered the campers together and told them, "I'm so sorry to tell you all this, but Ginny has passed away. I thought maybe you would all want to have a memorial service for her." Travis raised his hand, "Yes, Travis?"

"Well, you know how much she liked the campfires? Maybe we should have a campfire tonight and share our memories of her."

"That's a great idea."

That night, in addition to the campers, the entire staff showed up. Oma sat between Tucker and Murray. Each camper and counselor took a moment to say something they remembered about Ginny. Then Dennis had the children each write a message to her and, one by one, they tossed their messages into the flames. The pieces of paper burned bright white for an instant and then wisps of smoke rose into the air as the paper sizzled. Everyone became quiet after that, until Oma spoke up.

The flurry of activity around the camp and seeing the children every day, had somehow helped her to regain some of her memory. She looked at the fire and said, "When I was a little girl, we had a bonfire every year for the Epiphany." She looked around at all the faces who were now watching her carefully and explained, "The Epiphany comes after Christmas. It is when the three wise men arrived to present baby Jesus with their gifts. Well, on that night, we would burn our Christmas tree and the sparks from the evergreen branches would reach up into the dark night sky, just like this. But before we took down the tree, we children, my bruder and I, would search through the branches to find any sweets our parents may have hidden there. The treats sort of represented the gifts the wise men brought. Then as the tree burned, we would sing, *O Tannenbaum*, and we would dance. One time, my friend Rebekah was there, and we danced together. That was the last time we burned a Christmas Tree. There were no more Christmas Trees after that one."

The children had become used to Oma not speaking anymore and so now they gave her their rapt attention. Maisy asked, "Why were there no more Christmas Trees?"

Oma's head shook with age as she said, "Because the war came."

Then Maisy picked up a large evergreen branch from the pile of tinder and added it to the campfire. In silence we watched the sparks fly and listened to the crackle and popping as the fire consumed it.

Oma's shaky voice started to sing,

"O Tannenbaum, o Tannenbaum

Wie treu sind deine Blätter

Du grünst nicht nur zur Sommerzeit,

Nein, auch im Winter, wenn es schneit.

O Tannenbaum, o Tannenbaum,

Wie treu sind deine Blätter.

It seemed a fitting tribute to Ginny. There wasn't a dry eye around the campfire as everyone joined in to sing the song in English,

"Oh Christmas Tree, Oh Christmas Tree,

Thy leaves are so unchanging.

Not only green when Summer's here,

But also when it's cold and drear,

O Christmas Tree, Oh Christmas Tree,

Thy leaves are so unchanging."

CHAPTER FORTY-NINE

PRESENT DAY

On the night of the play, the activities cabin was crowded with visitors. Oma sat up front and sang along with every song that was sung. It was great to see that she was having another good day. Being around the children all summer really seemed to have improved her cognitive abilities.

The parking lot filled up with people eager to see the play, and soon the audience took their seats. I saw Olivia arrive accompanied by a woman who worked at the orphanage. Dennis and I made our way to her and I gave her a huge hug. I said, "Olivia, I'm so sorry about Ginny." Her chin quivered just a bit before she said, "Thank you. She's not in any pain anymore." Olivia looked from me to the woman who had accompanied her, "This is Miss Porter, she says it's time for me to let go of my pain too." Dennis smiled, "Very good, Olivia. And I think coming here tonight is a great way to do that." She nodded her head in agreement.

The children put on a wonderful show, and at the end, they all lined the stage. They had seen Olivia sitting up front in the audience, so they called to her to join them. Olivia ran up onto the stage and linked arms with her old friends. Together they all took a bow as the audience roared with cheers.

Oma clapped and waited for the room to empty before she stood to go. I was about to help her, when a man from the back of the audience approached her hesitantly.

In a thick German, he said, "Hello, Issy."

Although the man was close to 80 years old himself, he still had some brown hair mixed into the gray. His eyebrows furrowed and then he smiled at Oma and said, "What? Do you not remember me?"

Oma looked at him blankly as Bonnie eyed him warily.

"Issy, it is I, Markos."

She looked at him and repeated his name in wonder as an old memory slipped back into her tired brain, "M-Markos?"

"Ja, Issy. Do I look so different that you cannot recognize me?"

Tears of joy filled Oma's eyes, "Markos! I never thought I would see you again!"

He was the same little boy she and Rebekah had found holding onto his dead mother's frozen hand. But now he stood towering over her. He reached out and gathered Oma into his arms.

I said, "Please, come back with us to the house. I'm sure my grandmother would like to talk with you. With all the excitement out here, she won't be able to hear you very well."

As the counselors took over the care of the boisterous campers, I ushered Markos back to Oma's cabin along with Tucker, Murray, and Maria. Markos explained who he was, while Murray and Bonnie flanked her on either side.

Maria made coffee for us all and we sat down at the kitchen table. I said, "Markos, Oma has told me all about you. But as you can see, her memory comes and goes now. Please tell us, whatever happened to Friedrich and Vera?"

"Ah, they stayed in Germany and Friedrich opened a shoe store in Nuremberg. They kept me with them and raised me."

Oma asked, "Did they ever have any more children?"

"No, I'm afraid they did not." She shook her head sadly, "I remember the baby they took for her arms."

Markos nodded, "Ja, Issy, I remember him too."

Curious, I questioned him further, "When did you come to America and how did you find Oma?"

He took a sip of the coffee and said, "I came briefly for business in 2005. I have always had it in my mind to try to find Issy and Rebekah. I knew they wanted to come to America. They used to talk about it all the time." His hands shook slightly as they moved, and as he spoke, his facial expressions changed in dramatic fashion, "I never forgot that they made me memorize the address for her Onkel Peter." He recited, "2130 Fourth Street, Brighton Beach, New York." Then he continued, "But by the time I got there, her Onkel Peter didn't live there anymore. The man who answered the door told me to check with the house across the street. He said the people who lived there were close friends with Peter. So, I crossed the street and I told them I was a friend of Issy and Rebekah.

It seems this neighbor across the street was the bruder of Rebekah's husband. He told me that Rebekah had passed away and that Issy had moved to Tennessee. He gave me her address, but I wasn't able to travel here on that trip because I was set to return to Germany the next day. But I knew that someday I would come back to find her. I'm afraid it has taken me this long to get here."

I said, "The man you met in Brighton Beach must have been Sasha."

Markos nodded, "Ja, that was what he said! His name was Sasha."

Oma repeated the name with a smile, "Sasha."

Jace turned to Tucker, "Sasha would be your father's brother."

Tucker nodded with a smile, "That's right, he would be." Having never really known a blood relative, he was now understandably eager to meet this Sasha.

I turned back to Markos and explained, "Tucker is Rebekah's grandson."

Markos reached out his hand and grasped Tucker's in his. He said, "Rebekah had a very kind heart. She used to rock me when I was afraid. She always made sure that I knew she was there. When she and Issy left the refugee camp, I missed them both terribly. But I knew that Vera needed me. I stayed with her and Friedrich. I even started to call them Mutti and Vater. I was very lucky to have them."

I asked, "So, Markos, what have you been doing all this time?"

"I married and had two sons of my own. They have their own families now, in Germany of course. My wife and I always said we would travel together to America; I wanted her to meet Rebekah and Issy. But we never got around to it. Now she is gone, so I am traveling on my own."

I said, "Well, you are welcome to stay here tonight. We have an extra room. You can stay as long as you'd like."

"Thank you, that is very thoughtful of you. But tomorrow I have to move on. I have a rail pass and am seeing the country by train. I want to see Memphis and Elvis Presley's home, Graceland. After that, I'm crossing the Mississippi River and heading south toward New Orleans."

Murray responded with relief, "Sounds like you have quite a trip planned. I guess you have to keep moving." I smiled at Murray; he was making it pretty obvious that he didn't want to share the little that was left of Oma with any other man. Not even with Markos.

The next morning, Oma was still feeling well and seemed to be having another clear day. She helped me make a big break-fast for Markos with her favorite German sausage and cheesy scrambled eggs. It felt so good to have her beside me in the kitchen again. It seemed like old times and I treasured every moment. After breakfast, Markos said his goodbyes and gave Oma a giant bear hug. Oma waved as he got into his car and called out to him, "Tell Friedrich and Vera I said hello."

I didn't remind her that they were long dead by now. It was best to let her think she had remembered things correctly. Markos nodded to her and put the car into gear and drove away.

The following day was the last day of camp and I hugged

Haylie as I said goodbye. She said, "I'll miss you, Jace." I held onto her tighter than I should have, but truthfully, I didn't want to let her go. "I will miss you too, Haylie."

I didn't want to get her hopes up, so I never told her I was looking into the adoption process for myself. It seemed, from what I had learned so far, that my effort to adopt her would have a greater chance for success if I were married.

CHAPTER FIFTY

PRESENT DAY

On the first of September, leaves had fallen on the ground and it was raining when Oma decided to walk outside on her own to get the mail. It was Maria's day off and I was taking a shower. When I came out of the bathroom, I saw the front door was open to the screened-in porch. I called out, "Oma?" But there was no answer. The only sound was Bonnie whimpering at the front door.

I grabbed a jacket and stuffed my feet into my boots. As I opened the porch door, I saw something lying in the road near the mailbox. I ran toward the road, but Bonnie raced out of the door ahead of me. I found Oma lying there unable to get up. "Oma! Are you okay?" She cried, "Oh Jace, I'm glad you found me." I tried to lift her, but her weight was too much for me. I gently helped her into a more comfortable sitting position on the ground, took off my jacket, and wrapped it around her. She wasn't even wearing shoes. I ran back into the house and called Tucker on my cell phone before grabbing some blankets and a chair to bring to Oma. It only took Tucker ten minutes to get there. Together, we lifted her onto the chair. An ambulance pulled up a minute later. Tucker said, "I called them, I thought it was better to be safe than sorry."

The paramedics lifted Oma and placed her on a stretcher. Bonnie protested as they brought Oma into the ambulance. I wrestled Bonnie back to the cabin before locking it up. Then I rode in the ambulance, while Tucker followed with his car. In the emergency room, we waited with Oma until an orderly took her up for X-rays. The doctor met with us after. He announced, "She's broken her hip and she will need to be admitted."

I said, "All right, but can I stay with her tonight? She doesn't know where she is, and she gets confused. She has dementia," I explained.

The nurse calmed my fears, "She will be kept medicated tonight and will not be conscious. Go home and get a good night's rest, she will need you tomorrow after the operation when she starts her recovery."

On the drive home, Tucker asked what had happened. I was taking a shower. Oma has been so good lately; I thought it would be okay to leave her for just a few minutes." I shook my head, "It's all my fault."

He said, "You can't say that. She *has* been clear-headed this summer. You didn't know. You can't be there every minute, it's impossible."

"I know, I know, but still, I feel as if I should have been there."

When we got back to the cabin it was almost midnight. Tucker said, "Is it all right if I stay here tonight?"

"Please do. I'd feel better if you were here."

The stress had gotten to both of us and I was glad for his strength and comfort. I looked up at him with my hair covering half my face. He gently lifted the stray strands and tucked them behind my ear. Then he tilted my chin up toward him as he lowered his mouth onto mine. He hadn't kissed me again since the night we were alone in the dark sitting by the fireplace. This kiss started out gentle, but then it became more demanding. I stopped fighting against my own desire and I opened my mouth to his. His body trembled as it pressed against mine.

In a husky voice he said, "I love you, Jace," and then he gently kissed my forehead. His kisses continued, leaving a trail across my face and all the way to my ear. His hands softly traveled from my shoulders and down my back. I felt a deeper yearning awaken in me. It had been gone for so long. I pulled him toward the bedroom and we fell onto the sheets and into each other's arms.

To taste his lips and to feel his skin against mine sent my senses reeling. When he pulled me on top of him and he slid inside of me, I thought I was going to burst with joy. Again he said, "I love you, Jace." And this time I replied, "I love you too, Tucker."

Afterward, we lay in each other arms and I felt as if I would die if I ever lost him. Now that I had given myself to him, I wanted to be reassured he had meant every word he said. "Tucker, do you really love me?"

He looked intently into my eyes, "Jace, I have loved you since the moment I first saw you and that was a very, very long time ago. I remember your visit with your grandmother. I remember you looked like an angel and I thought my heart had broken when you left without ever knowing how I felt. I was just an orphan kid, but you were beautiful. I had never seen a girl as beautiful as you were. When I saw you again last year at camp, I just about fell over. I couldn't believe it was you again and that you had come back. But then I found out that you were broken. I tried to tell you how I felt, but you weren't ready to hear it. I want you to understand, having you in my life has filled this emptiness that I have carried with me all of my life. I don't want to be alone anymore. I want you to be with me, always."

I smiled then as the memory finally came back to me. I said in surprise, "I remember now!" I remembered the blonde boy with hazel eyes. I admitted, "I too have felt very alone. But having you in my life has made me feel that I can live again. You don't have to wait any longer, Tucker. I'm here and I don't ever want to leave again."

We made love once more and then fell asleep in each other's arms.

The next morning, we dressed and headed straight for the hospital. Oma was wheeled into the operating room at 9 a.m. and by noon, she was in recovery. The doctor warned us that it was going to be a difficult recovery, and he was right. It took a while for the anesthesia to wear off, and when it did, she was very confused. She didn't know where she was or who we were. She continuously tried to get out of bed in spite of the broken hip. We were terrified she would fall again and do further damage to herself. So, we took turns staying with her, 24 hours a day in the hospital. Even with medication and the hospital staff nearby, her confusion and mood swings were hard to manage. She couldn't remember why she was in pain and it was torturous to watch her suffer. The pain medication was given to her freely, but still it did nothing to appease her.

A few weeks later, she was sent to rehab. The change in venue caused additional confusion. She was there for another four long weeks and then finally, she came home again to Bonnie's delight.

She settled in at home and Maria came each day to help. I brought her to rehab three times a week, but she could never remember how to do the exercises and her frustration was breaking her. To tell the truth, it was breaking me, as well. When she would turn her anger and frustration on me, I did my best to soothe her. Bonnie didn't understand what was happening either. She had missed Oma terribly and didn't understand why Oma swatted at her when she tried to cozy up next to her feet.

One afternoon, out of desperation, I sat her in front of her easel and placed a paint brush in her hand. It took a moment, but then she dipped the tip of the brush and started to paint the scene that lay before her. She painted Bonnie, sitting comfortably by the fire place next to the old spinning wheel. I found that her talent had withstood the onslaught of her disease. Her natural instincts took over and what appeared on the canvas was beautiful. It relaxed her too. It brought a sense of peace and comfort back into her life.

By December, Oma was able to walk pretty well with the aid of a walker to help keep her balanced. Her memory was worse than ever, but physically, she was much better. That was all we could hope for now. She enjoyed petting Bonnie and Bonnie remained ever loyal.

I decided to plan a Christmas holiday with all the German trimmings from Oma's childhood, hoping it would bring back some of her memory again. Tucker and I combed the Internet to find just the right decorations. We found advent pyramids, nutcrackers, and German lace ornaments. Tucker said he would make some glass-blown ornaments just like the vintage ones we had seen on-line.

Murray and Maria both stayed with Oma while Tucker and I went in search of the perfect Christmas tree. White overhead lights were strung across the lot to light our way as we critically judged the symmetry of the trees and tested the needle retention. Christmas music played gaily over the loud speakers, while families enjoyed hot chocolate as they waited for their trees to be secured to the tops of cars.

"I think we found it!" I exclaimed, as Tucker held a beautiful Frasier fir upright so I could get a better look at it.

He instructed, "Good, then stand by it while I get someone to help us."

As I watched him walk away, I thought of all that transpired for us to be here together at this moment. It really was a miracle that Oma had found him all those years ago. I was sure Rebekah was in heaven looking down on us and smiling with approval. Then I thought of Brian and frowned. The guilt I felt for his death was what had made it the hardest to move on. I reminded myself, loss is one thing, guilt is another. But I had learned that I do not control the universe, and there is a power much greater than I which turns the wheels of fate. If I hadn't come to visit with Oma, Tucker and I would never have had a chance to share the experiences, both good and bad, which had led us to where we were now. His hat was turned sideways as he came back with

349

one of the young workers who took the tree to give it a fresh cut.

I reached up to fix Tucker's hat and set it right on his head. He smiled broadly down at me and gave me a kiss. He said, "You look beautiful with pine needles stuck in your hair." And proceeded to pick them out before I playfully pushed him with both hands. He warned, "Now, now, don't go getting physical with me or I might just have to get physical with you too."

"Is that a threat?" I asked.

"No, it's a promise." He replied.

I smiled, "Well, then," and I grabbed onto his coat and pulled him toward me, "I think I'll collect on that promise when we get back to the cabin."

On the way back home, we sang along with the Christmas songs on the radio. I had never heard him sing before and was surprised by his beautiful voice. I complimented him, "You could have sung professionally."

He imitated Marlon Brando and said, "I could'a been a contender."

"You still can, you know, you could go on one of those television shows where you can be discovered."

"Now what would I want to do that for, when all I want I already have right here." He reached for my hand across the car seat and held it in his.

Back at the cabin, Oma sat on the sofa and watched us decorate the tree. The glass-blown ornaments that Tucker had made were breathtakingly beautiful. He had hand-painted them with intricate scenes of the German countryside and people riding on horse-drawn sleighs through the snow. The last thing I added was a glass pickle. Murray poured us some of his homemade hot cinnamon apple cider and we relished the warmth we felt. We were a family.

On Christmas morning, it was just the three of us, and Bonnie, of course. We gathered once again by the tree. Bonnie was busy munching on a new rawhide bone when Tucker handed me a small box. As I opened it, I saw the sparkling diamond ring inside and tears spilled down my cheeks. He knelt beside me and asked, "Jace, will you marry me?"

I wrapped my arms around him and said through my tears, "Oh yes! Yes! Of course! Yes!"

Oma smiled, when she saw Tucker slip the ring on my finger, "That is good, Jace."

I was startled because lately she had a hard time remembering my name. I sat down next to her and let her have a better look at the ring, "Oma look, Tucker and I are going to be married." She patted my hand and smiled at the ring on my finger. She said, "I love you, Jace." She puckered her lips for a kiss and I kissed her, "I love you too, Oma."

Tucker came over carrying a larger package which he handed to Oma. "This one's for you, Oma."

She carefully untied the ribbon as her hands shook slightly and then neatly unwrapped it to find a simple black box. She lifted the lid and saw the doll inside. Her face was perfect, the blue eyes and bow shaped mouth, the hint of pink blush on her cheeks. No cracks marred her sweet complexion. Oma lifted the doll out of the box and held her closely and cried, "Oh, Catrina, you came back to me! I've missed you so much!"

I asked Tucker in amazement, "How did you do this?"

He said, "I took the doll from your room and I made a cast of her face. Working with porcelain is not much different from working with glass. Then I painted her face to match the old one."

I was stunned, I exclaimed in wonder, "I didn't even notice she was gone." Tucker looked at the smile on Oma's face and said, "By the way, I found this tucked into the doll's apron." He took out a small dog carved out of wood. He handed it to Oma and she looked at it intently. She showed it to Jace and said, "I'd forgotten he was in her apron. That's the dog Opa carved for me." Then she frowned, "I always wanted to give it to Rebekah, but I never did. It's too late now, isn't it?"

Tucker said, "That's all right, Oma. You could give it to me now. Then I would have something that was made by my great-grandfather." Oma brightened up and said, "Ja, that is right! Did I tell you, Tucker? You are Rebekah's grandson." And with that, she happily handed the small carved dog back to its rightful owner.

I hugged him and buried my face in his shoulder, "Thank you, Tucker, for making this the best Christmas ever!"

CHAPTER FIFTY-ONE

PRESENT DAY

That June, in the little chapel in Gatlinburg with the majestic Smoky Mountains as a backdrop, I stood waiting in the vestibule. Just in front of me, Oma sat in her wheelchair with both Catrina and a basket of pink rose petals in her lap. At Oma's side, Bonnie stood quietly, with a wreath of forget-me-nots and baby's breath around her neck. Haylie stood behind Oma, ready to push the wheelchair. Haylie was my bridesmaid and she wore a simple sleeveless blue dress that matched the flowers in Bonnie's wreath. Lexi, my maid-of-honor, stood behind me, holding the trail to my gown. And on either side of me, stood my parents, waiting to escort me down the aisle.

Oma turned to me and pointed to my mother. She whispered, a bit too loudly, "Who is that? She looks familiar."

My mother cried, "Mama, it's me, Lily."

Oma smirked, "Oh, that's good. You must come and visit me

more often." My mother's cheeks blushed red and she agreed, "Yes, mama. I promise, I will."

The organ music began, and Haylie pushed Oma's wheelchair forward. Oma reached into her basket and tossed the petals as we proceeded. The little chapel was full of friends and relatives. Maggie, Dalton, and Olivia were there, along with Miss Porter, from the orphanage. But then my attention was drawn to the man standing at the front of the chapel, patiently waiting for me to reach him. Tucker looked more handsome than ever. Oma had once called him towheaded, like his grandfather, Stephan. With his light blonde hair, those warm hazel eyes, and deep dimples, he made my heart leap as I neared him. Cole stood beside him as his best man.

Haylie turned Oma's wheelchair toward the left at the first pew and parked it next to the aisle. Then Haylie took a seat with Bonnie beside her. My father lifted my veil and placed my hand in Tuckers. The minister asked, "Who gives this woman?" He responded, "My wife and I do." Then my parents took their seats beside Haylie, Oma and Bonnie.

When it came time to exchange our vows, Tucker smiled down at me as he said, "Jace, I promise to love and cherish you for the rest of my life. Through all the joys and sorrows that await us, together, we will face them all. My heart has been yours since the day I met you. Now I am glad to share all that I have, or will ever have, with you. And I promise to do all that is within my power to bring a smile to your face every day of your life."

I faced him now and spoke my own words, "Tucker, I promise to give you my whole heart and soul and to treasure every moment that we have together. I promise to never take you for granted. And I promise that for as long as there is a breath in my body, I will continue to nurture the love between us."

And with that, the minister announced, "I now pronounce you, husband and wife. You may kiss your bride."

The church erupted in applause as the organ music started up again and we walked back down the aisle together.

After the ceremony, we threw a party back at the camp under a giant tent. I was thrilled when it was Lexi who caught my bridal bouquet. "You're next!" I exclaimed. Then Cole grabbed her in his arms for the next dance. Soon, Tucker stood up and tapped his glass to get everyone's attention.

"Thank you all for being here to share this very special day with Jace and me. Knowing that she is now my wife, I can only tell you how blessed I feel. Our story is an amazing one and shows just how strangely life weaves itself until our dreams can finally become a reality. But today, Jace and I have more to be thankful for than just our marriage. Haylie, can you come up here and join us?" Haylie ran to stand next to us, so proud to be my bridesmaid. Then Tucker announced, "This morning, we signed papers which will make it official. Haylie, you are now our daughter."

Haylie looked at me as if she did not quite believe what she was hearing. So, I said, "Haylie, today we signed adoption papers, you are ours now." Haylie looked toward Miss Porter as if to make sure that it was true. Miss Porter nodded, and Haylie wrapped her arms around us, embracing us both. Then, in her excitement, she hiccupped between tears of joy, "You mean, *hic*, you mean, *hic*, I don't have to go back to the orphanage anymore?"

I nodded, "Yes, sweetheart, that's what I mean. This is your home now. And you don't have to say goodbye to your friends either, because you will be able to see them every summer when they come back to camp." Maggie, Dalton, and Olivia screamed with joy.

Dennis shouted out, "What did I tell you, Haylie?" She laughed thinking of the time he told her that someday the right parents would come along for her. Everyone stood and cheered as we took her with us to the center of the dance floor. Tucker put an arm around each of us, and together, we began to dance. The song the band was playing was *Edelweiss* from *The Sound of Music*. Haylie started to sing, her sweet voice was joined a moment later by Oma's trembling voice on the sidelines.

Murray was sitting beside Oma's wheelchair when a man approached them. The man asked Murray, "Can she stand?" Murray said, "Yes, but please be careful with her." Sasha extended his hand to Oma and helped her stand. She let him guide her slowly across the dance floor. I smiled at them as they danced together, Issy and the youngest brother of Andrei. When the dance ended, she looked up at him in confusion, and I heard her say, "Andrei, is that you?" Although Sasha's hair had turned white, it was not so different from his natural color, and she knew those hazel eyes.

Sasha smiled, and remembering the words his older brother always said to her, he replied, "Yes, Issy, and you are still as beautiful as ever. As beautiful as that porcelain doll of yours."

"Ah, it is you!" The music started up again and together they continued to dance. Oma looked younger than she had in years. Her silver hair in braids around her head like a crown. Her crystal blue eyes sparkling with happiness. Murray stood on the sidelines and let her have this moment. He knew, as well as the rest of us, that this moment, as precious as it was to Oma, would soon be forgotten.

Later that night in our hotel room, I looked at my husband and couldn't help but be amazed at how happy I felt. I said, "Tucker, I feel so lucky to have you in my life." He held my hand and led me over to sit on the side of the bed. His smile, his face, his touch, all just had a way of melting me. It seemed my fears and worries disappeared with him by my side.

He shook his head and said, "Jace, with all that we have learned from our own lives, and from the story that Oma has told us, you should know that our love has nothing to do with luck. You and I are both survivors, who came from survivors. Life happens as it is supposed to. We each have shown that we have the strength to learn from the past, and because of that past, we understand how important it is to find joy in the present."

I thought about what he was saying, about the children who were hidden during the war, about those who had been executed at the hands of evil, about those who had suffered in concentration camps, and those who had their homes and families taken from them, and I knew that he was right. All the suffering of the past could not be changed, but we could make sure that those who suffered did not do so in vain. We could spend our lives feeling sorry for ourselves, or we could help those around us to have a better understanding of the past and, in turn, find peace. There was no doubt in my mind which was the better choice. That was when I decided I would take Oma's story and turn it into a book for others to read.

I kissed my husband and, as he wrapped his arms around me, I knew I had finally found my home.

ABOUT THE AUTHOR

Author Theresa Dodaro holds a BA in liberal arts from Stony Brook University, where she studied English, history, and secondary education. She worked in publishing and marketing until she put her career on hold to raise her children.

She grew up in Baldwin, New York, and currently lives on Long Island with her husband. Now that her children are grown and have started lives of their own, she spends her time writing novels, blogging, and conducting genealogical research for herself and others.

Theresa is the author of the previously published, Tin Box Trilogy (The Tin Box Secret; The Hope Chest; and Reawakening). She enjoys meeting with her fans at book talks and signings, and especially loves to meet with book clubs to discuss her books. Please check out her websites: www.theresadodaro.com and www.raisingdrama.com.

To set up appearances at events, you can contact Theresa at thetinboxtrilogy@gmail.com.